Two
Minutes
To
Midnight

Willow Salix

DragonCat Press

Copyright © September 2016, Willow Salix
Original Cover Art by Soxsational Cover Art
Published by DragonCat Press
ISBN :978-0-9955073-0-2

To Joan and Albert, the most supportive, loving and caring, grandparents ever to live. Thank you for believing in me and encouraging me to be whatever I wanted to be and do whatever I wanted to do. I just wish you were here to see this.

This book has been a long time coming and now it's finally here and I have few thanks to give to those that have helped along the way.

Firstly, to my amazing grandparents (again) for giving me my love of reading and writing, giving me the freedom to fuel my imagination.

To my family, Spider and G, who have helped make this book possible by putting up with my crazy writing bouts and sudden yelling of plot ideas at random times, yet still support me.

And lastly, to my friends who help keep me sane by listening to my rantings and story ideas and never thinking I'm crazy.

To my Diamond Bitches – Cristina, Kat and Tasha (my witch, Valkyrie and Dragon), who have helped me by reading, checking and supporting my writing and helping keep me cheerful even on my darkest days. As we always say, Good friends are like Diamonds, you have to search through a lot of crap to find a real one.

To Jay, the Demonish that every witch should have, who doesn't even question why he gets random messages asking how he would describe the scent of death.

To Z, my Demon, who provides me with my sanctuary online and are always there when I need her. Ready to listen, hug and tell me I'm awesome.

I couldn't do it without you all. Thank you.

Prologue

Logan McGregor had had a long day. He was tired, aching down to his bones and desperate to get home to his wife and their children. It was always the same during the harvest, everyone working from dawn to dusk, trying to reap the most to get the best payment possible.

He allowed his thoughts to wander as he negotiated his way through the woods in the growing dark, thinking about nothing but dinner and a restful night's sleep.

As the trees finally gave way to the well-worn path that lead to his little cottage he picked up his pace, his tiredness lessening at the thought of his wife greeting him at the door with a hot meal and a mug of ale.

Glancing up, he spotted his house in the distance and began to jog. As he neared he noticed with a start that the house was in darkness. He paused, looking carefully at the window for the candle his wife, Alcina, always lit to guide him home in the dark. He began to run towards his house, panic setting in. Alcina *never* forgot the light.

He didn't bother to push open the little gate that surrounded his small plot of land, instead vaulting over the fence and rushing to the door.

1

His heart skipped a beat when he finally paused to catch his breath at the threshold; the door was open a crack.

With a trembling hand, Logan flung open the door, uncaring of the way it crashed back against the door frame.

"Alcina," he called out, looking around frantically for his wife and children. Not a sound reached his ears.

Logan slowly entered the house, the inside lit up by nothing but the flames in the hearth.

Looking around wildly, his gaze swept over the room, coming to rest in the corner where his children slept. His breath came out in one long rush as he saw, to his relief, that his children were curled up on their mats, covered snugly with a blanket. Seeing this, his panic began to fade, giving way to relief.

He chuckled quietly to himself. His son and daughter were sound asleep, Alcina would not stray far from her beloved children, therefore she must be very close. Maybe she had gone down to the stream that ran behind their house to fetch more water.

Logan made his way across the room. It was his custom to kiss his children goodnight, no matter how late he arrived home. Squatting down, he gently pulled back the blankets, bending his head to bestow a kiss on their foreheads.

His children stared blankly up at him, eyes wide open, mouths hanging slackly, blood pooling around their heads. Logan drew back, unable to believe what his eyes were seeing. He scooped Mary up into his arms, hoping that it was all some kind of joke and that the children would suddenly burst out laughing and Alcina would rush in from outside and tease him for being foolish enough to be tricked by the little devils.

Mary's little body was floppy and unresponsive, her arm drooping lifelessly down by her side. Her head was turned to the side, showing the gaping wound on her neck. It looked like her throat had been ripped out by some savage beast.

2

Turning to look at Thomas, Logan saw that his son had met a similar fate. Anguish welled up inside him and a primal yell tore from his throat. He dropped to his knees, cradling Mary's tiny body to his chest, tears of grief pouring down his face.

Logan didn't know how long he knelt there, clutching his daughter tightly; finally, he stirred and crawled back towards the bed where his son still lay. He gently placed his daughter down beside her brother, and without thinking he pulled the blanket back up over their small bodies, as if not wanting them to get cold.

Outside a scream of terror broke the silence.

"Alcina!" Logan yelled, recognising his wife's voice, he leapt to his feet and raced out of the door in the direction he thought the scream had come from. He looked around wildly, his eyes darting from one direction to another, searching for his wife. He could not see her.

"Alcina, my love, where are you?" he bellowed, cupping his hands around his mouth in an attempt to amplify the sound. He was met with silence, hearing nothing but the wind blowing through the trees.

Logan collapsed to his knees, sobbing anew. His children were dead and his wife had disappeared, what was he to do?

He dropped his head into his hands and tried to take a deep, steadying breath, but the air was suddenly forced out of his lungs by a great weight crashing into his back. An arm wrapped around his neck and began to squeeze, constricting his throat and cutting off his air. Logan began to struggle, thrashing from side to side, trying to dislodge the body on his back.

His lungs were burning, crying out desperately for oxygen. The strength slowly left his body and his struggles lessened, blackness began to form behind his eyes and his vision faded.

Logan felt his life slipping away from him, his limbs became laden, and his head rolled back on his neck. The last thing he felt as he slid into oblivion was a sharp pain in his throat.

Chapter 1

"The current rise of sea levels during the last century was recorded at a rate of 1.8mm per year. This has recently increased dramatically, due to our current era of Satellites. It has now increased to a staggering 3.1mm per year. This is, of course, all due to the thermal expansion of water and melting from the continental ice sheets." Leif picked up his glass of water and took a sip, no doubt gearing up for yet another fact or lecture.

"Did you know that each year 8mm of water from the entire surface of the oceans falls on the Antarctic ice sheets as snowfall? Topaz, are you listening to me?"

She glanced up sharply, bringing her attention back to the man seated opposite her. He was definitely not her type, with his greasy hair in stringy, mud brown dreadlocks and his horrible jumper. His glasses kept slipping down his nose as he talked and rather that push them back up with his finger, as most normal people would do, he instead would wriggle his nose and tip his head back slightly until they returned to their original position. This had given her an interesting, if disgusting, view right up his nostrils on several occasions already.

She let her psychic vision come in, un-focusing her eyes and squinted at his aura. Just as she had suspected. It was a bright lemon yellow, which indicated that he liked to be in control and feared losing respect. Well, he had certainly done that. She closed her sight down and caught his gaze.

"No, I didn't know that, how fascinating," she paused as she spotted their waiter working his way over to the table. The young man looked happy and eager to please. She guessed that he must be new, just wait until he had a few awkward customers. That would take the shine off. She had had a few of them in her time. She didn't need to look at his aura to see that he was a happy person who was always ready to please.

"Are you ready to order?" he asked with a bright smile, his order pad ready in his hand, pen poised over the paper.

Topaz decided to let Leif go first and waved him on. She liked to have time to decide. He picked up his menu and looked up his selection.

"Yes, I'll have the nut roast, with roast potatoes, peas and carrots." The waiter nodded and wrote down the order, before turning to see what Topaz wanted to order.

"Now," Leif carried on regardless of the fact that Topaz had opened her mouth to speak. The waiter turned back to him. She rolled her eyes behind his back, childish she knew but it made her feel better.

"Are the vegetables organic? I can't eat anything else. And the potatoes are they vegan? Have they been cooked in a separate tray to the others? Also the gravy, does it contain any meat juices?"

He looked up at the waiter expectantly, who shifted uncomfortably under his questioning gaze, looking like he was back at school and had just had a surprise exam sprung on him, with no time to study. Damn, Topaz felt sorry

6

for him, he was going to get a crash course in difficult customers right here, right now. She wiggled slightly in her seat, turning her head to look out of the window, sending the universal, He's-nothing-to-do-with-me, I-just-met-the-guy, message out to the rest of the diners and wait staff.

"I don't know, Sir, I'm sorry I only started here yesterday. Would you like me to go and ask for you?" The poor lad was almost sweating under Leif's stare.

"Well obviously I would or I would not be asking, would I?" Leif scowled at the waiter and made a shooing motion with his hand.

"Very good, Sir." The waiter turned on his heel and scurried away in the direction of the kitchen.

Leif turned to Topaz, coughing to get her attention. Sighing under her breath, she turned back to her date. He immediately launched into a torrent of abuse at the expense of the poor waiter.

"Can you believe that he doesn't know how the food is prepared? It's just not acceptable; I shall be having a talk with his supervisor when we leave."

Topaz was shocked by his attitude. There was no way in hell that she was going to let him get away with being a jerk all night. She tried appealing to his good nature, not that she was convinced he even had one, it was either very deeply buried or he'd misplaced it somewhere. She leapt to the waiter's defence.

"Oh no, don't do that, It's not his fault. He said he only started here yesterday. Cut him some slack, he-" Leif held up his hand, cutting her off mid-flow and shocked, Topaz blinked. *Oh no, he didn't just hush me*, she thought, and even as she glared at him, his face settled into lecture mode. *Here it comes, brace yourself, Tope, my girl, block your ears*, she mentally instructed herself, resisting the urge to stick her fingers in her ears.

"Topaz, my dear, you are too soft. These people should know their job. How do you expect the service to improve if

7

you do not tell them what is lacking? Now he will know for future reference, won't he?" Leif smiled triumphantly at her, pleased that he had made his point, taking her stunned silence as agreement. *These people? I think he just insulted me too,* she thought in amazement.

She spotted the waiter returning to their table, and the poor lad didn't look happy.

Leif looked up as the boy approached and Topaz wanted the ground to open up and swallow her whole. She glanced down at her feet, half hoping that a chasm had conveniently appeared that she could throw herself into. No such luck. The diners on the neighbouring tables were listening in unashamedly.

"Well?"

"I'm sorry, Sir, I asked Chef and he said that the potatoes are all cooked together and the vegetables are not organic. As for the Gravy, it is made with beef stock."

"And what are you planning on doing to rectify this problem?"

"We would like to recommend the salad, Sir, it is organic." Topaz covered a snort of laughter with a cough and tried to look innocent of any wrongdoing but didn't succeed.

Leif looked like he was about to offer yet another of piece of his mind, no doubt about to berate the poor man on his poor service and the skills the Chef was lacking. Deciding there and then that enough was enough Topaz leaned over the table to whisper fiercely under her breath, beyond annoyed with his rude behaviour.

"Just take the salad." She added a glare for good measure.

Leif sighed loudly, admitting partial defeat. "Very well, I'll have the salad, but no cheese on it." He handed his menu back to the waiter.

"And for you, Madame?" The waiter turned to Tope. She bestowed a dazzling smile on him, trying to make up for

Leif's rudeness. Leif took a sip of his water, avoiding looking at her.

"I'll have the steak please," she answered the waiter, ignoring Leif's shocked intake of breath and his subsequent chocking, as he coughed up his mouthful of water. "Medium to well done, with the vegetables and potatoes." She handed the menu back to him with another smile.

"Very good, Madame, an excellent choice, it is our speciality, very popular." He winked at her and walked away to deliver their orders.

Topaz turned back to her date to see him gathering his things and standing up from the table. She allowed him to do so without comment. She didn't want to spend another second in his company and was not about to stop him if he decided to leave.

"I'm sorry, but I can have no future with someone who would partake in animal flesh."

"We had a future?" she muttered under her breath, but Leif continued with his rejection speech. She let him ramble on, stifling a yawn, bored now, propping her elbow on the table and resting her chin in her hand.

"You're not what I thought you would be, Topaz Thompson, I'm very disappointed, you are nothing like Summer Rain said you were." He turned his back on her and walked away, pausing at the front desk, no doubt to complain about the potatoes and then left.

Topaz let out a sigh of relief. "Screw you and the horse you rode in on," she grumbled at his retreating form, resisted the urge to cast a small spell, just to freeze his vocal cords for the next day or two; personally she felt that she would be doing the whole world a big favour.

This had to have been the worst date of her life so far, and she had had some bad ones. The waiter, seeing Leif leave, made his was cautiously back to the table.

"Would you like me to cancel the orders for you?"

9

She looked up at him. "Yes please, and could you bring me the bill for the drinks we had? The cheap git didn't even leave enough to cover his cider." Topaz wasn't in the mood for food now, she wanted alcohol and lots of it, drowning her sorrows was the way to go.

"Certainly, Madame," he leaned down and said in a low voice. "I am sorry about your date."

"What, that he was a pompous, arrogant arse or that he left me alone to foot the bill?" She smiled to show that she was fine with it and that she had had a narrow escape. She dreaded to think what he would have come up with to complain about if they had gone on to see the play as they had planned.

"The first one."

Topaz smiled a little wider at his answer and nodded in agreement.

"So am I, and you should be grateful that you didn't have to listen to his lecture on global warming. Don't worry about me, my girlfriends are in the bar across the street and I think I might join them."

While the waiter fetched her bill, she dug out her mobile phone and called her friend Geena, a member of her coven, the 'Summer Rain' Leif had referred to. The phone connected and began to ring.

When Geena finally answered, the background noise made it obvious that she was out on the town.

"Topaz, honey. How's the date going? Isn't he just fabulous? As soon as I met him I knew he would be just perfect for you."

Topaz was stunned, but not into silence. Did she not know her at all?

"Perfect for me?" she hissed into the phone, trying to control her temper and not disturb the other diners any more than they already had. "He was unbearable. He was rude, judgemental and a know-it-all. He didn't let me get a word in edge ways and when he kissed me hello, he sniffed me,

10

SNIFFED ME, Geena, then he proceeded to complain about the fact that I had showered and lecture me on the waste of water." Her voice had risen to a shrill yell and she took a deep breath to calm herself down. "Remind me never to agree to go on a date with someone you meet and think is perfect for me, ever again."

"So you didn't like him?" Geena asked innocently, but Topaz detected a hint of a giggle in her voice.

"I like him about as much as you like polyester," she answered, putting the phone down on her so called friend's reply. She dropped the phone back into her bag and yanked out her purse, glad that for once she had stopped on the way home to get some money out of the bank. She sighed deeply.

What had she learnt? Never let your friends set you up on a blind date, it's more trouble than it's worth. That, and the fact that all the men she met seemed to be losers of the highest degree and she was doomed to die alone with nothing but cats for company. Roll on old age.

As the last student finally left to go home, Topaz relaxed back into her chair and swung her feet up on the desk, a naughty luxury she never normally allowed herself to do. It was the end of term and it had begun to feel like it would never get there. She was looking forward to a nice relaxing break at home. She had lots to do, rooms to decorate and lessons to plan for her new students. Nowhere to go, and nobody to see, she could please herself, it was going to be fantastic. Topaz couldn't wait to get out of there.

Don't misunderstand, she loved her job teaching at the adult college. She had been on board right from the start and had seen it prosper and gain respect from others in their field. Athena's Academy was no ordinary college. Athena's specialised in all things weird and wonderful. Set up 10 years ago by her friends Andy and Clarissa Johnson, two of the world's best known psychics. They dealt with the world of the supernatural. Andy gave lessons in spiritual healing and Clarissa in Meduimship. Other classes included Tarot Reading, Ghosts and Haunting's, Angels and Supernatural Forces.

Topaz taught Mythology and Folklore, specialising in Supernatural creatures from myth and legend. She had always had an interest in the supernatural world from a very young age. Becoming a Wiccan in her last year at school and reading up on every subject she could lay her hands on, eventually changing her name legally from Sarah to Topaz, her chosen Wiccan name.

She had drifted from one low paid job to the other for a few years before meeting Andy and Clarissa on a ghost hunt. They had gotten talking and they had been impressed with her knowledge. They had invited her to their house the next night and then explained about their new project, Athena's. She had loved the sound of it and had agreed to join their staff straight away, that had been 9 years ago and she hoped that she was now a valued member of their staff.

Athena's was not just a college, they ran a web site dedicated to their work and published a twice yearly newsletter. Topaz often went on fact finding trips and wrote articles for the magazine.

Her thoughts were interrupted by a soft knock on the open classroom door. She looked up to find Andy lounging on the door frame. He was your average looking man, average height, medium brown hair cut short, warm brown eyes and an open, cheery face. There was nothing average about his talent though, and his average looks had been a great advantage to his work; people warmed to him almost immediately, making him a very popular medium for first timers. He always came highly recommended and was booked up months in advance.

Topaz smiled at him as he entered, grabbed a chair from the ring of chairs that formed her teaching space, she liked to sit in with her students as much as possible, spun it round and straddled it. She waited for him to settle himself comfortably before speaking.

"Hey, Andy, how's it going? Looking forward to our holiday?"

"Yeah, I am, we have a few of our regular clients scheduled in but that's it. You got any plans?" he asked innocently. She was not fooled for a second, Andy was up to something. He had that look on his face, that I'm-about-to-drop-a-bombshell-now look. Topaz saw her plans for the holiday fading before her eyes. But she was feeling generous today and decided to hear him out. Get the bad news straight away and get it over with, kinda like ripping off a plaster, do it quick and it's done. She had a quick look at his aura and didn't like what she saw. It was his usual gold colour but was pulled in close to his body, shielding from her. *Damn*, she thought, *this man knows me too well*.

"OK, spill it, what do you want from me?" Blunt, her? Never.

"We have a mission for you," he began and Topaz groaned, she didn't want to go on yet another fact finding trip.

"Oh, Andy, not again. Can't you get someone else to do it? I just want a nice, quiet holiday at home. I don't want to go rushing off on some wild goose chase yet again," she whined, because that's what most of them were, wild goose chases, normally engineered by a sad person with too much time on their hands. Pick on the ones with the radical ideas, it's not like they have feelings or pride. OK, she was mentally ranting again, a bad habit of hers.

"We can't send anyone else, we need you," he looked at her pleadingly and she sighed and waved him to continue, might as well hear him out before she said no. "We need your special skills."

Special skills my butt, she thought, flattery would get him nowhere, she had fallen for that one too many times. But

13

damn her pride and curiosity, now she just had to know. She tried not to sound too suspicious when she answered.

"What for?" OK, that did sound suspicious, even to her ears.

"We have been contacted by someone, a man named Mason Barrett." The name didn't ring any bells.

"And?"

"He is a member of our online community and has been following our work, yours in particular. He has decided that he is fed up with all the rumours circulating about his kind and wants to set the record straight. He knows you are the authority on all things Supernatural and wants you to write the article for him. He wants you to visit with him."

"Well what does he want me to do? What is so special about him?" Andy's words came back to her. "What do you mean his *kind*?"

Andy looked at her for a second, seeing if he had hooked her yet, then cocked his head towards the door. Topaz waved her hand in its general direction and it slammed shut.

Once the door was closed he leaned forward to look her in the eyes. OK, she'd admit it, now she was very curious, it must be something big for Andy to be this cautious, he was normally so open, inviting anyone around at the time, to chime in with their opinion.

Andy finally opened his mouth and spoke.

"He's a Vampire, Tope."

She burst out laughing, she couldn't help it. He'd been suckered in again.

"Oh, Andy, you've been got good. A Vampire? A real un-live Vampire? Yeah right. No one has ever met one. It's probably some wanna-be goth guy that stumbled across our website and decided to make trouble."

Andy just looked at her, waiting for her hysterics to end. "We think he's for real."

"Why? What makes this time so different to the dragon sighting?" That one had been embarrassing, she had travelled all the way to Cornwall to find a bloke with a private collection of lizards. "And what about the unicorn that turned out to be a pony with a plastic horn stuck on for their daughter's birthday? I'm not being laughed at again, Andy, no freakin' way."

"He gave us his name, place of birth, everything. It all checks out."

"So what?" Anyone could look up public records, especially now everyone was looking into their family trees.

"The records are from 1890."

That stopped her for a second, while her mind raced to catch up. Could it be true, a Vampire? She had dreamed of meeting one for years, having always been fascinated with the creatures. The idea of them existing was too good to be true. It had to be a wind up, someone's idea of a joke.

"Anyone could have looked up old birth records, Andy."

"Yes, but he provided the information of his death too."

Topaz felt a little chill run down her spine at this comment.

"What did you find out?" She hardly dared to believe.

"He died in 1910, apparently in a fall from his horse. There was a photo of him in the records, a family photo taken the year he died."

She could feel herself getting more excited by the second, but tried to control it, she didn't want to get excited about some loser with a Vampire fetish.

"How do you know it's him?"

"He sent me a photo of him taken 3 weeks ago in the bar he works at, he looks exactly the same, except his hair has changed." She knew she was openly gaping at Andy by this point but didn't care.

He pulled a photo out of his pocket and handed it to her. She looked at the picture of a young man. He was very good looking, with black hair, swept back from his face. He had sculpted cheek bones, so sharp you could cut yourself on them. His nose was fine and straight. He had a cheeky,

15

flirty smile on his face and just visible under his lips was a pair of wicked looking fangs. She looked back up at Andy, disbelief written all over her face.

"Are you serious? Really and truly serious? He's a real Vampire? Like with fangs, who drinks blood? That kind of Vampire?"

Andy was chuckling by this point; he knew he had her attention now. He knew she would do anything to know if he really was a Vampire. And he knew that she would have to find out for herself, believing no one else. Supernatural creatures were her life's work. His aura swelled before her eyes. He was no longer shielding, he knew she wouldn't yell now.

"Yes, that kind of Vampire. He wants to do an interview with you. He said in his email that he liked the articles you wrote on werewolves. He liked the way you handled their situation and how you portrayed them in a good light. He wants people who matter i.e. our members and staff to know the truth. He thinks you're the one to do it."

That had been a good article even if she said so herself, she had researched lycanthropes extensively and put together a pretty convincing argument for them being real, too bad all her adverts for a real Were to come forward had met with failure, but she still dreamed of one day meeting one.

"Well, yeah, I guess I could understand that. I'm kinda flattered. What do I have to do, where do I meet him?"

"That's the catch, he lives in Scotland, Edinburgh to be exact. You have to travel to him. He wants you to meet him on Monday night at Night Walkers, the bar he works at."

"Monday! He wants to meet on Monday? But it's already Friday. I can't get everything sorted out and get to Scotland in 3 days." Topaz had jumped up and began to pace back and forth behind her desk, waving her arms around in the air above her head, doing a good impression of a demented windmill.

16

Andy watched her with amusement for a few seconds before deciding she had suffered enough.

"Calm down, love, it's all sorted. We've booked you tickets on a flight to Edinburgh leaving Sunday lunch time. That way you will have time to settle into your hotel and explore before you have to meet him on Monday night. And as he doesn't want to meet until midnight." She made a face at this, how clichéd could you get?

"You will have all day Monday to yourself. Think of it as a holiday with a little work thrown in. You can go home tonight, relax, pack on Saturday and make arrangements to have someone pop in and water your plants and be off on Sunday, no problem." Andy looked pleased with himself.

She looked at him, trying to look stern but failing, she was so excited to be meeting a real Vampire. Damn, she would be disappointed if he turned out to be a fake. Topaz shook her head to dispel the negative thoughts. Andy had done his best, sorting out everything for her so she wouldn't have to.

"Looks like you've got it all planned out, don't you, Andy? Bit sure of yourself aren't you?"

"Just to make it easier for you, Topaz. It was purely a selfless act, I assure you." He laid his hand on his heart and adopted a sincere expression. She wasn't fooled for a minute.

"You are so full of bull, Andy, but I love you anyway." She walked around the desk and gave him a big hug. "This is so big; can you imagine it? Real Vampires, just like I always dreamed. I have been trying all my life to prove that they exist and all I ever got for my troubles was ridicule. Well not this time, this time I'll have proof."

"Hang on a minute, darling, there's another, little teeny, catch." He held up his thumb and forefinger, leaving about a millimetre gap between them. "You can't try to go public with your article. We have to keep it just for us. Not for the mainstream population. It's one of his conditions, something about not being allowed to go public yet, he said he would

17

explain more to you when you meet. Anyway, I had to promise that the information would be kept locked on our website, only people with the right clearance, namely our members, will be able to access it. And it will be locked so it cannot be copied or distributed without our knowledge."

Topaz saw her dreams of worldwide notoriety fading before her eyes. All her hopes of silencing the sceptics that had made fun and belittled her, were shot to pieces. She took a deep breath and forced herself to think rationally, she would know the truth, and the people who mattered most would know, that would be good enough for her.

"OK, Andy, I'm in. I'll go. I'll meet the guy and do an interview. I'll bring back our proof, I promise." She gave him a kiss on the cheek and another hug. He grinned at her.

"You get off home; I'll pick you up at eleven Sunday morning, to take you to the airport. I'll bring your ticket with me, and all of your hotel information." He broke their hug and headed to the door, his bright gold aura almost blinding her now, and she quickly closed down her psychic sight.

"Thanks, Andy, I really appreciate this." She waved as he left and sank back down into her chair. Her head was spinning. A real Vampire. Could it be true? Damn, she hoped it was.

"Shit," she muttered to herself. This holiday might just change her life.

Chapter 2

Topaz stood at the window of her hotel room and looked out. The cheap bed and breakfast she was staying in would never win any style awards, but it was clean and comfortable, that was all she needed; she wasn't that comfy with posh anyway.

The window looked out onto a charming street. She could easily imagine a horse and carriage trotting down the road. After gazing out for a good ten minutes she moved away from the window and over to the bed where she had laid her case.

She sighed, having put it off long enough, she opened her case and started to unpack, not her favourite job. She began to think through the days to come as she sorted out her clothes. First she had to get some dinner, that was a must, she hadn't eaten since breakfast and it was now after six. After that she had planned to check out the bar the supposed Vampire, worked at. She didn't want to talk to anyone tonight, just wanted to get an idea of what to expect. She wanted to take a look at the area, see what the bar was like, if it had a dress code and more importantly, how easy it was to get back to the hotel. If this meeting turned out bad, or Mason tried anything, she wanted to have an escape route. Paranoid? Her? Never.

Determined that she was going to relax a bit while away, she had booked a bus tour around the city for Tuesday morning.

Happy with her plans and finally unpacked, Topaz set up her altar (very subtle, just a candle, a sea shell, a stone and a small incense cone) on the dresser. She never felt completely comfortable anywhere without some kind of work place. She grabbed her bag and headed out of the room and down to the front desk.

The little old lady who had shown her to her room earlier was still there, sitting in a chair, watching a small television behind the desk that was showing a soap opera.

She waited patiently for the lady to spot her, it didn't take too long. She tore herself away from the action on the screen, a couple arguing over who was the real daddy, and stood up with a smile, straightening her house coat as she did so.

"Hello there, lass, Is your room satisfactory? You needing anything?"

Topaz smiled back, she always had a soft spot for oldies, before answering.

"Yes, thank you, the room is lovely, I'm just a little hungry and wanted to ask if you could recommend a good restaurant, not too expensive, in the area of Market Street?"

"Aye, of course, there are some lovely ones all around there. What do you fancy?"

"Just something simple. Like maybe pizza or a pub that offers food?"

"Yes, well there's a Pizza Express out that way, I think, and a couple of nice pubs. I would recommend just heading out and seeing if anything takes your fancy. Just to warn you though, we do lock our doors at midnight, so if you're going to be out later than that I shall have to give you a key

20

for the front door. Just no bringing anyone home with you. We don't allow that sort of thing here."

She said 'that sort of thing' like she was talking about drowning kittens or something equally as disgusting. Pre-marital sex, the evil of the world. As a Witch, Topaz didn't hold with that idea, if you liked someone, do what came naturally, not that she had had much chance to get down and natural with anyone recently.

She shook her head to dispel her thoughts and smiled at the stern look on the lady's face. Like Topaz was going to be lucky enough to get any action, her love life was drier than the Sahara.

"I wouldn't dream of bringing anyone back, I'm here on a research trip, not a singles holiday. I'm not planning on being out too late, but can I take a key just in case?" The lady looked a little happier at the thought that she was only here for research. She cheerfully handed over the key and the number for a local cab company, along with a street map, obviously content that she would not be turning her home into a knocking shop any time soon, and waved her out the door.

Pretty soon Topaz was happily wandering down the road, heading in the general direction of Market Street. She loved to look around, spot interesting shops to come back to and watch the people going about their business.

She had decided to head that way for a number of reasons, one being that Waverley Bridge was just off of it, which was the place her bus tour departed from in the morning and two, it was close enough to Victoria Street, the location of the bar Mason, the Vampire, worked at. Market Street was going to be her marker, she decided, the place she would head back to if she got lost, which was a strong possibility, given that directions were not her strong point. It was not a very complicated plan, but it was a plan none the less and she was going to stick to it.

21

It took her a long time to make it to her destination, more because she kept stopping to look around, snap off a few photos and consult the street map, than actual distance. Well, she was supposedly on holiday after all.

Once on Market Street, she found a small pub, near to the turn off for Victoria Street, which looked cosy. She had a quick look at the menu on the door out front and decided that it was the place for her, good simple food and reasonably priced. What more could a low paid educator wish for?

She took a table near the window after she had given her order of lasagne and chips -waist line be dammed, she was on holiday and was going to be bad- to the bar maid while she ordered herself a coke. She watched the people walking past the window as she waited for her food to arrive. She had only been in town for a few hours but already felt comfortable. All the people seemed very friendly; she was looking forward to her tour the next day.

Soon her food was placed in front of her by a smiling young man. She thanked him and began to eat. It was delicious, the chips were chunky and crispy, just how she liked them and the lasagne was juicy with a generous amount of cheese on top, browned nicely. *Oh cheese, you were sent to tempt me,* she thought to herself.

After eating as much as she could and now feeling pleasantly full, she paid for her meal and, leaving a generous tip, headed back out in search of Victoria Street and the club.

She gazed up the street at the bar. There was a long line of people waiting outside, none of which seemed to be gaining access to the inner sanctum. They were all dressed in various degrees of Goth, almost all of them sporting paper white faces and lots of eye liner, men included. Damn, she felt under dressed.

Night Walkers was big, the outside was painted dark red, while the windows were blacked out, giving you no clue as to what the inside held.

Suited bouncers guarded the entrance, wearing black sunglasses even at ten o'clock at night. They stood with their hands clasped in front of them and stared ahead, turning only to tell someone that, no, they could not come in, the club was full. She took a moment to study their auras, looking for a clue that might help her and was shocked by what she saw. Their auras were a mess, a jumble of colours, swirling around like a rainbow in a tornado. They made her dizzy just to look at them. She had never seen anything like it before, but she had never been one to let a little thing like that put her off.

She girded her loins and slapped a flirty smile on her face, it never hurt to be friendly, and tried to stroll confidently up to the entrance, acting like she belonged there even if she did stick out like a sore thumb. One of the bouncers glanced at her with interest, her smile was working.

"Hello, darling, are you lost?" He smiled back at her, flashing a lot of teeth. So much for blending.

They both had dark hair, slicked back and from what she could see of their faces around the sunglasses, she could tell they were both breathtakingly handsome. Muscles strained the shoulders of their jackets. You definitely didn't want to mess with them.

She smiled a bit wider before answering. "No, I'm not lost, I'm supposed to meet someone here tomorrow night, and just though I'd check it out before hand, you know, get a feel for the place."

The bouncers smile slipped a little.

"Sorry, love, no can do. This place is members only unless you're invited. Also you don't meet the dress code." He gestured behind him with his thumb, at the waiting crowd.

23

"Well, what am I going to do then?" Topaz asked. She was beginning to think that the whole trip was one big wind up, and that it was, as she had suspected, some goth play acting. No one had told her that she had to be a member of this stupid club just to get in to meet her contact. Her smile must have slipped a little, the disappointment showing on her face, as the bouncer seemed to feel sorry for her.

"Well, if you say you are meeting someone here," he paused and cocked an eyebrow in question.

"Oh, I'm meeting Mason, the bartender," she hurriedly supplied. He nodded before carrying on.

"Well, give us your name, and come back tomorrow night, in the right clothes of course, and well check with Mase. If he says yes, you're in. If not, sorry, you've had a wasted trip."

"Is that it, my only option?" she asked. He nodded. She sighed, defeated.

"In that case, my name is Topaz Thompson, and I guess I'll see you tomorrow night then."

Having no other option, she turned away and headed back the way she had come, it looked like she would not need the use of her key tonight after all.

Nine o'clock the next morning found Topaz -well rested after her enforced early night- standing outside an alternative clothing store, waiting for it to open. She had passed the shop the night before on her way back to the hotel. A dress had caught her eye, and knowing that she needed to dress the part for the Vampire bar to let her in, she had made a note of the opening time and come back. Its name of High Vampage

Movement inside the shop dragged her attention back to the present and she moved away from the wall she had been leaning against and stood up straighter. The closed sign flipped round to open and the lock clicked back. She immediately pushed open the door and went in -no point putting it off- startling the shop assistant standing behind it.

The assistant looked completely at home in the shop. She was small, about 5ft 3 at her guess. She had short, spiky black hair with indigo tips. She had one of those small, dinky little faces that always reminded Topaz of a pixie. Her eyes were heavily lined, big black streaks that started on the inner corners and swept out into a dramatic flick. That helped with the decision; she figured it was as good a place as any to start her, very reluctant, transformation.

She didn't like dressing in black, it was a matter of principle. Being a witch meant that people expected her to wear a pointy hat and carry a broom stick. She didn't like to feed misconceptions like that. The girl looked tough and scary as hell.

"Holy shit," the girl clutched at her chest, "you scared the crap out of me."

OK, maybe not that scary. She had a light Scottish accent, a girly, sing-song kind of voice totally at odds with her appearance.

"Oh, I'm so sorry, I didn't mean to startle you." Topaz reached out a hand to steady the girl. The girl smiled.

"That's OK, no harm done. It's just that most of our customers come in after midday, I'm not used to people waiting to come in. I was just going to make a cup of coffee, would you like one?" Topaz immediately revised her opinion of her and decided she was her new best friend.

Topaz nodded, she had only had one, very small, cup in her room before she showered, and she normally needed at least a bucket full to start her day.

"I'd love one, I've got a feeling I'm going to be in here a long time." She followed the girl over to a door at the back of the shop to look at the rack of tops there.

"How do you take your coffee?" the girl called out.

"Milk, two sugars if you have it," she replied, fingering a top that was so see-through she suspected she would get arrested if she wore it in public, and glanced around at what else was on offer. The sight did not instil her with confidence.

"Here you go," the shop assistant was back, handing Topaz a steaming mug full of golden coffee. She took an appreciative sip and groaned, closing her eyes in bliss.

"Oh, thank you, I need this."

The girl moved over to the counter and put her cup down.

"Right, let's get down to business, my name is Veronica, call me Ronnie, how can I help?" She held out her small hand to shake.

"I'm Topaz," she took the tiny hand in her own, and tried not to crush it as they shook, "and I find myself in need of an outfit for tonight. Nothing too mad and it must be comfortable."

Ronnie whistled. "You don't want much do you?" She laughed "I can tell that it's not your usual style, and that you probably don't live around here."

Topaz looked down at herself in her favourite long floaty skirt and peasant blouse and laughed too. Yeah, she could take that.

"Right and right. I could never carry off what you're wearing," She gestured to the girl's corset and skinny 'Morticia Addams' style skirt. "I'm visiting for work."

"What kinda work do you do that you need this get up?"

She debated over what to tell Ronnie but decided a watered down version of the truth was the best way to go, she was a terrible liar, she'd get nervous and begin to stammer.

"I teach at a college and help out with their website. I'm looking into popular Vampire culture and have been invited to a club in town by one of our members."

"No kidding," Ronnie looked impressed. "What website, sounds like my kind of thing."

"It's the website for our college, Athena's Academy."

26

"Wow, I know it. I'm a member. Wait, did you say your name's Topaz. Are you Topaz Thompson?"

"Guilty," she confessed. Ronnie looked at her as if star struck.

"Oh my God, I love your stuff, I've read it all. And you're working here? What club you going to?"

"Night Walkers, It's just down the road from here."

Ronnie began to bounce on the spot, jumping up and down and clapping like a cheerleading seal.

"I'm going there tonight. We have to get you something fabulous to wear, follow me." She abandoned her coffee and grabbed Topaz's hand, dragging her across the shop to a rack of dresses. She pulled one out and held it up against her, before stepping back to look at it. Topaz looked down at the dress, it looked like it belonged on the bride of Dracula. She shook her head.

"It's not really me," she said gently, not wanting to offend.

Ronnie looked at her again and nodded her head in agreement.

"Yeah, maybe a little less, well... just less." She turned to peruse the rack again before heading off in another direction. Tope followed with a sigh, this was going to take a long time.

After what seemed like hours, and many unsuitable dresses later, Ronnie held up a dress that took Topaz's breath away. Now *that* she could pull off. It was black, with a long floating skirt attached to a corset style top, the sleeves were also floaty, made of the same silky material as the skirt. It reminded her of a medieval gown and came with a lovely cloak, in a deep purple velvet. Black ankle boots would complete the outfit. She grabbed it in joy and rushed into the changing room, she *had* to try this one on.

She pulled back the curtain of the dressing room and stepped out. Ronnie took one look at her and began to clap her hands, wolf whistling in appreciation. Topaz could get used to that.

27

Tope turned to the mirror and struck a dramatic pose. She looked so good, the dress hugged her in all the right places and hid the bits that she hated. The top pushed up her boobs and cinched in her waist, the skirt swishing around her ankles like a dream. It would look fantastic on the dance floor.

"That's it, that's the one. It's perfect, very you. It fits you like it was made to measure." Ronnie whirled away like a tornado and raced over to a counter full of cosmetics.

"Now you just need the right makeup. A nice purple to match the cloak I think, and some eyeliner, dark lipstick. You're going to look fabulous." They looked very scary to Topaz, who began to back away which stopped Ronnie in her tracks.

"Hang on just one bloody minute, I'm not wearing all that, I wouldn't have a clue what to do with it."

"Don't worry, I can help. I'll come by your hotel later and we can get ready together, we'll have such a great time." Ronnie looked so excited she didn't have the heart to say no. Topaz heaved a deep sigh and resigned herself to the fact that she was going to have extra company that night, no getting out of it.

"OK, OK. Ring it up, I'll take it." She returned to the changing room and wriggled out of the dress, pulling on her own, more comfortable clothes.

By the time Ronnie had rung up and wrapped all her purchases her purse was considerably lighter. She hoped it was all going to be worth it, as she would probably never go anywhere to wear it again. After arranging with Ronnie to meet later at her hotel, she headed off to Waverley Bridge at a quick trot, she only had ten minutes to catch the tour bus or wait another hour for the next one.

The tour had been wonderful. The guide had been very knowledgeable, making the history of the city very interesting, funny and enjoyable. He pointed out all the

28

popular landmarks and the journey had gone by very quickly. Topaz had enjoyed it immensely. She had stopped on her way back to the hotel to pick up a pizza to share with Ronnie while they were getting ready.

Laying the pizza box on the little table in the corner of her room, she decided a shower would be just the thing to make her feel fresher after the bus trip. It had been an open topped, double-decker bus and the fumes from the other cars and buses had made her feel grimy, the smell seeming to cling to her hair and skin.

She stripped off her dirty clothes and folded them carefully before tucking them into her suitcase.

She gathered up some clean underwear that would work under the dress and turned on the shower, letting the water run till it came through hot.

She was just rinsing the conditioner out of her hair when a knock sounded on the outside door. Grabbing a towel from the rack, she wrapped it around herself toga style and ignoring her dripping hair, she rushed out to answer. The lady owner was standing there, her hands on her hips and a stern look on her face. Ronnie was standing behind her, she waved cheerfully at Topaz over the lady's shoulder, seemingly unconcerned with the hostile welcome.

"Oh, Mrs Baker, is something wrong?" Topaz asked worried, had something happened back home, had Andy called looking for her, was her house still standing?

"Aye, my dear, there is. I found this," she turned to Ronnie and raked her with a gaze full of distain, "person, coming in through me reception and heading for the stairs. When I questioned her she said that she was meeting you in your room. I told her that Miss Thompson would never associate with the likes of her, that you were a good, God fearing girl." She wound down and gave Ronnie another scowl, before turning to Topaz again. Ronnie smothered a giggle. Tope smiled sweetly at the old woman, trying to diffuse the situation.

"Mrs Baker, this is my friend Ronnie. I did invite her up, she's helping me get ready for a night out. Thank you so much for seeing her up. Now if you would please excuse us," she gestured down to her towel, Mrs Baker immediately squawked in alarm, only just noticing her state of undress, "I need to get dressed. I'm getting quite cold standing out here in the hall."

Topaz glanced about meaningfully, as if looking for someone coming down the hall. The realisation that she was standing in nothing but a towel hit Mrs Baker and she practically shoved Ronnie through the open door, before turning on her heel and trotting off down the stairs, back to her beloved reception desk.

Topaz shut the door behind her and leaned against it. She risked a glance at Ronnie and regretted it instantly. One look at her face had her bursting out laughing.

"Oh, she hated you," Topaz pointed out. "She must think you're the devil incarnate, dressed like that." Ronnie looked down at herself, she was clad in yet another corset, this time red, and a very short, puffy black skirt that reminded Topaz of a tutu. She had on black and red, stripy stockings and knee-high boots with a wicked stiletto heel. Her make-up was even darker than before. She shrugged in acknowledgement.

"Yeah, I guess I might look a little scary to her. You wait until she sees you later, your 'God fearing' little Topaz image will be gone for good."

Topaz shook her head in exasperation, she could tell that the night was going to be interesting in more ways than one.

"I'm going to get dry, help yourself to pizza, I got plain as I didn't know if you ate meat." She had a quick flash back to Leif, the disastrous date, and felt a shudder of revulsion run over her skin.

She shut the bathroom door behind her and slipped into her dressing gown. She plugged in her hair dryer and began to run it over her wet locks.

As she worked her mind wandered to other bad dates she had had over the years. There was Charlie, the body builder. That had turned her off straight away, she didn't like bulging muscles. He had been sweet enough but was as dumb as a brick. She needed someone who could keep up with her mentally.

Next came Jake, an accountant, he had given her some good advice on her mortgage but that was it.

Bob had been almost as bad as Leif in the environmental stakes, he had insisted on having a picnic in a local park, which was fine until he had stopped her feeding the ducks- something she loved to do, childish as it was- and had wanted to keep all the rubbish to recycle at home, explaining that he would wash out all the little pots and re-use the tinfoil. She was all for doing her bit for the environment but that was just being cheap in her opinion.

She sighed, why couldn't she just meet a decent man for once? One who treated her well but let her know her own mind? One who could accept her intellectual pursuits and support her work. One who took care of his appearance without being vainer than a male model. Was that too much to ask? Apparently, the answer was yes.

She thought about her first love, the man, well, boy really, who had dumped her and broken her heart. She had met Bradley (Bradders to his friends) at school, and they had dated for about a year, until Bradley got into a college 200 miles away. Not that far away if you were willing to work at a long distance relationship, but far enough away that he felt the need to dump her, telling her that he didn't want to be tied down and to drive off into the sunset, his new life beckoning. She pulled a face at her reflection in the mirror, the face she always pulled when she thought about that situation.

Last she had heard, he had moved back to their old town with a wife and 3 kids in tow. His promising career had been cut short when his then girlfriend, now wife, had got pregnant and he had to drop out of University. He was now an assistant manager at the local supermarket. She had had an evil rush of pleasure upon hearing that. Remembering that made her expression brighten considerably.

She chuckled to herself as she switched off the dryer and began to run a brush through her hair. It was a vibrant shade of red that hung in glossy curls down to her waist, it was her pride and joy, and all natural, thank you very much. She sprayed it liberally with anti-frizz spray and was good to go; she rarely did anything complicated with her hair, either putting it up in a simple ponytail or leaving it down.

She entered the bedroom to find Ronnie sprawled out on her bed watching T.V. Topaz looked into the Pizza box and found that she had left her exactly half of the pizza, good girl. She plucked a slice from the box and took a big bite. She was starving and was determined to eat before she went out, she hated to drink on an empty stomach. It was still warm, delicious and she ate it with relish, feeling the cheese hit and stick to her hips with every mouthful, unfair, but that was life. She shrugged her shoulders and took another slice, flopping down on the bed next to Ronnie, the pizza box on the duvet beside them.

When she was finally done eating and had washed her hands, she stood before Ronnie, who was still on the bed and threw up her arms dramatically.

"OK, do your worst." Ronnie looked up and raised one eyebrow at her theatrics, in silent question.

"Do your worst? What do you think I'm going to do to you? Shave you bald and pierce your nose?" She shook her head. "Amateur, go get your pretty dress on and then I'll do your makeup."

Topaz grinned at her and grabbed the dress from where she had hung it on the wardrobe door. She slipped into it in the bathroom and did a little model pose when she came back out.

"Very nice," Ronnie said with a smile of approval. "Sit your butt down here and let me work my magic." She pointed to the one and only chair the room possessed, which she had set in front of the bed where she was still sitting.

Topaz sat down and relaxed back into the chair, trying very hard to ignore the scarily dark colours Ronnie had laid out next to her on the bed. She closed her eyes and let Ronnie work her 'magic', sweeping powder over her face and colour onto her eyes. No blush obviously, those goths liked to be pale. She felt lipstick being painted onto her lips a second before Ronnie announced, "There you're done, take a look."

Topaz's heart leapt in her chest, oh Goddess, what did she look like? Ronnie was a lovely person but her own make up was in no way subtle.

"It's not that bad I promise," Ronnie giggled, correctly reading her expression of dread.

Tope got up from the chair and turned to look in the mirror. Her mouth dropped open when she saw her reflection staring back. Ronnie had used a dark plum colour on her eyelids, surrounded by a pretty lilac. She had outlined her eyes with kohl and added mascara to her lashes. It looked wonderful, and the colours made the green of her eyes pop. The powder made the most of her already pale skin, leaving it looking flawless. This was so not her, but she liked it.

"Wow, Ron, I look amazing. You are so fabulous."

Ronnie preened, pleased with the compliment.

"Yeah, I know. I am pretty great." She glanced at her watch. "What time are you meeting your guy?"

"I don't have to meet him until midnight, so we have a bit of time before we need to be there."

"Well I say we go and have a drink before we head over."

Topaz picked up her bag and draped the cape over her shoulders. "Sounds like a plan, let's go."

33

They arrived at Night Walkers just after eleven, still giggling over the reaction they had received from Mrs Baker. They had breezed down the stairs, looking forward to their night out. Mrs Baker had taken one look at the dress Topaz was wearing and had crossed herself before announcing that she would pray for her soul. They had beat a hasty retreat after trying unsuccessfully to explain to Mrs B that Topaz was just dressed up for a night at a theme club, her frantic praying ringing in their ears.

Ronnie took charge and marched right up to the doors, ignoring the line of people waiting to get in. The bouncers smiled when they saw Ronnie.

"Hey, girl, not seen you for a few weeks. Where you been?" Topaz recognised the one who had spoken to her last night.

Ronnie smiled at the guy. "Oh, I've been around, just been taking a little break, recuperating, you know how it is," she winked cheekily, a suggestive leer on her face. Goddess, Topaz loved this girl, she was so glad she had met her.

"Yep," he stepped aside and opened the door for her, the sound of rock music floated out. "In you go."
Ronnie turned to Topaz and slipped her arm through hers.

"I'm taking my friend in with me, she's meeting with Mason inside." The bouncers looked at her.

"You the girl who came by last night?" She nodded. "You cleaned up well. We spoke to Mason when his shift finished last night and he vouched for you. You're in. Enjoy your night." He turned to Ronnie. "Explain the rules to her, she's your responsibility until Mason gets here, he seems to be running late."

Ronnie nodded and smiled. "No problem, Dane, I'll see that she behaves," she grinned at him and breezed through the doors. Topaz smiled at the bouncers and followed Ronnie inside.

Once inside she looked around in amazement. The inside of the club looked like a really cool Halloween party. The walls matched the outside, red walls and black paintwork. Framed pictures of movie Vampires adorned the walls, and plastic bats hung from the ceiling. Curtains hung from the walls, and she suspected that they lead to private rooms. People milled about in all manner of outfits, ranging from serious goth to jeans and t-shirts.

"Well that sucks," she muttered to herself, "I had to dress like an idiot to get in here." Ronnie giggled in response.

"Only new members or visitors are required to dress this way, older members get to ease off a little. Where are you meeting Mason?"

"At the bar. I guess I just have to wait there for him." She glanced at her watch. "I've got about 40 minutes to wait." Ronnie immediately grabbed her hand and began to tow her across the room to the dance floor.

"Good, you have time to dance with me for a bit then."

Ozzy Osborne's Bark at the Moon, began to play, sealing the deal. Topaz had a secret passion for classic rock music and she loved this song.

They danced along happily for a few songs until the DJ spoke over the sound system. "Ladies and Gentlemen, the dark hour is upon us." Iron Maiden's Two minutes to Midnight, began to blast out. Tope looked at her watch 11:59, she tapped Ronnie on the arm and pointed to her watch.

"I'm going to go meet this Mason guy, are you coming?" Ronnie shook her head.

"I'm gonna stay here, I've just spotted the guy I'm here to meet up with. I'll catch you later." She gave her a hug and danced off into the crowd. Topaz watched as Ronnie reached the side of a very handsome man. He smiled when he saw her and took her hand, leading her off the dance

35

floor. She watched them make their way to the back of the room and disappear behind one of the hanging curtains. Shaking her head in amusement she headed off to the bar.

Finding an empty bar stool, she sat down and waited for the busy bartender to get to her, which by the looks of it could take a while.

The bartender was dressed like he was the love child of Captain Jack Sparrow and Adam Ant. He was wearing one of those puffy shirts, tucked into black leather jeans. A colourful bandana was tied around his head, keeping his dark blond hair out of his eyes. He was chatting, flirting and laughing with every customer, shaking the cocktail shaker enthusiastically, making his gold hoop earrings jiggle around.

While she waited she studied the cocktail list, it had two sides to it, one said Mortal, while the other said Immortal. She ran her eyes down the Mortal list.

They all seemed in keeping with the club's theme, Death in the Afternoon, Corpse Reviver, Vampire, Wolfram, Zombie, Bloody Aztec, Dracula's Kiss, and a Black Cat, to name but a few.

She had already decided on a Tequila Sunrise, so out of curiosity she studied the Immortals list. They had all the same as the Mortal one but in each drink one ingredient had been substituted for blood and some of the names had been altered.

At the bottom was a list of blood types they carried. She put the menu down and chuckled over just how far they were prepared to go. It was a well thought out list, she could tell that great care had been taken over picking the drinks and working out the blood substitutions. They were certainly taking the Vampire idea to a whole new level. She guessed that people who ordered a drink from the Immortal side got an extra shot of something or a few extra cherries.

She took a quick squizz at the bartender's aura, a bad habit she knew, while she waited for him to finish up with his

36

other customers. She opened her third eye a little and focused on the man as he mixed up another cocktail, shaking it vigorously along with several parts of his anatomy. She did a quick double take and looked again, opening her mind a little more but she had been right the first time.

The man had no aura to speak of, there was a very faint blue line around his body but that was it. Either the man was a very strong psychic that kept his aura guarded or he was dead. She chuckled at her own little joke and closed her eyes, shutting down her third eye and that part of her that allowed her to see magic.

Chapter 3

Logan McGregor was sitting behind his desk trying to concentrate on the paperwork in front of him, but it felt like he was fighting a losing battle. He had been alright until about half an hour ago, then his focus had suddenly gone. He didn't know why but he felt restless, like something was stirring the air around him. When the phone on his desk rang he snatched it up almost immediately, grateful for the excuse to leave the accounts he was struggling with.

"Aye?" He answered the phone in his usual impatient manner.

"Logan, its Damian." Damian Durriken was his club manager, he handled everything Logan himself didn't want to deal with, drink orders, staff rotas and all that tedious stuff.

"Damian, is there a problem?" Damian rarely bothered him with trivial matters.

"Maybe, maybe not. It's Mason. He didn't show up tonight. Normally he's quite good about arranging cover or calling if he's not going to make it in."

Logan was a little concerned by this news, Damian was right, Mason was not the sort to leave them high and dry. He had always been a bit of a wanderer, disappearing for weeks on end, but he always let someone know to arrange cover for his shifts.

"Who is covering for him now?"

"Avery is working the bar tonight so we're OK at the moment, but I will have to sort something out for tomorrow just in case. I just wanted to let you know."

"Good man, call me if you need anything else." They said goodbye and Logan hung up. Never one to let anything go without checking, he turned to the computer screen sitting on the desk next to him, it was linked up to the club's security cameras, currently focused on the dance floor.

It was a busy night; the dance floor was almost packed to bursting with gyrating bodies. He pulled up the camera feeds on his computer and flicked over to the one that covered the bar area.

Sure enough there was Avery, working the bar like a pro, serving drinks and, from the cheeky smile on his face, flirting with most of the female customers. They all seemed to like and respond to the ex-pirates charisma and unique sense of style. No matter how much they tried they just couldn't get him to completely drop his pirate image and the result was an eclectic blend of new and old.

As he watched, Avery turned to a lone woman sitting on one of the stools that surrounded the bar. He leaned forward to take her order but then leaned closer at her gesture, allowing her to speak into his ear. Avery shook his head and turned to fix her drink. Logan zoomed in closer, curious.

It was unusual to see someone sitting alone at the bar. The woman had long curly hair that reached right down to her waist. She turned on her seat to look about her as she waited for her drink.

Catching sight of her face, Logan sucked in a great lungful of the charged air. Her face was one he had not seen for over four hundred years. He stared at her, almost mesmerised. He zoomed in closer until her face filled the small screen. It was uncanny, if he didn't know better Logan would have sworn that he was looking at his wife, his *dead* wife.

His darling Alcina, the love of his life. He had forgotten over the years just how beautiful she had been. His heart ached with the loss but at the same time his body reacted as it always had, hardening almost instantly. He shook himself out of his reminiscing. He had to meet her.

Jumping up he headed for the door and practically raced down the corridor that lead to the main club area. Flinging open the doors he strode up to the bar. His eyes quickly found her, and damn she was breath taking. His legs carried him forward of their own accord until he found himself standing behind her. He had to speak to her, introduce himself, get to know her. Focusing on the couple sitting next to her, he sent them the mental message that they desperately wanted to dance.

As soon as they vacated their seats he slid into the one next to the girl. She turned to look at him. She was even lovelier close up; her hair was a rich, vibrant red that he itched to run his fingers through. Her eyes were a dazzling green and her skin was pale and flawless.

The dress she was wearing showed him a little of what must be an amazing body that she had hidden away. The corset of the top had lifted her breasts up, almost presenting them for inspection. He gave them due attention before letting his gaze travel down to her gently rounded hips, full but not overly big, and her pert bottom. He stifled a small moan as a mental picture of what she would look like without the clothes popped into his head.

The air around Topaz suddenly seemed to vibrate with some unseen energy, making her turn in her seat.

She looked with interest at the man who had taken the seat next to her and instantly wished she hadn't, he was gorgeous. He had long, dark brown hair, tied back into a pony tail and warm brown eyes, flecked with gold. He had a nice straight nose and a strong jaw sprinkled with just a hint of stubble. He was wearing black jeans and a red shirt that hugged his chest like it had been painted on. She fought the urge to reach over and run her hand across his chest. She leaned back casually on the stool, pretending she was stretching her back and risked a quick glance down to his butt. It was tight and firm, just the way she liked it.

"Damn," she breathed.

He caught her looking and smiled at her. His smile was open and warm but had a cheeky quality to it that did all sorts of interesting things to her insides. She felt her breathing quicken as he leant forward towards her. Instinctively she leaned in too, closing the distance between them. He bent closer to speak into her ear, the volume of the music making conversation difficult.

"Hello, beautiful, my name is Logan, you must be new, I haven't seen you here before have I?" He held out his hand for her to shake. He had a deep Scottish accent that seemed to rub itself against her skin, making her shiver. She was pretty sure she would marry him right this second if he asked her.

She blushed slightly at his compliment, *he called me beautiful*, she silently squealed to herself and tried to answer him, but her throat had closed up and her mouth was dry, her tongue sticking to the roof of her mouth. He smelt so good, his scent wafting up her nose with every breath she took. She took another sniff and suppressed a shudder as desire zipped through her.

41

There was something about the man that she couldn't quite put her finger on. She took a sip of her drink and tried again, this time successfully. She put it down and took his hand in hers. Instantly she knew where the electrifying energy had come from. He radiated power and confidence. The power seemed to travel down her hand in waves, sinking into her skin and wrapping itself around her like a caress. She savoured it for a moment before speaking.

"Well, thank you, I'm flattered as it's not a bit true. I'm Topaz, it's nice to meet you. You're right, I am new, I'm just visiting, I was supposed to meet someone here but he didn't turn up."

Logan scowled a little at this, she was meeting someone? He was alarmed at the stab of jealousy that shot through him at the thought of her with someone else. He didn't know anything about her but it felt right to be sitting here with her, they had a connection.

He smoothed out his face, locking his emotions up tight. He had no claim over her, but he didn't have to like it.

"Well I come here a lot," he watched her rake her eyes up and down his body, obviously taking in his clothes. When she raised one eyebrow, he chuckled. "Who were you meeting, maybe I know him." And if he did he was going to warn him off. She smiled back, and the smile lit up her face.

"I had arranged to meet up with a man named Mason, he works the bar here. It was work, not pleasure I'm afraid and I guess he skipped out on me. Avery here," she gestured to the man further down the bar, still serving and flirting outrageously, this time with two good looking men, "said that he didn't come in tonight. I'm a bit disappointed though, I travelled all the way from London to meet him."

Logan smiled at her, relieved that she was not meeting a boyfriend or worse yet, another Vampire. He didn't like the thought of her being a Donor and allowing someone to feed from her. He made up his mind right there and then that he would make sure she would never be tempted to give herself to anyone but him.

"Well, Mason's not in today, but I'm sure it has nothing at all to do with you. No one in their right mind would stand you up." She felt her face flush at his compliment.

Logan waved at Avery to attract his attention, at the same time sending him a mental message to not mention who he was. Avery cocked an eyebrow his direction but remained silent, finishing off the drinks he was pouring and sliding them across to the waiting men.

Logan turned back to her; she had been watching the milling crowd with interest. She was particularly amused by the amount of people who had gone all out with the Vampire theme. Some were sporting fake fangs that flashed in the light when they spoke and others had gone as far as to paint puncture marks on their necks. If nothing else came out of this trip she would have some interesting stories to tell the guys at work. Catching sight of Logan looking at her, she turned back to him with an apologetic smile.

"Sorry, I was people watching, it's a bad habit of mine. Did you say something?"

He chuckled, the sound rumbling deep in his chest, a primal sound that almost made her melt. "Aye, I asked if you would care for another drink. I was hoping that I could make up for your wasted trip and enjoy the pleasure of your company tonight."

She stared at him, was he serious? How could a good looking man like this want to spend time with her? She dipped her eyes quickly down to his left hand, no wedding ring. But that didn't mean that he wasn't taken. How could he not be? Every man she ever dated was a loser, why would Logan be any different. She weighed up her options, she was only visiting here after all, what harm could it do? If a good looking *adult* man wanted to spend time with her, who was she to complain.

43

Logan watched the indecision on her face, fascinated by the play of emotions that showed in her expressions, her face like an open book. He waited patiently for her to get through thinking. Finally, she nodded.

"Yes, thank you, a drink would be lovely. I did come with a friend but she seems to have disappeared, so company would be great."

Avery made his way over and stopped before them.

"Yes, Sir, can I get you a drink, and maybe one for the fair lady?" He wiggled his eyebrows at Topaz, earning him a low growl from Logan. Avery looked at him in surprise. Topaz was oblivious, unable to hear much over the loud music, her hearing not being as acute as theirs.

Logan struggled to control his temper, Avery didn't know any better, he had only just met Topaz, how was he to know how Logan was feeling? That this woman here could very likely be his Soul Mate? He could feel their connection already, pulsing gently between them like a low voltage electrical current. He was already aware of a sense of wonder, and a little suspicion, coming from her, she was obviously not used to such attention. He would have to remedy that. He smiled at the thought of all he would like to do to woo her.

"The same again for Topaz and I'll have a scotch please, Avery, no ice."

Avery nodded, "Coming right up."

While they were waiting for their drinks, Logan decided that if he wanted to get to know Topaz he would have to get her talking. She had said that she was meeting Mason for work, he would start with that.

"So, what kind of work brings you here?"

She pulled her attention back to the man sitting next to her. She was surprised, most men she dated never wanted to talk about what she was interested in. She stopped

44

herself right there. She should not be allowing herself to think about dating Logan, she was going home in a few days. Work was a safe topic.

"I'm a teacher at an adult college. I specialise in folklore and the supernatural. Mason contacted our website and wanted to meet me. I'm researching popular Vampire culture in these modern times. People's impression of Vampires has changed a lot in the last century, I wanted to explore the reasons behind it. They are no longer feared as they once were; now they are seen less as scary monsters, and more as objects of fantasy. Why is it so popular now, that's what I want to know?" Logan nodded his head, appearing to agree with her. "I mean look around," she swept a hand out, gesturing to the swarming crowd. "Everyone here is either dressed like one or displaying signs of wanting to be with one. They are living the fantasy."

Topaz was a very interesting woman; her perception of the modern Vampire culture seemed accurate. He had given up his wanderings -as most Vampires did eventually- and decided to settle back in his native country of Scotland, buying the club so that he and his kind would have somewhere safe to meet, relax and be themselves, for just the reasons she had highlighted. He had made the bar as clichéd as he could, playing up the Vampire angle so that they could flash their fangs without worrying about mortals.

Topaz had been right when she had said that Vampires were popular, he had watched with fascination as mortals had lost some of their fear for his kind and began to offer themselves as willing Donors. The things he could tell her about Vampires would boggle her mind, but she obviously didn't know what he or some of the patrons of the bar, were. He stored away the fact that Mason had contacted her to worry about another time, tonight was for them alone.

"That is a very interesting topic. I hope you do well with it." He downed the last of his scotch and set down the glass.

45

He had been sitting next to her for too long, the scent of her skin was calling him and he was desperate to be nearer to her. The music had changed, settling into a slower pace. He stood up and offered her his hand.

"I would very much like to dance with you."

She looked down at the hand in front of her, it was a very nice hand, long and slender but strong, then up to the man himself. He was tall, about 6ft 4" at her guess, she was tall for a woman at 5ft 10" and was used to looking down on people. She liked to date taller men but rarely found one. She also loved to dance and the thought of being held in his arms was doing all kinds of crazy things to her hormones. What the hell, she was on holiday, why not have a little fun? She nodded and placed her hand in his.

He smiled and gripped her hand as she stood up, before letting go and placing his hand on the small of her back to lead her to the dance floor, the feel of his warm hand resting on her spine was wonderful. Aerosmith's I Don't Want to Miss a Thing, had just begun to play as he gently took her in his arms. She relaxed into his embrace as his arms circled her waist and rested on her hips, urging her closer to him.

She slid her hands under his arms and rested her palms on his back, one near the base of his spine and the other up between his shoulder blades. She held him close as they swayed from side to side, turning in a small circle, conscious of the other dancers.

Logan breathed in her scent and felt his body relax, she felt so good in his arms. He urged her a little closer and smiled as she uttered a small sigh and melted into his embrace.

Her soft curves were nestled snugly against his hard muscles, her breasts pressing against his chest with every breath she took. He stroked his hand up her back, feeling the tingle of awareness from his fingers as they caressed

46

her soft curls. He felt rewarded when she shuddered with pleasure at his touch.

She leaned against Logan's hard chest, tucking her head under his chin, their bodies fitted together as if made for one another. She had never felt so safe and comfortable in someone's arms so soon after meeting them, but with Logan, it just felt right to be held by him. She felt so happy all of a sudden and strangely enough it didn't feel like it was all her.

She racked her brains, trying to figure it out. All she could think of was that Logan must be a projector, someone that had almost non-existent shields and projected his every emotion out to anyone who was able to receive it. Either way he was happy to be there and that was all that mattered to her.

She relaxed against him, lowering her own mental shields a little, instinctively, as she did so. Normally she kept them sealed tight while in a crowd, finding that she would pick up on the atmosphere which she found off putting. She snuggled closer and wrapped her arms around him a little tighter.

Logan smiled as he felt her move closer of her own accord. There was something special about her and he felt a deep longing inside him, one that had not stirred for many years. After living for over four hundred years sex became boring, never being able to be close to someone. Vampires and other supernatural creatures were always looking for their Soul Mate, the one special person who would complete them and make them whole, someone to share the rest of their long lives with. Logan had travelled around the world in search of his, but they had always paled in comparison to his Alcina.

Topaz stirred in his arms and he realised that the song had ended. He had lost all sense of his surroundings, letting

47

his mind wander. He sensed her withdrawal and guessed that she thought that their dance was over, but he was reluctant to let her go. He wanted so badly to keep holding her, he also wanted to taste her, a deep yearning in his soul.

She pulled her head back and looked up at him, her full lips seeming to beg to be kissed. He had waited so long for her, he knew that now, she was the one he had been waiting for. The gods had been kind to him, she was so like his wife, that he felt the hurt he carried deep inside him ease a little.

Unable to resist he ran his fingers lightly down her face, pleased when she placed her hand over his, holding him in place and leaned into his caress. He cupped her chin and lifted her head so he could look into her eyes.

"You, are so beautiful." Unable to help himself, he leaned his head down and brushed his lips lightly across hers, a sweet loving gesture that had her sinking back into his arms.

She couldn't believe it; he was kissing her. Her mind went blank, blocking out all thoughts but the ones of the man who was holding her like she was the most precious thing in the world. She felt him increase the pressure of his lips on hers as he urged her closer to him.

Her body was crying out for him, the instant attraction she had felt on first seeing him making her want to wrap her arms around him and beg for him to take her home. She was surprised at herself; she never reacted to men this way. She had only felt mild attraction before, but this, what she felt for this man, was something else entirely. There was something mesmerising about him, something she couldn't name. He just felt right, like she had known him all her life. Like he was especially for her.

She gave into her body's demands and wrapped her arms around his neck and pulled him closer. His tongue ran tentatively across her lips and she opened her mouth to his silent command for access. Immediately his tongue filled her mouth, rubbing softly against hers. She sighed into his mouth, he tasted better than she could ever have imagined. He was sweet like fresh rain with just a hint of mint, and the scotch he had drunk, all mingled together.

Logan's hands slid down her back, making her shiver under his touch, to rest on her behind. He cupped her cheeks and urged her closer, pulling her against his groin, and his growing erection. Well, at least that proved he found her as attractive as she found him.

She felt him pressing against her and snuggled closer, moaning against his lips as her breasts scraped against his chest. He growled and broke the kiss, leaving her panting, to kiss his way down her neck. She shuddered as his lips burned a trail down her skin, followed by a slight scrapping of his teeth on her sensitized flesh.

Logan fought the need to sink his teeth into her. She tasted so wonderful, soft and sweet. His body was crying out for him to taste her properly. He ignored the urge and moved back up to her succulent lips, kissing her softly, before pulling away to look at her.

Her lips were swollen and wet, her cheeks flushed and chest heaving with her rapid breathing. No one had ever looked so amazing to him.

She looked around her, trying to calm her racing heart. She didn't know how long they had been standing there, making out like a couple of teenagers but the dance floor had pretty much cleared and people were beginning to head out of the door. She looked around for Ronnie, who had still not returned with her companion and begun to wonder just what was behind those curtains.

Logan watched her look around her, obviously looking for her friend. He saw that the club was winding down and soon she would be leaving. He didn't want to let her go; he had waited many lifetimes and only just found her. He had the sudden, cave man like urge to gather her up in his arms and take her to his apartment upstairs, locking her away from the world while he proved to her just how special she really was.

She looked at Logan, not wanting the evening to end but knowing it must. She had a sudden, over whelming need to throw herself back into his arms and beg him to take her back to his place. This was all wrong, she didn't act like this. She was no virgin; she had had boyfriends before but didn't make a point of going home with men after one dance, even if the kiss had been the hottest of her life. She took a deep breath and let it out.

"I guess I had better go, my friend will be waiting for me. Thank you for the drink and the dance. You were very good company and certainly saved my night." She gave him a smile and crossed her fingers behind her back, hoping that he would want to see her again.

He smiled back. "I'm glad I lived up to your expectations," he took her hand and held it gently in his. "I would very much like to see you again. Are you busy tomorrow night?"

She thought for a second, she had wanted to come back to Night Walkers if she could, just in case Mason Barrett did turn up, but now she had a much better reason. She had to see him again; she didn't think she could live without knowing what could be. He could be the perfect man for her, the man of her dreams. Was she willing to let that go? The answer was, Hell no, she was not. She paused for a moment, unsure what to say. She didn't want to jump at the chance and seem too eager, but then she was never very good at being subtle. She took a deep breath and jumped in feet first, as was usually her way.

"I don't have any plans for tomorrow, I will need to come back here to see if Mason turns up, but we could meet up and do something after, if you want to that is." She looked up at him.

He smiled. "I understand, your work is important. I'll arrange for the men on the door to let you in tomorrow night, wear whatever you want," he grinned down at her, raking his eyes up and down her body unashamedly, "I take it that this is not your usual attire?" He cocked his eyebrow in question. She grinned back, she couldn't help it, he made her feel happy just being in his presence.

"You're right, I would be more comfortable in my own clothes, so that would be great if you could arrange it." She gave him a flirty smile. "Do you have anything in mind for after my meeting?"

He smiled back, wider this time, a smile that held many promises, and then took a step forward, taking her back into his arms and pulling her close. It felt so natural to be in his embrace that she instantly slipped her arms around his neck and pulled him down to her. He leaned down to whisper in her ear.

"I have a lot of things in mind," his hands slipped down to her waist to urge her closer to his body, unable to resist she gave a small hip wiggle, grinding their lower bodies together. He growled and gave her ear a gentle nip, sending a shiver of pleasure down her spine. "Don't tease me, woman."

She giggled. "I know what's on your mind, Mister, but I have to tell you I'm not easy, you will have to work very hard to impress me. Do you think you are up to the challenge?"

Logan pretended to think long and hard about her statement, stroking his chin in a classic huh-let-me-think gesture before answering.

"I definitely think I'm up for your challenge. You just get your bonnie self," his hands roamed up her back and pulled at the laces of her corset top, "in here tomorrow and I promise you won't be disappointed." He nipped lovingly at her neck again. The feel of it caused little zips of pleasure to run through her. There was something slightly dangerous about him that she couldn't quite put her finger on, yet

51

instead of making her fear him, it had the opposite effect. It made her feel safe, it made her want him all the more.

"Mmm, I like how you think," she snuggled closer and raised her head up for a kiss.

He obliged, ghosting his lips over hers before he twisted his fingers lightly in her hair, changing the angle of the kiss. She felt his tongue sweep softly against her lips, begging for access. She immediately opened her mouth, desperate to taste him again. Kissing him felt like nothing she had ever experienced before, and again the feeling of having known him forever hit her hard. After what seemed like an age, they finally pulled apart.

Not wanting to let go, they just stood there, holding each other tightly. She rested her head on his shoulder and breathed him in.

"I don't think I can wait for tomorrow," he whispered in her ear, his breath tickling her skin. She felt the same and again fought the urge to invite him home with her. She pulled herself together before she did something stupid.

She glanced up and saw Ronnie waving at her from across the room. The man that had been with her was nowhere to be seen. She gave Topaz a big thumbs up and a cheeky smirk and received a scowl in return before she turned back to Logan.

"I'm sorry, baby, but you'll just have to. My friend is waiting for me, I have to go."

Logan sighed dramatically. "You are a hard woman, Topaz, but I know you're worth it."

"Just you remember it," she teased lightly.

"I will," he promised solemnly. Ronnie beckoned her over from the door; she had her coat on and was holding Topaz's cloak, ready to go. Tope held up her finger, indicating she would only be a minute.

"I have to go, Logan, I don't want to, but I can't leave my friend alone, we came together, so we go together. It's part of the girl code."

"Aye, I understand, until tomorrow."

She nodded and turned to leave but was restrained by a hand on hers. Logan pulled her back round to face him and gave her a quick, but very hot kiss. She was slightly breathless when he let her go.

"To remember me," he explained with a wink before turning and walking away. Like she could ever forget. She watched him cross the dance floor and disappear through a door marked EMPLOYEES ONLY. So he worked here too. She had wondered how he had so much sway over the bouncers on the door.

"Hey, girl, looks like you had a good night," Ronnie appeared at her side, smiling widely. Topaz tried to be stern but couldn't hold back her grin. She gave in and jumped on Ronnie, giving her a huge hug.

"I know, isn't he lovely? He wants to see me again, tomorrow night actually."

"Way to go," Ronnie gave her a high five.

She glanced at her watch, and gasped when she saw the time.

"Ronnie It's nearly five am. How did it get so late?"

She gave her a cheeky grin. "Well, I think you were busy, time flies when you're having fun." Topaz gave her a light punch on the arm and she wobbled dramatically, almost like she was drunk.

"Cheeky cow, come on, let's go home." She yawned widely. "Now I know how late it is, I'm suddenly really tired." Ronnie nodded, yawning too.

"I know the feeling, I feel drained." She giggled and swayed slightly on her feet. Topaz caught her arm to steady her.

"Damn, Ron, how much have you had to drink?"

"Not much, just two vodka and cokes."

"Well you can't handle your alcohol then. Come on, let's get you home." She suddenly remembered that she didn't know where she lived. She had felt so comfortable with her

53

that she forgot that they had only met today. "Where do you live, Ronnie?"

Ronnie looked at her, her eyes a little unfocused. "I live on the next street to your hotel." Topaz nodded and steered her towards the door.

"Everything alright, love?" the bouncer asked as she dragged Ronnie forward.

"Yeah, my friend has just had a little too much to drink, any chance of catching a taxi round here?"

He nodded and waved his arm in the air, she looked in the direction he waved and spotted a row of taxi's sitting by the curb, waiting for a fare. A taxi pulled up almost immediately and the bouncer helped her get Ronnie into the back seat. She thanked him before climbing in herself. Ronnie roused herself enough to rattle off her address, thanks in part to a well-placed elbow jab to her ribs. She scowled at Topaz before leaning back against the seat and closing her eyes.

Soon they were pulling up outside Ronnie's house. It was a nice house, small but comfortable. Topaz paid off the taxi and helped her wobble to her front door. She perked up enough to let herself in and say good night, after making Topaz promise to come to the shop the next day, she was on the late shift, which was a good thing as she doubted she would be up early in the morning. Tope muttered a quick shield spell that she hoped would protect Ronnie from damage should she bump into anything or stumble on her way up the stairs.

She waited outside until she saw a light go on upstairs, her bedroom, she guessed. Satisfied that she would be alright, she walked the block to her hotel and let herself in with her key, creeping up the stairs so as not to wake Mrs B. That would be a fate worse than death.

Chapter 4

Topaz was bending over a big black pot, stirring the bubbling broth inside it. She put down the wooden spoon and moved away from the fireplace.

She looked down at her feet as she walked, which were bare and filthy. She lifted her skirt for a better look, her legs were not much better, they were streaked with dirt. She rubbed the material of the skirt between her fingers; the material was very coarse, not like her usual clothes. She looked at the skirt more carefully; it was a muddy brown colour and seemed to be made of a kind of woollen cloth.

Now she was really confused. She looked around the room, noticing her surroundings for the first time. She was standing by a plain wooden table, around which wooden stools were arranged. Wooden plates and bowls were laid out on its surface, a candle stick the only decoration. Bundles of herbs hung from the ceiling beams and around the fire place. A broom stood in one corner and an old, bound book sat on top of the fire surround.

The room was tiny and very dark, the only light coming from a small window across the room. Blankets were piled up in one corner. She could hear the sound of children's laughter coming from outside, mingling with the background noise of squawking chickens and grunting pigs. She moved over to the door and looked out. She could see two children, a boy and a girl, both dark haired, playing together, chasing the chickens round a small yard.

She was about to go out and join them when she woke up. She could hear a loud droning noise coming from the hallway outside her door. It took her a few moments to realise it was the sound of a vacuum cleaner being pushed up and down outside, its sound burrowing into her sleep deprived brain. Groaning, she pulled the duvet over her head and tried to block out the offensive noise. It soon became apparent that it was not going to work, there was nothing for it, she was going to have to get up.

She stumbled into the bathroom to turn on the shower. She returned to the bedroom to grab some clothes, simple jeans and a t-shirt today, catching a glimpse of the clock. Damn it was late. She went into panic mode; she had to meet Ronnie for lunch.

After a quick shower and shave, she got dressed and brushed out her hair, which she had put up to keep dry. Thrusting her feet into low heeled boots she grabbed her bag and keys and headed out of the door.

She had missed breakfast being served by a good 3 hours, it was now just after midday, and she was feeling it. She was starving and more than ready to eat. She hurried down the road, reprimanding herself sharply every time she got distracted and began to browse the shop windows. She made it to High Vampage in under twenty minutes, slightly puffed out and in desperate need of a cup of coffee.

Ronnie was waiting for her outside, looking perky and well rested, the cow. There was Topaz, hiding behind her sunglasses and feeling like she had an elephant taking up

56

tap dancing in her head. In contrast, Ronnie was all fresh faced, sparkly eyed, made up perfection. Some people just made you sick, without meaning to she scowled at her. Ronnie took one look at her face and correctly judged the situation.

"Coffee, let's go get you some coffee." She took her arm and led her into the nearest café.

Only when she had a cup of strong black coffee clutched in her grateful hands and had taken her first sip, did Topaz feel ready to communicate like a normal person.

"Sorry, I'm not meaning to be such a grump, Ron, I just didn't sleep very well last night, I had a really strange dream." She took another fortifying sip of the black gold.

Ronnie waved away her apology. "That's OK, I woke up feeling crappy too, but I drank about a pint of orange juice and had lots of toast, so I feel much better now that I've made up a bit for what I lost last night." She said this so casually that it took Topaz a while to process what she had said, her brain still decidedly fuzzy and only firing on two cylinders.

"Lost, what do you mean lost? You didn't say you lost anything or I would have helped you look." Ronnie looked at her like she was mad.

"Last night," she prompted, "when I met up with Derek, you know what we were doing, right?"

"No, you went back into one of those little rooms didn't you?" Topaz racked her poor caffeine deprived brain. "I guessed that you just wanted a private drink, away from all the noise."

Ronnie blushed slightly. "Well, you could call it that."

Now she was seriously confused, what the hell was she blabbering on about? Topaz must have been staring at Ronnie in bewilderment, because she looked around, as if looking to see if anyone was listening in, before leaning forward to talk to her in a low voice.

57

"Derek fed from me last night, I'm a Donor, didn't you know?"

Tope tried to make sense of what she said but comprehension failed her. She shook her head, confused.

"What do you mean, feed him? What's a Donor?" Ronnie looked at her, shocked.

"You really don't know?"

She shook her head again. Ronnie sighed and got up from the table; she grabbed her hand and dragged her through the door at the back of the café that led to the toilets. After looking under each stall, checking if they were alone, she turned to face her.

"OK, here goes. You know that Night Walkers is a Vampire bar right?"

Topaz nodded. "Yeah, of course. People who like the idea of being Vampires all dress up and party there."

"Not quite." The tone of her voice implied she thought that Topaz was being particularly dense.

"What do you mean, not quite?" Topaz was beginning to worry. She leaned against the wall, suddenly feeling weak, a headache beginning to bloom behind her eyes.

"It's a real Vampire bar, Tope. I thought you knew," one look at her startled face must have told Ronnie the truth. "You didn't know? I assumed that you did, you were meeting up with Mason after all."

"You know about Mason?"

"Of course I do. Mason is a Vampire. I know you didn't tell me the real reason you were meeting up with him, but I really thought you knew." It was Ronnie's turn to look bewildered.

"I did know about Mason, but I didn't know anyone else did. I thought I was meeting up with one Vampire, ONE, not a whole bloody pack of them." Topaz's legs gave out and she sank down the wall to collapse onto the floor in a heap, massaging her temples. "Are you seriously telling me that not only do Vampires exist but they have their own club? Do

58

they have a freakin' secret handshake too? And what do you mean you're a Donor?"

Ronnie squatted down next to her on the floor.

"I'm a Donor, I feed the Vampires," she shot Topaz a look that implied she was being deliberately difficult, like a petulant child that kept asking why.

"*Feed* them?" Topaz's brain had begun to short circuit; she just couldn't wrap her head around what she was being told.

"I feed them, let them drink from me." Ronnie swept her hair back from her neck, revealing two neat puncture marks on her otherwise flawless skin.

"They bite you?" Ronnie nodded. "Then they what, drink your blood?" She nodded again. "And you let them? They don't force you or anything?"

Topaz had heard all sorts of legends about Vampires. About their ability to cloud your mind, make you forget them feeding from you. She looked at Ronnie's neck again. Sure, she had known what they did to survive in theory, but when it was thrust into her face like this, she just didn't know what to think.

"Yes, they bite me," Ronnie informed her patiently, "and yes I let them. I like it. We all do." She got the feeling that she may have had this talk a few times before.

"We? You mean there are more of you?"

"What, Donors you mean?" Topaz nodded. "Sure, there are loads of us. You didn't think I could feed them all by myself did you?" Ronnie giggled.

"To tell you the truth, I hadn't thought about it at all. Why would I?"

"Well, not all vamps feed from us. Some of them hunt the old fashioned way; others drink only at the club or get their blood delivered from blood banks. And others rely on their partners."

Ronnie was saying this all so casually, like it was an everyday occurrence, as simple as popping to the shop for a pint of milk.

"I just don't get it, I mean of course I *get* that they need to feed, everyone does. But why do you let them snack on you? What do you get out of it?" Topaz's mind jumped back to last night, recalling how weak and wobbly Ronnie had been. "Was that why you were ill last night? Did they do that to you?" She could feel herself getting angry on her behalf.

Ronnie sighed. "Yes, that's why I was weak, I'm sorry, I really thought you knew."

"No, Mason contacted my organisation, saying he wanted to talk to me. I thought that he was the only one, just hiding out, living his life, working in a bar, I assumed that he chose Night Walkers as a good place to hang out where no one would look twice at a man who was a Vampire. I wasn't even sure that he was for real. I mean Vampires, that's not something you hear every day." She was beginning to babble now, working up to a good freak out session. Ronnie must have sensed this. She made soothing noises and calm-down motions with her hands.

"Please, Tope, calm down. It's all right. Nothing's wrong, no one forced me to do anything. I like it, that's why I do it."

Topaz didn't understand. What was to like about being someone's take-away dinner?

"What do you mean, you like it? Doesn't it hurt?" She assumed having two bloody great fangs chomping on your neck would hurt like crazy.

"Nope, it feels amazing," Ronnie leant forward, like she was going to tell the biggest secret in the world. "It's like the best sex ever."

"You have sex?" Tope screeched out, shocked. Ronnie giggled.

"No, we don't have sex, I'm not like that. It's hard to explain, but it's like you can feel them feeding, right down deep inside you. It feels orgasmic." She looked like she was having a great flash back, her eyes had glazed over and her breathing become a little shallower. Topaz backed away a couple of inches, feeling uncomfortable, wondering if she was about to jump her bones. She liked her a lot but she just didn't bend that way.

As Tope was waiting for Ronnie to snap out of it, a woman walked into the bathroom. She took one look at them both sitting on the floor, Topaz flattened against the wall like she could push through it and Ronnie's expression that of a playboy cover girl and turned right back the way she came. It suddenly dawned on Topaz that they were sitting on the cold, hard floor in a public bathroom. She needed a few minutes to puzzle things out in her head. Her stomach rumbled, reminding her that she had yet to eat anything. She couldn't think well on an empty stomach.

Ronnie looked at her, apparently done fantasizing. Jumping up, she reached down to help her up. "Come on, let's go order some food. We can talk more later."

Topaz nodded, glad she was letting it go for now, she needed time to process all this new information. She scrambled to her feet and followed her back to their table.

They got lots of funny looks as they sat down, not that she could blame them, they had been gone a long time. She didn't want to begin to imagine what they thought they had been up too.

They ordered their food and sat in silence while they waited, Topaz thinking through everything she had just learned and Ronnie waiting anxiously to see how she would react.

Being realistic, she wasn't as shocked as she thought she was, she was just being dramatic, feeling like she should be shocked and reacting like she was. She knew Vampires existed, she was here trying to prove it for pity's sake. She was all prepared to meet one, even looking forward to it. What difference did it make if it was one or a hundred? She had been preaching to people for years to give them a

61

chance, talking about how they were not monsters, just misunderstood. Ronnie was the thing that had gotten to her. She just hadn't expected someone to willingly allow themselves to become food, it was like a chicken walking into KFC, spreading its wings and saying 'cook me'.

She was jerked out of her ponderings by the arrival of the waitress bringing their food. She tucked into her scrambled eggs, bacon, sausage and toast with gusto, hoping food would help her headache. Ronnie began working on her toasted sandwich. When Topaz had eaten enough to take the edge off of her hunger, she decided Ronnie had suffered enough. She swallowed her mouthful and laid down her knife and fork.

"OK, I don't get what you do or why you do it, but it's your life. You're an adult, you are perfectly capable of making your own decisions. If you choose to do it, then so be it. Just don't expect me to join in."

Ronnie put down her sandwich to grip her hand across the table, looking relieved.

"Oh, Topaz, I'm so glad you said that. I didn't want you to hate me or think less of me, you're like my idol. You know so much about everything. I'm just sorry you found out like this, I really did think you knew." She looked at her. "It's not as bad as you think it is, you know. We are highly respected. We have rules that they have to abide by."

Topaz had gotten over her dramatics and was now very interested.

"What kind of rules?" Her breakfast was still calling to her, her stomach feeling hollow and empty. She didn't want to be rude but couldn't help it. She picked up her fork and took another bite of egg and looked at her, waiting for her to elaborate.

"There are too many to go into now, but the main points are that we, as the Donors, have almost all the rights."

Topaz raised her eyebrows at that as she chewed thoughtfully. She had always imagined that Vampires would be the ones in charge, they seemed to be such a dominate species. Her mind was running over all the new things she was learning, thinking up ways to translate what she was hearing into useable information for her article. She wished desperately for her notebook and a pen to record it all.

"Everything is pre-arranged before the feeding," Ronnie carried on. "The bite area is chosen and agreed upon. Both parties are consenting, both adults, nobody gets hurt." She peered at Topaz meaningfully, emphasizing her point. She nodded to show she got it.

"The Vampire's personal details are never discussed with anyone, the same goes for the Donors. We have to register to be a Donor and are sworn to secrecy, I shouldn't even be telling you really, but you were invited in, so I guess you can be trusted." She looked at her sharply.

"Well, of course I can be trusted, I agreed before I came here that the information would be kept private." Ronnie nodded, apparently pleased with her answer.

"So, tell me about that bloke you hooked up with last night," Ronnie had obviously decided to change the subject. "You worked pretty fast, you were supposed to be talking to Mason, not picking up hot looking blokes, not that I blame you."

Topaz smiled at her, this was what she needed, a good gossip session about blokes, it would make a change for her to be talking positively about someone she had met.

"He introduced himself at the bar, Mason didn't show up, so he kept me company while you were indisposed," she glanced pointedly at her but her friend grinned back unashamedly. "He bought me a drink and then asked me to dance."

"Wow, a man who likes to dance, that's a rare find, I'd hang on to him. You are seeing him again aren't you?" She said the last like Topaz would be mad not too, fortunately, for once, Tope completely agreed. Logan was most definitely a keeper.

63

She nodded. "Yeah, he asked me to meet him tonight at the club."

Ronnie clapped her hands in glee. "You go girl, another date so soon. You must be doing something the rest of us aren't."

Topaz shook her head.

"It's nothing I'm doing, I promise you. My love life to date has been pretty awful to tell you the truth." Ronnie waved her to continue, a look of rapt attention on her face. "My friends keep setting me up on blind dates, all of which turn out to be disasters. I swear all the decent men seem to have been snapped up already. I haven't had a serious relationship in years."

Ronnie raised her eyebrows in surprise. "Seriously?"

She nodded, fiddling with her fork, and making little piles of eggs all around the edge of her plate.

"Seriously, I dated a lad from school, but he left to go to college. Since then it's been a few dates here and there and if we get to the second date, he always turns out to be a jerk."

Ronnie looked flabbergasted. "I just can't believe it, I mean, you're so great. How could they not want you?"

Topaz smiled at her compliment and her defence of her. They may have only just met, but she could tell that Ronnie would be a good friend. They would definitely be keeping in touch when she went home.

"What about you?" Topaz asked. "You got a love life to speak of?"

Ronnie grimaced and picked up the remaining half of her sandwich. "Not really. I have had boyfriends, but most of them don't like me going out without them, which I have to do for my Donor work."

Topaz nodded encouragingly, watching Ronnie's fingers shred the bread into tiny pieces. "I did date a fellow Donor for a while but it didn't last, he took the Donor thing too far." Topaz must have looked confused because she elaborated.

"It can be very sexual to be fed from, some Donors, when it's agreed upon, will engage in sex with their bleeder. I told him that if he wanted to do that then he would lose me. He chose the sex."

Topaz felt so sorry for her, without thinking she reached across the table and gave her hand a squeeze. Ronnie squeezed back.

"I do understand why he did it, I'm no saint, with the right bleeder it's amazing. But I only engage when I'm single. That didn't matter to him, my feelings didn't matter." She sighed. "So for now I'm laying off men. I'm free to please myself. If I want to indulge I do." She shrugged in a 'no big deal' gesture and waved her hand, as if sweeping it away.

Ronnie had finished with her sandwich and Topaz had eaten as much of her breakfast as she could, so she made no move to stop her when she called for the bill.

"I think we need to go shopping if you have a date tonight." Ronnie winked at her. She had learnt from picking out the dress yesterday, that resistance was futile. Giving in gracefully she grabbed her bag and threw some money down to cover her part of the bill.

They were soon standing outside a little shop that Topaz had previously overlooked in her wanderings, as it was tucked away in a corner of the street. The front window was plainly dressed with nothing but a mannequin in the window, dressed in a 50's style dress, and a few hat boxes with shoes on top. It was not her usual shop to say the least. Seeing the doubt on her face, Ronnie intervened.

"Oh come on, Tope, it's great in here, it's Edinburgh's best vintage clothing shop, I come here all the time." She grabbed her hand and proceeded to drag her into the shop.

Inside it was stuffed to the rafters with racks of dresses, tops and skirts from every era you could imagine, as well as piles of accessories. Topaz looked around in amazement at all the choice, her eyes already seeking out some things

65

she wouldn't mind trying on. Ronnie jabbed her gently with her elbow.

"See, I told you it was great." She looked suitably chuffed with herself.

"OK, OK. I give in, it's great." And it was, it had all the charm and personality that chain store shops lacked. They both turned when a short lady, maybe in her late 50's, bustled out of a door, previously un-noticed, at the back of the shop. She saw Ronnie and immediately threw her arms around her in a huge hug. Ronnie hugged her back, giggling. Pulling away Ronnie introduced her to Topaz.

"Hey, Margo, this is my friend, Topaz. She has a big date tonight and needs something fabulous to wear. Can you help?" She clasped her hands together in a begging gesture. Margo immediately went into work mode, raking her eyes up and down Topaz's body as if assessing her. Topaz in turn immediately started squirming, uncomfortable with this level of scrutiny.

"Humm," she walked around her, "size 14?" Topaz nodded dumbly, how did she do that? "Yes, I think I can help."

She was like a whirlwind, rushing from here to there, grabbing up clothes by the armful and depositing them in Ronnie's arms. Before long they had a huge pile of clothes for her to try on. Topaz took the pile from Ronnie and disappeared into the changing room. She discarded a few items right off the bat, bright colours and loud patterns were not her thing.

She decided to start at the beginning with a 1940's party dress; it was a deep red and had a boned bodice with spaghetti straps, covered in lace and sprinkled with rhinestones. The full pleated tulle skirt hovered on her knees. She came out and did a little twirl. Ronnie loved it but Margo didn't think it was quite right.

She tried on a 50's prom gown next, floaty skirt that hit her mid-calf, very grease; it had a fitted bodice that buttoned

66

up all down the front with tiny pearls and short sleeves. It was a baby blue colour that she thought clashed a little with her pale skin and red hair. She exited the changing room ready for inspection but her critics were less than impressed, seeming to agree with her, turning her around and sending her straight back in to try on the next one.

Lastly she tried on an 80's evening gown. It had a ruched bodice, no straps, and a multi layered skirt, handkerchief style, that flowed around her ankles like a dream. It was a gorgeous deep purple colour that she loved. She stared at herself in the mirror, gob-smacked. It was perfect, she was sure that this was the one for her. It fitted like it had been made for her, hugging her curves and displaying them to their full advantage. She stepped out from behind the curtain and did a slow turn, showing off the dress from every angle.

"Oh, Tope, you look amazing," Ronnie gasped. "That colour is perfect for you." Topaz looked at Margo, who had so far been very critical of everything she had tried on.

Margo studied her in silence for a few moments, nodding her head slowly before breaking out into a huge smile.

"Yes," she beamed. "That's the one for you." She bustled off still nodding, muttering to herself about shoes and handbags.

By the time they had finished, and Topaz had recovered from her dead faint upon seeing the final total, they were back at High Vampage. Ronnie had the late shift, four until ten. After making Topaz promise to call her later for a progress report, she sent her on her way.

Chapter 5

Topaz was primped and preened and ready to go by eight o' clock. The dress was still as amazing as it had been earlier. There was nothing worse than buying a dress in the shop and finding it was not as nice as you thought once you got it home. She had bought a pair of sexy, black high heels to go with it but declined on the handbag Margo had tried to encourage her to purchase. Margo had more than made up for the loss of the sale by showing her a gorgeous black velvet wrap which, unfortunately, was perfect with the dress. That had come home with her too.

She didn't stop for dinner as she had done the last night, not knowing if Logan would want to go out to eat. She therefore arrived at Night Walkers earlier than they had the night before. The line was nowhere near as long as it had been on her previous visits. She joined the end of the queue and patiently waited her turn. She didn't have to wait long. Dane the bouncer from the previous night came up to her.

"Hey, Topaz, what you waiting here for?"

She looked at him like he was daft. "I'm waiting to get in of course."

He shook his head chuckling. "You don't need to be waiting out here with these folk. Logan said to bring you in as soon as you got here."

She smiled at him. "Well, that is a pleasant surprise."

He turned and began to walk away, down the line of waiting people to the doors. People around them began to mutter in disgust as she followed him out of the queue. She smiled in a sorry-but-what-can-I-do way and grimaced when people began to mutter unflattering comments about her sexual promiscuity. She gave up being pleasant and scowled at the grumpy goths waiting to enter. It gave her a small amount of satisfaction to know that they had very little hope of getting in that night, or any night in fact. She was cool, they were not, she had to stomp on her childish urge to stick her tongue out or flip them the bird.

Dane and his friend opened the door for her and waved her on in.

It was still early and the club was practically empty, the music was low enough that she didn't think talking would be a problem. She looked around to see if she could spot Logan but didn't see him anywhere. She made her way over to the bar, deciding that she would wait there. Mason might be in and if so, she could finally do her interview, if not it was as good a place as any to wait for Logan.

Avery was working the bar again, this time sporting a classic three corner hat and a colourful waistcoat over his shirt. As there were so few customers to serve she didn't think he would mind having a quick chat. After receiving her drink she took the plunge.

"Mason not in again then?" She tried to sound casual, taking a sip of her drink, a black cat cocktail this time.

"Nope, still don't know where he is, no one has seen him in a few days. We're beginning to wonder if he's taken off."

69

"Oh, that's a shame. I was really hoping to meet him, he contacted me offering to help me with an article I'm working on."

Avery's eyes widened at her comment. "So you're the one who is so interested in Vampires?" He smiled at her, giving her a quick flash of his fangs. Well that explained his lack of aura, maybe her joke about him being dead was not far off the mark after all.

She was slightly taken aback by his forthright attitude but she nodded, if Ronnie came here all the time they must be nice and it's not like she was scared of him before.

"Yeah, that's me, but it wasn't really my doing. He contacted my organisation and asked for me to come and meet him. That's why I'm a bit annoyed that he's not here. This is my holiday I'm wasting."

A hand suddenly dropped down on her shoulder and a voice purred in her ear, making her jump out of her skin. "Not completely wasted I hope."

She spun round on her stool, her conversation with Avery completely forgotten. Logan stood before her looking so knicker-meltingly hot that she had to fight the urge not to jump into his arms right there and then.

He was wearing black jeans and a black shirt, open just enough to give a tantalising glimpse of the smooth chest underneath. Circling his neck was a thin leather thong on which hung two plain gold rings. He had left his hair un-bound tonight and it fell down past his shoulders, framing his face. It looked so silky that her fingers itched to caress the soft strands. He held out his hand and she took it, letting him help her up. The same tingling sensation fluttered down her arm. He smiled down at her and her knees went so weak, she was pathetically grateful that he still held her hand.

"So, where are we going tonight?" Topaz asked when she had sufficiently recovered her composure.

"Well, I had several ideas, but none of them felt right. They were all too stiff and formal, so I decided that we would just go out, wander around and see what takes our fancy. Let's be spontaneous," he grinned at her. She found herself beaming back, it was actually a great idea. She had been worrying about where he was taking her, worrying that it would be somewhere stuffy and posh, somewhere she would stand out like a sore thumb. Now she could relax and enjoy herself.

She gave his hand a friendly squeeze, not sure how to react now she was here. She desperately wanted to kiss him but he had made no move to do so, not even in greeting. She decided that going with the flow was going to be the order of the day.

"Sounds like a plan to me. Let's go."

He used his grip on her hand to pull her closer. Hauling her up to his side, he let go of the hand, instead dropping his arm to wrap it around her waist in an obvious display of possession. She smiled a small, secret smile of glee. No one had ever been so blatant before and she loved it, not that she would tell him that or admit it to anyone else, but maybe she might get a little action tonight after all.

He used his hold on her waist to steer her towards the doors. Avery gave her a thumbs up from behind the bar and she grinned back, giving him a little wave as they disappeared out the doors.

"I can't believe you actually wanted to watch that," Topaz giggled when the film finally finished. Don't get her wrong it was a sweet story but her professional brain was screaming the whole time, begging her to set the record straight. "It was so incredibly inaccurate. That was the whole reason I never wanted to watch it when they were first released. Give it a try you said, it'll be fun you said."

She was working up to a good rant, the kind of rant that had her friends shaking their heads in exasperation and

71

begging her not to make a scene. She paused at the thought, and looked at Logan. She didn't want him thinking the same thing and cause him to be embarrassed to be with the girl that was taking the film *way* too seriously (she would admit it, she did huff a fair bit during the showing). But instead of looking annoyed he just looked amused. His eyes were sparkling and he was biting his lip to stop from laughing. He waved her to continue.

"Carry on, I know you're desperate, let it all out."

She tried valiantly not to burst out with the one thing that had really bugged her but could hold back no longer.

"Diamonds," here it comes, "they glitter like diamonds! Sparkly Vampires? Where were the flames? The burning, the screaming agony?" She felt vaguely cheated somehow, stupid as that sounded. It's not like she wanted to see a Vampire go up in flames, but it was the principal of the thing. "And they survive without blood? What's that all about? What Vampire goes without blood?"

Logan snorted with laughter and she couldn't help but laugh too. By the time they finally stopped she was leaning against Logan and trying to catch her breath. Logan rubbed her back and encouraged her to breathe.

"Drink, I need a drink," she finally managed to splutter. Logan looked around for a second before spotting a quiet looking pub at the end of the road. He took her arm and steered her towards it.

They took seats in one of the cosy corner booths and Logan made his way to the bar to fetch their drinks. While he was gone, she sucked in a deep calming breath and took stock of the night so far.

In her mind it was going very well. She loved the fact that he hadn't tried to impress her by taking her somewhere fancy. He'd chosen a little independent theatre that showed films that were at least a few years old for a cheaper price. It was like stepping back in time, the seats were big and comfy, nothing like in modern cinemas where you had to fight over the arm rest. From the beautifully moulded ceiling hung chandeliers that wouldn't look out of place in a mansion.

They had snuggled a little during the film, his arm around her and her head on his shoulder. They hadn't needed words; she had felt so comfortable in his company. They had sat in silence, watching the film. She had never connected with someone as quickly as she had with Logan. She had loved the feel of his arm wrapped around her, flexing to hold her close every time she showed even a hint of wanting to move.

The scent of him had been teasing her nostrils all evening, causing some primal urge deep down within her to react. She had seemed to be aware of his every move; every breath he took caused his chest to rise and fall against her cheek. She wanted nothing more than to wrap her body around his and kiss his brains out, but aware of their surroundings she had managed to remain in her seat, content with playing her fingers across the back of his hand.

But now Topaz was feeling very wound up and in desperate need for some proper physical contact, preferably along the lines of kissing and light groping. She had never been this worked up before; her whole body seemed to be in overdrive. Her skin felt ultra sensitive and, very embarrassingly, her breasts were aching, as if they were reacting to the need in her and were expressing their own.

She began to imagine just what it would feel like to get as close to Logan as she wanted to be. She imagined him sitting next to her on the seat; she would fling her leg over his and climb into his lap, wriggling just a little to get comfortable before wrapping her arms around his neck and pulling him in for a kiss. Letting her hands wander over his skin while he did some exploring of his own...

Logan set her drink down on the table, cutting short her lusty imaginings, which was a good thing. Some pretty interesting visuals had been filling her head, causing heat to

73

pool down deep inside her, making her wet and achy, desperate for his touch. She squirmed in her seat as subtly as she could, squeezing her thighs together, trying to relieve some of the pressure.

"Are you alright, sweetheart?" he asked, sitting down next to her and taking her hand.

His question took her by surprise, but not as much as the endearment he had used.

"I'm fine, I was just thinking about the movie." She smiled and took a sip of her drink, trying not to focus on his hand holding hers.

Logan grimaced. "Are you still thinking about all the bits they got wrong?"

She shook her head. "No, I'm trying not to dwell," she said in a solemn voice. He chuckled and wrapped his arm around her waist pulling her closer to his side. She breathed in his lovely smell, all fresh and masculine. It made things inside her jump for joy, and begged her to crawl onto his lap and have her wicked way with him as she had thought about doing earlier. No, bad girl, she told herself, you will not act like a cheap hussy and make a spectacle of yourself in a crowded pub.

"So, tell me about yourself. You have told me all about your work, but nothing about you. I want to know everything." He slouched down in the seat so he could lean against the back, turning to give her his undivided attention. What more could a girl wish for? A man that actually wanted to learn about her. She leaned back against the seat, settling in for the night and began to talk.

Logan watched her talk. He loved how animated she became when talking about the things that she loved. They spoke about books, music, films, everything and anything. It seemed like they could spend a life time talking and still have more to say. She looked so sexy, leaning back in the seat, completely relaxed in his company.

74

His eyes travelled over her body, taking in her long legs, slim waist and hovering for just a second longer on her breasts. He forced his eyes back up to her face but found his gaze settling on her luscious lips. They were full and juicy, just begging to be kissed.

He remembered their kisses during their dance, her taste, the way she felt in his arms. Her body seemed to mould itself to his like she was made for him. He wanted another taste but didn't want to push his luck.

Fearing that they both might have been caught up in the moment the night before he had tried to keep things friendly all night, but it had proven to be almost impossible. Having her so close and not touching her was like some kind of exquisite torture. He loved the feel of her skin under his, it was so soft and touchable. He had contented himself with small caresses and simply enjoyed holding her, but he knew that it would not be enough, it would never be enough.

He let his mind wander, imagining all the wonderful things he dreamed of doing to her. He dwelled for a little while on the interesting images that had popped into his head while he had been waiting to order their drinks. Thoughts of her sliding onto his lap and allowing his hands to wander wherever they wanted while indulging in some very hot kisses. His body hardened in response to these thoughts and he shifted in his seat, propping his ankle up on his knee to try to hide the erection that was now straining his jeans.

Topaz was in the middle of telling him about her holiday to Spain with friends when a bell sounded.

Startled they both looked up as the barmaid yelled out that they were closing. Logan glanced at his watch and was surprised to see that it was one in the morning. He would have happily sat talking to her all night but suspected that she might be getting tired.

He stood up and shrugged on his jacket. Topaz did the same and picked up her handbag.

"Well," she began, "I guess I had better be off. Thank you for a lovely evening, sorry about bending your ears so much." She smiled apologetically at him. He shook his head.

"Don't be silly, you didn't bend my ears. I like hearing you talk." He took her hand and helped her out of the booth. "And I am not going to let you wander about the streets on your own at this time of night. I'm going to walk you home and I don't want to hear any arguments," he added sternly. She opened her mouth to protest but he silenced her with a quick kiss. Topaz was too stunned to argue and followed him meekly out of the door.

Topaz didn't know what to do. They were standing outside her guest house and Logan had held her hand the whole way home. They had chatted some more, perfectly at ease in each other's company. But now the night was over, the only problem was she didn't want it to be. She finally took the plunge and broke the silence.

"I had a wonderful time tonight, thank you." Now she was stuck again. She wanted desperately to kiss him goodnight but didn't know how to go about it. She felt so out of practice it was ridiculous. She shifted uncomfortably on the spot, waiting for Logan to respond. It wasn't the response she had expected. It was a hundred times better.

He stepped up to her and encircled her waist in his arms, pulling her closer. He lowered his head and captured her lips with his, kissing her softly at first before becoming a little more forceful. Her arms snaked their way up and around his neck as she wriggled closer against his body. His tongue swept into her mouth, caressing hers and driving her wild with longing.

She shuddered in his embrace as he ran his hands up her back. Their kiss intensified, passion bursting over them. She felt his erection press against her groin and she couldn't resist rocking her hips against his. They groaned in unison as he brushed against her aching centre. All the thoughts and feelings she had had during the evening came rushing back with a force so intense it was staggering.

Just as she was about to promise him the world if he would just take her now, he broke the kiss. Nipping at her lower lip and trailing his lips down her neck. Her neck was her weak spot, guaranteed to make her melt. She groaned softly and circled her hips against his again.

Logan growled against her skin, the sound rumbling through her like a wave. She had never heard anything hotter. She was suddenly desperate to taste him again. He seemed to sense this and raised his head, locking their lips together again.

The world around them seemed to melt away, leaving them with nothing but each other. After an age Logan pulled away.

"We had better stop." He didn't look to happy with the prospect, and to tell the truth neither was she.

Topaz swallowed and nodded her agreement, it had been a long night and Mrs Baker was pretty insistent that she didn't bring anyone home.

"Would it be OK if I picked you up tomorrow night for another date?" He slipped his hands down to her butt and gave it an affectionate squeeze. She backed up into the caress and ran her hands down his chest until she reached the waist band of his jeans. Sliding her thumbs into his belt loops and pulling him close again.

"Most definitely." She lifted her head in offer and he obliged, giving her a soft kiss. She moaned gently as he broke the kiss to whisper in her ear.

"I wish we were somewhere a little more private, preferably with a nice soft bed." She pulled back to look at him. He had that cheeky smirk on his face that she loved.

"I wish that too, unfortunately Mrs Baker doesn't allow guests."

"Well, maybe next time you can walk me home."

She giggled at his nerve and pretended to consider his offer.

"That sounds like a good plan, I'll have to give it some serious thought." Deciding that this was a good time to leave, giving them both something to think about -and she would be doing a lot of thinking- she pulled out her keys and waved goodbye.

Logan stood and watched from the street below, waiting for her light to go on, signalling that she was in her room. He absently touched his lips as if he could still feel hers on them. It had taken all his self-control to break their kiss and let her go inside, but he didn't want to push her into anything she didn't want to do. He was pretty sure that she would like to join in with all the things that he dreamt of, but it had to be on her terms. He was a patient man, he had waited over 400 years for her, he could wait a bit longer.

A light blinked on overhead and he looked up, hoping to catch one last glimpse of her. What he didn't expect was an ear-piercing scream to rent the air.

Logan was rushing to the front door before he could even think. Of course, it was locked, but with only a moment's hesitation he lifted his leg and planted his boot on the door. The lock shattered and the door burst open. Logan raced up the stairs, memories of his beautiful Alcina's death running through his head. He couldn't lose Topaz as well, he just couldn't.

Chapter 6

Topaz hadn't bothered turning on the hall lights as she came in, not wanting to wake anyone up. She had muttered a very quiet, "lend me a light to guide me," and conjured up a small glowing ball to light the way. Maybe if she had turned on the lights, she might have had prior warning and not screamed like an idiot. Her light had vanished as soon as her concentration had waned, not that you could blame her.

She stood there in shock, complete and utter shock. Some sleaze bag had broken into her room. HER Room, with HER stuff in it, HER stuff that was currently spread across the entire room.

Logan rushed in, closely followed by Mrs Baker and Mr Baker, whom she had previously never seen before.

Logan immediately took her in his arms and hugged her.

"Are you hurt?" Logan began running his hand up and down her body, checking for injuries.

It took her a moment to register that he was in her room.

"Wait, what are you doing up here? How did you get in?"

"That's exactly what I want to know. What happened in here?" Mrs B was standing there, hands on hips, glaring at them. And trust me for a woman wearing a dressing gown and curlers in her hair, she could pull it off. "I told you no men up here."

Topaz shook her head.

"I didn't bring him in. I got back and found my room like this. Someone must have broken in." Her voice wobbled as she looked about in despair. Everything she had brought with her was now scattered here, there and everywhere. She couldn't help it and began to blub like a baby, tears streaming down her face.

Logan gathered her into his arms again and kissed her head.

"It's OK, darling please don't cry. We can fix it."

"But it's all my stuff, someone touched my stuff." She was getting past crying and rushing head-long into, right royally pissed off. "Someone put their dirty, filthy, hands on my things," she looked around again, "and they riffled through my undies. That's it I'll have to burn them. And my…" she gestured to her scattered altar, unwilling to elaborate on what it was with the Bakers in earshot.

"I'll buy you anything you want to replace them, I promise." Logan soothed.

"That's not the point I," she broke off as she was interrupted.

"Calm down, my dear. I think the first thing we have to do is call the police." Mr B stepped forward with a mobile phone in his hand.

"That's right, husband, you call them." Mrs B nodded her head in agreement, as if it had been her idea.

Topaz's legs suddenly went weak and she dropped down onto the bed. Logan knelt before her, his hand on her knee as Mr B spoke into his phone, explaining what had happened and reciting the address. Topaz placed her hand over Logan's.

80

She leant forward to whisper in Logan's ear.

"How did you get in? I locked the door behind me."

He squirmed slightly and looked a little guilty.

"I might have broken down the door." She gaped at him.

"You what?" She shook her head in amazement, bloody men. "Why did you do that?"

"You screamed. I was worried, I had to get to you. I'm sorry. I'll pay for it to be fixed. Don't worry your wee head about it."

She couldn't help but smile at him, her annoyance vanishing, he was so sweet. No one had ever worried about her like that. Most men she dated would have run away when she had screamed, not come charging in to rescue her. She felt that now familiar arousal beginning to build inside her but she pushed it away, this was neither the time nor the place.

"Don't worry about it, no real harm done. Thank you for rushing up to save me." Without thinking she leaned forward to bestow a quick kiss on his lips but was interrupted by a loud cough behind them.

They both turned to look. Mrs B was glaring.

"The police will be here any minute," she informed them. They heard the sound of the doorbell chiming downstairs. Damn, they were quick here. Mr B tottered off to answer it.

A bellow of rage came floating up the stairs. She guessed he had seen the door that Logan had crashed through. Seconds later thumps were heard as they charged back up the stairs.

Mr B looked mad enough to spit, his face had gone beet red and if she squinted just a little she thought she could see steam coming out of his ears. She blinked away the visual and tried to pay attention to the police officer that had accompanied him. He looked like he was in his fifties, his hair was going grey and he wore glasses. He looked quite business like, with a slightly stern look on his face. He cleared his throat and waited for their undivided attention.

81

"Hello, my name is Inspector Jackson, who can tell me what happened here?" he pulled out a slim, black notebook and licked his pencil. Topaz watched fascinated, she didn't think people really did that.

Mrs B pushed her forward.

"Well," she paused. "I got back about fifteen minutes ago. I said goodbye to Logan outside and let myself in with my key. Then I …"

"Wait a moment, young lady," the inspector said. "Did you just say that you let yourself in with your key? So the front door was locked?" Topaz looked at Logan; she knew where this was going.

"Erm… Yes," she finally answered.

"Then what, pray tell, happened to our door?" Mr B broke in.

Logan stepped forward, and took her hand and gave it a squeeze, letting her know it was alright.

"Actually, I broke the door. I heard Topaz scream and I was worried. I kicked the door open and ran up to help her."

"You broke my door?" Mrs B was fuming with rage; Topaz half expected the wrath of God to strike them down in the form of a lightning bolt.

"Aye, and I'm very sorry about it. I'll pay for any damage of course." Logan smiled in a reassuring way that they didn't seem to buy.

"Anyway, what happened next?" the inspector wanted to know, clearly used to dealing with people who went off topic.

"Then I came upstairs and opened my door, I flicked on the light and saw all this," she finished. Not very exciting but that was about it.

"Did you see anyone?"

She shook her head.

"No, I'm sorry, it was dark and I didn't want to turn on the light because I didn't want to wake everyone up."

"In the morning we'll come back and ask the other guests if they heard anything, they may be able to help," Inspector Jackson informed them.

"There are no other guests at the moment," Mrs B told him. "Topaz is our only resident. We don't even live on this floor."

"Well, can you tell me if anything is missing?" he asked Topaz. "It might give us an idea what we are looking for, or why they chose this room."

She glanced around, trying to run an inventory in her head to work out if anything had gone, but everything looked to be there. Then she spotted it, her empty laptop case, dropped on the floor by the bed and partially hidden under the blankets that had been yanked off and thrown onto the floor. She ran over to it and picked it up, as if looking at it didn't prove that it had gone, she had to really check for herself. She slid her hands down into all the pockets. Her note books and all her discs were also gone.

"My laptop," she quietly announced, "and all my notes." The inspector looked at her curiously. "I'm here on a research trip and had made a few notes about what I had found. I wrote them up rough in my notebooks and then copied them onto my laptop."

Logan took the bag gently from her hands and slipped his arm around her waist.

"Don't worry, darling, we'll get you a replacement."

"Anything else missing?" the inspector interrupted, clearly wanting to pack up and go home to bed. It was now after two.

Topaz shook her head. "I don't think so, it looks like they just messed everything up. I didn't bring anything else of value with me. No jewellery, not much money, only my laptop."

The inspector made one last note, then closed his notebook and slipped it into his inside pocket. "Well, I would say that it's just a simple case of thieves targeting tourists.

83

We've had it happen before, they pick someone out and follow them to their hotel and wait for their chance. They probably loved the fact that you came back so late." Mrs B's disapproving glare was back with a vengeance.

"We'll send someone round later to dust for prints but I doubt any will show up, these people normally use gloves. We haven't caught any of them yet." He looked at them, as if daring them to comment or argue. They wisely kept their traps shut. "You'll have to stay in another room for tonight. Avoid contaminating any evidence and such like."

Topaz nodded her understanding, she had suspected as much. Just her luck. She knew she should have stayed at home. This whole trip had been a waste of time. Mason hadn't turned up and she had no Vampire to interview. Logan squeezed her waist and pulled her a little closer to his side, as if he could read her thoughts. She smiled up at him. Well maybe not a complete waste of time. She leaned her head against his chest, uncaring as to what people thought. She had had enough tonight.

"Well, I'll be off now," the inspector broke in. "I think I have all the information I need. Someone will contact you all in the morning." He said his goodbyes and Mr B followed him down the stairs.

Mrs B turned to Topaz, her expression grim.

"I'm sorry, Topaz, but we just can't have this sort of thing happening in our home," she shook her head to drive home the point. "You can stay here tonight but will have to find a new hotel tomorrow."

Topaz was dumbstruck, the nerve of her. She exploded both barrels.

"Wait a minute, are you saying this is my fault?"

"Well it's never happened around here before you got here. And you brought that girl inside." She said 'girl' like it was a piece of shit on her shoe. "She probably told all her friends about us. We're just lucky that they stopped at your room, they could have taken my good china." She turned to level a look at Logan. "And now you bring home a man who broke down our door. It's just not good enough. We thought you were such a nice girl." She sighed dramatically, as if her faith in mankind had been wiped out with Topaz's very birth.

Topaz was about to give her a piece of her mind when Logan stepped in.

"Mrs Baker, I have apologised for the door, and offered to reimburse you. There is no need to make personal comments to Topaz. She won't be taking that room," he hugged her close, "she will be staying with me for the remainder of her stay." He handed her a card from his pocket. "Here is my card, kindly forward the bill for the repairs and call us when the police are done with the room. We'll come by to pick up Topaz's stuff then. Goodnight."

He silently gathered her altar bits and slipped them into his jacket pockets, glaring at Mrs B as if daring her to protest, before putting his arm around her.

Leaving Mrs B gaping like a guppy, her mouth opening and closing, but no sound coming out, he swept Topaz out of the open door.

Once outside he let her go.

"I'm sorry about that. I didn't mean to make decisions for you. I just couldn't stand hearing her say those things about you." He took her hand in his and looked at her. "I didn't mean to push you into anything you might be uncomfortable with. I have lots of space and three spare rooms, you can choose any one you wish. And if you aren't comfortable we can find you another hotel tomorrow."

She smiled up at him, he was being so sweet. She took his arm and wrapped it around her shoulders, snuggling close.

"I accept your offer of a room, thank you." Logan beamed down at her as he pulled his mobile out of his pocket and proceeded to call for a taxi.

85

Chapter 7

"You live here?" Topaz asked in disbelief as they pulled up outside Night Walkers. "Do you rent a room above the club?"

Logan shook his head. "No, I don't."

He paid off the cab and led her around to the back of the club, which was down a long, dark alley way. Pulling a key out of his pocket, he opened the back door. Inside was a corridor with lots of doors, which she took to be offices and store cupboards. She guessed that it led out to the main floor of the club. Logan unlocked another door directly in front of them, pulling it open to reveal a staircase. He started up the stairs and she had no choice but to follow him. Logan unlocked yet another door at the top of the stairs. Security must be a big thing for them.

"Welcome to my home," Logan swept his arms out in a mock theatrical gesture and stepped aside to let her into his apartment.

She just stood there, staring around her, stunned. The place was amazing. It was huge. The main living room was open plan. The seating area was full of comfortable sofas grouped around a glass coffee table. The kitchen area was off to the left of the room, separated by a breakfast bar. A dining table sat in one corner and a piano in the other. The floors were polished wood, with a few rugs scattered around. Book shelves covered one entire wall, with books of all shapes and sizes arranged neatly in rows. Ornaments and curios were dotted here and there on the shelves between the rows of books. A hallway at the end of the room obviously led to the bedrooms. She was desperate to see what else there was.

"Wow," she finally spat out. "How many people do you share with?"

Logan flopped down onto one of the couches.

"None, it's just me."

She was now officially confused, but hey it didn't take a lot.

"But you said you didn't rent above the club?"

"I don't."

"Am I just being really dense here?" she crossed her arms in a defensive pose.

Logan rolled his eyes and stood up, grabbing her gently and pulling her down next to him on the sofa.

"I don't rent this place, I own it."

"But what about the club downstairs, I assumed you worked there? Don't tell me you own that too?"

Logan looked a little sheepish, refusing to meet her eyes.

She was speechless, and that didn't happen to her often. She felt like she was missing the big picture, like he had something else to tell her and it was staring her right in the face, but she just wasn't getting it. She was turning everything over in her head, trying to figure it out. Logan seemed uncomfortable about something, but she still couldn't put her finger on it.

Logan waved his hand as if brushing away her questions and said oh-so-casually, "don't worry about all that now. Let me get you a drink while you take a look around. Go pick your room." He stood up and made a shooing motion with his hand before heading over to the kitchen.

Curiosity was getting the better of her; she was desperate to check out the rest of the place. Slowly she stood up, almost waiting for him to follow her, call her back, offer her the grand tour, anything, but he didn't.

She wandered slowly down the hall and opened the first door she came to. It was small bedroom, decorated in pale pinks. The bed was a single, off to one side, under a window, a wardrobe and chest of draws were also in sight. There was another door in the room, which opened to reveal a bathroom. It was obviously a guest one as there were no personal items in the room. There was a toilet, sink and a small cubicle shower. Several bottles of shower gel and shampoo sat on a shelf, but all were un-used. Towels were folded neatly on a rail on the far wall.

Another door led to the next bedroom. This one was much larger. It was decorated in pale blues, with a matching bedspread and curtains tying the whole room together. White furniture was dotted around, a chair sat under the window and the chest of draws had a mirror on the wall above it. The room was calm and peaceful. Topaz liked it instantly and decided that this was the room for her.

She was about to head back to the main room and inform Logan of her choice when curiosity reared its ugly head again. She just had to see his bedroom. You could tell a lot about someone by the state of their bedroom and she desperately wanted to know more about Logan. If he turned out to be a slob who only owned three pairs of underwear, all of which he wore for a week at a time, she wanted to know.

He was just so mysterious. He knew almost everything about her, yet she felt like he was holding back a big part of himself.

Her feet carried her down to the end of the hall. For some reason she knew that was where the master bedroom would be located. She headed to the door right at the end, ignoring the other two doors that were also down there.

She paused for a second and listened intently, she could hear Logan banging around in the kitchen. She didn't like to snoop but it was so tempting. And he had told her to explore, she reasoned. She took a deep breath and turned the handle, opening the door quietly.

Her breath came out in a gasp as she looked inside. The room was done out in much the same way as the club downstairs. Rich red, textured wallpaper covered the walls tying in nicely with the black woodwork. Heavy black curtains hung at the windows. Her eyes travelled past the built-in wardrobes to the bed. Great Spirit, the bed. It was huge. Most definitely a king size. Black silk sheets covered it, and a mound of pillows perched on top. Unable to resist she reached out a hand and stroked the soft material. It felt wonderfully cool under her fingers.

"Do you like my room?" a deep voice asked room behind her. She jumped about a mile in the air and spun round so fast that she lost her balance and stumbled. Logan caught her in his arms and held her as she regained her composure.

"I'm sorry, I didn't mean to startle you. Are you alright?"

She put her hand on his chest to steady herself and instantly wished she hadn't. Hard muscles pressed against her palms.

Logan looked concerned, a frown creasing his forehead.

She tore her eyes away from the bit of chest that was visible and shook away her mental image of what the rest would look like.

"I'm fine, I just turned round too quickly and got dizzy. I'm sorry, I didn't mean to snoop."

She realised that she still had her hands on his chest and that he had made no move to remove them. Her body was tingling just being near him, his power seeming to flow over her skin. All the feelings that had built up earlier during their kisses flared back into life and demanded immediate attention.

"I'm sorry, I should have warned you that I was there. You had a big shock earlier, I didn't think." Logan was talking again, but she barely registered his words. She was too busy focusing on his lips, his lush, kissable lips. He was right, she had had a shock. Her privacy had been invaded and her things riffled through. Now hordes of police would be looking through her stuff too. It suddenly hit her like a sledgehammer. Her laptop, her notes, everything was on that computer.

Without knowing it, tears had begun to slide their way down her cheeks again. Seeing them, Logan gathered her into his arms and held her tight. She sobbed into his shirt, her shoulders heaving, as Logan stroked her back softly and whispered comforting nonsense into her hair.

Finally, her crying fit began to wind down. Logan stroked the hair away from her face and urged her head until she was looking at him. With a gentle thumb, he wiped away her tears.

"I hate to see you cry," he whispered, kissing her wet cheeks.

"I hate for you to see me cry," she countered. "It makes me feel weak."

"You, my love, are anything but weak. You are strong and beautiful. You are kind and loving, wise and knowledgeable. You are perfect. My woman could never be weak." That made her smile a little.

"Your woman?" She teased whilst trying to decide if it was sweet or just annoyingly male. "I'm my own woman, thank you. I earn my own money and I…"

Logan silenced her with a kiss so hot she almost melted. She surrendered to the soft pressure and opened her lips, allowing his tongue to slip inside. The kiss started off slowly, soft nibbles of lips and loving caresses, their tongues sliding against each other in a sensuous dance. Logan broke off to kiss his way down her neck, nipping lightly at her skin. He found that sweet spot and sucked gently. She moaned and felt her legs turn to jelly. Logan slid his hand down her back, smoothed over her butt and travelled down further, sparks of desire igniting everywhere his fingers touched.

She was just wondering what he was up to when he suddenly swept her legs out from under her, scooping her up into his arms. She let out a little girly meep sound, wrapped her arms around his neck and hung on tight, trying to keep her balance.

Logan looked towards the bed and raised one eyebrow in silent question. His eyes were hungry, running over her body like he wanted to devour her. She thought about it for all of half a second. So what if he thought she was easy. This felt right and she was going to follow her heart, not her head that sounded suspiciously like a mix between Mrs B and her granny.

In answer Topaz leaned forward and kissed him, lapping softly at his lips. He growled and shifted her in his arms, pulling her around until she was facing him. He pulled her close and cupped her butt in his hands. She had two choices, dangle there like an idiot or hold herself up. She went for door number two. She tightened her grip on his shoulders and hoisted herself up, wrapping her legs around his waist. Logan closed his eyes and moaned as she inadvertently brushed against his groin as she settled herself, but seeing his reaction she did it again on purpose, giving a seductive little hip wiggle while she was at it.

"You had better cut that out or you'll be in for a very disappointing night," he warned her with a growl. she responded by nipping at his neck in much the same way as he had done to her, scraping her teeth lightly down his flesh before licking the sting away.

91

Logan's head lolled back, giving her better access, which she took full advantage of. She sucked his skin into her mouth and bit down gently.

"Do you have any idea how much I want you?" he moaned into her ear.

"About half as much as I want you," she answered. She slid her hands down his back, scoring lightly with her nails, until she reached his jeans. She began tugging at his shirt, trying to untuck it. It gave up the fight with little difficulty and she sighed with pleasure when she was finally able to run her hands over his bare skin. His skin reminded her of the silk sheets, he was slightly cool to the touch and so soft. Keeping one arm wrapped around his back for support she allowed her other to roam its way down his side and up across his chest. It felt even better than his back. His muscles rippled under her touch as she traced her fingers all around.

"Not fair," he murmured "you're touching bare skin. I want bare skin, I *need* bare skin."

"Who's stopping you?" she replied cheekily. In response he took a few steps forward, making his growing erection rub against her and let her legs drop down so she was standing before him, next to the bed.

"That's a lovely dress," he commented. "You look stunning in it," he heaved an exaggerated sigh. "Unfortunately it has to come off." His hands travelled up her back and eased down the zipper.

Gravity did its thing, thanks mostly to the lack of shoulder straps, and the dress slid down her body to pool at her feet on the floor. The look on his face was worth the extra effort she had put in earlier that day while getting ready. She stood there in nothing but her black and purple lacy panties, stockings and black high heels. A bra had been out due to the design of the top and her nipples stiffened immediately under a combination of his heated looks and the slight chill in the air.

92

"Beautiful," he breathed. He took a step towards her and raised his hands, not quite touching, as if waiting for permission. Topaz appreciated the gesture but her breasts were practically aching with the need to be touched. She also wanted to touch him almost as desperately. She leaned forward and slowly unbuttoned his shirt, running her tongue lightly over all that wonderful skin she was exposing. Logan dropped his hands to his sides and stood very still, letting her work at her own pace, his hands clenched into fists as if he was fighting for control. She loved that about him, he never wanted to rush her, never seemed to think just about himself.

She rewarded his patience by lifting her head and claiming his lips. As she kissed him she slid the shirt down over his shoulders and off his hands. Once his hands were free, she did the one thing she had been wanting to do from the first moment she saw him. Reaching up she ran her fingers gently through his hair, stroking the strands that were just as soft and silky as she had imagined, its heavy weight resting in her palms. She tightened her grip just a little and urged him closer.

His hands slid up her ribs, fingers dancing over her skin, working their way up. His fingertips skimmed around her breasts, not quite touching and she moaned in frustration and pressed closer to him, rubbing her nipples against his chest, the sensation making her shudder in his arms.

"Are you determined to make me lose what little control I have left, lass?" he asked. Her answer was to run her hands down his chest, toying with the dark sprinkling of hair, and un-pop the button on his jeans. He sucked in a deep breath as she eased down the zip and discovered, much to her delight, that he wasn't wearing any underwear. She was about to ease the denim down over his hips when he grabbed her hand to stop her.

93

She looked up at him questioningly. Was he backing out? Because damn she was not going to give this up without a fight and a major pouting session.

"I want to touch you," he whispered. He used his grip on her hand to turn her back towards the bed. He let go of her hand and placed both of his on her hips, before picking her up in his arms and laying her gently on the cool sheets. They felt so good against her heated flesh, like a cool kiss that she sighed with pleasure at the sensation.

Logan crawled onto the bed next to her and leaned over.

"I want to feast on you," he whispered, his voice husky with desire. "I want to lick and taste every inch of your luscious skin." He laid a gentle kiss on her neck and she shuddered, need rolling through her. "I want to take my time exploring you," he kissed a little path down her neck to her collar bone. "I want to feel you shudder in my arms and make you so wet, before I bury myself deep inside you." She groaned at his words and closed her eyes to enjoy the images they invoked. He took full advantage.

She almost leapt off the bed when he bent his head and gently licked one of her nipples. He lips closed over the peak and sucked, his hand sliding up her ribs to cup her other breast. She arched into the caress, trying to push herself closer. It seemed like she had been waiting her entire life for this moment and now that it was here, she was desperate for him to hurry up and make love to her.

"Patience, my love," he murmured against her skin. "We have all night." She groaned at the thought. On the one hand she wanted this moment to last forever, didn't want it to end because then she would have to face reality, think about going home, back to her life. She didn't like that idea, didn't want to leave Logan. But on the other hand she was desperate to feel him inside her, filling her, making love to her. She groaned in frustration, not knowing what she wanted.

94

He nipped at her nipple, scraping his teeth against it softly. OK, she definitely wanted to speed this up. She sank her fingers into his hair and used it to gently pull him up for a kiss, at the same time rolling over and throwing one leg over his hips to pull him closer.

She ground herself against him, making her desires very clearly known.

"You are such a demanding wee thing aren't you?" he growled against her neck, cupping her breasts in his hands and squeezing lightly.

She nodded, almost beyond words. "I want you," she managed to get out. He bent his head and kissed her, hard and equally as demanding. She melted against him and wrapped her arms around him, trying to get closer.

Logan rolled them over so she was lying on her back with his body cradled between her legs. Logan kissed her neck, a soft brush of lips that made her shiver, kissing and nipping, running his tongue lightly down her skin. He paused at her collar bone for a second before continuing down. He swirled his tongue along her ribs and swept a path down to her belly. Her skin contracted with his every touch, her muscles jumping as tingles of energy tickled her skin.

His hands followed the path of his mouth, smoothing over her skin, his fingers caressing and stroking, stoking the fire that was building inside her. He eased off and slid down her body until he was kneeling between her legs.

He ran his hands lightly up her leg, his fingers sliding over the silky stockings. He slipped his fingers under the lacy top, and kissed her skin, then slowly rolled the stocking down, kissing every inch of flesh he uncovered.

The feel of his lips caressing her skin was driving her mad. Images were floating through her head, images of what he was going to do to her later, how he would put that mouth of his to good use. He reached her ankle and slipped off her shoe before easing the rolled up stocking off her foot, tossing it over his shoulder, uncaring as to where it landed.

95

She tried to pull him up her body for a kiss but he hadn't finished tormenting her.

With agonizing slowness, he started on her other leg, easing down the stocking and following its path with soft kisses. By the time the stocking had sailed over his shoulder to join its partner on the floor, Topaz was writhing on the bed, her breath coming in shallow pants, desperate for him to touch her again. She lay back on the bed and closed her eyes, praying she would survive this night because she knew that she might very well die if he didn't fuck her soon.

His fingers caressed her through the thin lace of her panties making her gasp and lift her hips, urging him to slid inside and give her a more satisfying touch. As if he knew what she wanted he slipped his fingers under the waist band of her panties and eased them down. She lifted first one leg then the other. He caught her foot in his hand and pulled them off, dropping them on the floor without a second thought.

She tried to pull her leg back to settle it beside him on the bed but he held on, wrapping his hand around her ankle, his head lowering, he flicked his tongue against her ankle bone, licking lightly. She instinctively tried to pull away from him but he wouldn't allow it.

"Relax, baby," he crooned between kisses. She tried to do as she was told and laid back against the soft pillows taking a deep breath. Logan was steadily working his way up her leg and, even though she knew what was coming, it did nothing to prepare her for it.

Her back arched as he parted her moist flesh with his thumbs. She let out a strangled gasp as his tongue swept over her folds in a long, lazy stroke. Every muscle in her body strained as he set to work, driving her wild. His tongue delved and tasted, licked and sucked. The sensations he gave her were unlike anything she had ever experienced before, the pleasure so intense it made her head spin.

She clutched at the sheets, needing something to hold on to as the pleasure poured over her. Logan lifted her legs, resting them over his shoulders, opening her wider. Her hips were lifting of their own accord, grinding against him.

The pleasure began to build inside her, seeming to flow out from every point he touched. She felt him shift his position and gasped as he slid one long finger inside her, her muscles clamping down on the digit as he began to ease it in and out. The combination of his tongue sweeping over her, twirling around her swollen clit before sucking lightly and his finger working her was too much. She felt her orgasm build but was unprepared for it.

Her legs began to shake as the pleasure radiated out, sweeping through her whole body, she writhed and wriggled on the bed, trying to pull away, the pleasure almost too great to stand. But Logan held on to her, gripping her hips in a firm grasp, working her mercilessly, he feasted on her flesh, winding her higher and higher.

The pleasure peaked and she cried out, her body fragmenting, seeming to break into a thousand pieces, her spine bowed, her neck arching as her hips circled on their own, chasing his tongue, thrusting his finger faster in and out of her sheath as she rode the pleasure he produced in her, her moans and whimpers filling the air. Finally, her body went limp and she flopped down onto the sheets, her skin damp. Logan eased back, slowing his movements to light caresses, bringing her gently back down. She shuddered and shook, trying to calm her racing heart, her breath coming out in shallow pants.

Logan lowered her legs and crawled up the bed to settle beside her, wrapping his arms around her as he cuddled her close to his side until her body gradually stilled. She snuggled into his embrace, turning her head for a kiss. He lowered his lips to hers and kissed her softly. She could taste herself on his lips, and far from being unpleasant, the kiss deepened. Their tongues met and twinned against each other, caressing and exploring.

She felt her body begin to respond to his kisses and, even after the earth shattering climax she had just enjoyed, she was still aching for him.

Topaz broke the kiss and leaned into his chest, kissing the soft, cool flesh, it felt as soft as silk under her lips and she couldn't resist giving it a lick, tasting him. She ran her hands over every square inch of flesh she could find, sculpting his muscles and curves like she could memorized them and take them back home with her.

She reached the waist band of his jeans and tugged impatiently at them, wanting them off. She was desperate to get her hands on him, to give him back some of the pleasure he had given her.

Logan moved and crawled off the bed to stand beside it, tall and impressive. She drank him in with her eyes, starting with his gorgeous face, his eyes shining with passion, looking more gold than brown now. His hair was mussed up and framing his face where she had run her fingers through it so many times.

A very male smile curved his lips, making her smile back. Her eyes wandered down, flicking over the necklace with the two rings that he wore, they felt very familiar, like she had seen them before somewhere but she put the thought aside to puzzle over later. Her gaze travelled lower taking in his broad shoulders and sculpted chest, down lower over his abdomen to his slim waist. His hands followed her eyes, coming to rest on his hips as if in invitation.

She sat up and scooted to the side of the bed, dangling her legs over the edge. She reached out her hands, which was now trembling ever so slightly, and slid her fingers into the waist band of his jeans. They were still open at the button from where she had released it earlier, she took a firmer hold and tugged them down, easing them over his swollen erection. It sprang free, standing proudly to attention. She stared at it with a mixture of excitement and horror. He was huge. She stared at it some more, completely awestruck. That was so not going to fit.

She blinked and refocused as Logan kicked off his jeans and took her into his arms, urging her back onto the bed. He lowered his head to her breasts again, his lips closed over one nipple, he began to suck on it gently, before he drew back to lick it, his tongue rasping against the hard peak.

Topaz arched against him and wrapped her arms around his neck, pulling him closer and lifting her breasts up for easier access.

Her hands roamed over his shoulders and down his back, raking her nails over his soft flesh as he nipped playfully at hers. He arched his back and growled into her flesh. Noticing and liking his reaction she did it again then allowed her hands to keep wandering while he was distracted by her breasts.

He stiffened against her as she finally reached her goal. His eyes drifted closed and he raised his head, releasing her nipple to moan deep in his throat as she wrapped her fingers around his erection, squeezing gently before sliding her hand along his full length.

He moved against her, rocking his hips to encourage her to stroke him harder. She complied, softly at first and then a little more. Logan began to moan and she felt him swell in her hand. How was that even possible? Did he have a bicycle pump attached somewhere? They were definitely going to have problems very soon; she was damn sure about that.

Logan reached down and pulled her hand away from his cock. She looked up at him, wondering if she had done something wrong. It had been rather a long time since she had done anything like this and she was rather afraid that she may have been a little too rough, a little too eager.

"You have to stop, baby or I'm going to explode and I want to make love to you." He ran his fingers softly down her face, as if to reassure her that she had done nothing wrong and she leaned into the caress lifting her head for a kiss. She just couldn't seem to get enough of his kisses.

He kissed her while urging her to lie back on the bed, nudging her legs apart so he could kneel between them. He bent to kiss her again, distracting her so he could run his hand down her body. She jumped as he touched her damp flesh, his fingers parted her folds and dipping inside before slipping back out and spreading her juices over her flesh. They explored and caressed driving her wild. He worked at her, making her pant and writhe beneath him until she was beyond desperate to feel him deep inside her.

"You're so wet, you're almost ready for me." He sank his fingers into her again, causing her to arch back off the bed in pleasure. She didn't want to wait, she couldn't wait. She was so glad she had kept up with her contraceptive pill because there was no way she wanted to stop and worry about condoms.

"Please, baby," she begged wrapping her legs around his waist to pull him closer. "I want to feel you, all of you, deep inside me, please don't make me wait anymore."

He positioned himself at her entrance, still rubbing her in small, tingling circles. She lifted her hips, begging him with her body to hurry. He flexed his hips and began to ease into her, an inch at a time, before pulling back out, working her open. She had a moment of apprehension, what if he was too big?

"You're so tight, baby," he groaned as he sank into her another inch.

"Oh, Great Goddess," she moaned. "You're so big."

"Relax, baby," he soothed. "We'll fit. We were made for each other." He flexed his hips again driving into her with long, slow thrusts. She gasped and moaned, her mind recalling his sweet words.

She cried out as he finally entered her fully. She felt stretched open and full to bursting but it felt amazing.

100

"You feel so good," he groaned as he began to move, slowly at first, working away some of her tightness, easing through the muscles that were gripping him. His shaft grew slick with her juices, reducing the resistance. He began to move more smoothly, speeding up slightly.

She lifted her hips and began to meet his thrusts, urging him on. She needed him to quit being gentle and fuck her.

He pulled back and slipped his hands under her butt, cupping her arse and lifting her up, then surged back into her, filling her, deeper, harder than ever before. He moved within her causing little gasps of pleasure to come spilling out of her mouth with every thrust.

She felt the heavy weight of another orgasm build up inside her and managed to gasp out her plea.

"I'm close, so close, come with me."

"I will, baby, I will," he promised and used his hands to move her where he wanted her, changing the angle until he found that sweet spot inside her that made her come apart in his arms. He stroked over it a few more times, long, deep thrusts that made her groan with pleasure.

One more thrust and her orgasm hit her like a tidal wave. She screamed her pleasure to the world in one long scream. Logan thrust again and his body shivered above hers, a shudder of pleasure that went all the way down his body, it threw his head back, closed his eyes and bowed his spine. She felt him empty himself into her but was too far gone to do more than hang on. Their bodies were still quivering with aftershocks as she clung to him, pulling him close and kissing his neck.

After what seemed like an age he pulled out of her slowly, causing her to writhe under him, and rolled off. He settled on his side and pulled her into his arms so she was spooned against him. She could feel his now semi-flaccid member nestled against her butt and gave a half-hearted wriggle. He smacked her butt lightly and she giggled.

She cuddled into his embrace and closed her eyes. He kissed her neck softly and began to stroke his hand up and down her side in a soothing, loving caress. She yawned out loud, suddenly feeling so tired.

"Go to sleep, my love," he whispered into her ear and much as she tried to fight it, her eyes grew heavy and she drifted off, safe in his embrace.

Chapter 8

She was back in that house, her dream house, it all seemed so familiar to her. Yet again, the sound of children playing outside caught her attention.

She stood at the open door and looked out, watching the children. She knew now that they were hers. She didn't know how she knew, she just did. She was holding a small bunch of herbs, bound with string in one hand and a small stone in the other.

She heard footsteps behind her, but didn't turn round to see who it was, she already knew.

Strong arms crept around her waist, holding her tightly to a firm chest. A chin came to rest on the top of her head and she snuggled into the embrace, slipping the herbs and stone into her apron pocket.

She linked her fingers with his and looked at their joined hands. They both wore plain gold wedding bands. She knew this was her husband, the father of her children. She felt safe and loved as they stood there in their little house.

Soft kisses trailed down her neck and she leaned her head back to give him better access. She closed her eyes in pleasure and turned in his arms. Lips descended onto hers and gave her the most tender, loving, gentle kiss she had ever experienced.

She opened her eyes and met his warm brown ones, smiling up at her husband. She ran her hands up his back and over his shoulders to pull him closer. Her fingers twinned in his soft brown hair as she pulled him down for another kiss. She wanted to stay there for ever, enclosed in his arms.

"I love you, Alcina, my beloved wife," he whispered in her ear, running his finger down her cheek in a loving caress.

"I love you too, Logan, my darling husband," she whispered back and snuggled closer, resting her head against his chest and closing her eyes.

Topaz awoke from her dream in utter confusion. She was lying in Logan's arms, her head pillowed on his chest. She snuggled closer for a moment, the feelings of love that she felt in the dream still strong within her. She thought back over the dream, trying to make sense of it. Obviously she was having some kind of fantasy dream in which Logan starred as her husband, whatever that meant. She levered herself up out of his arms and turned to look at him, ready to apologize for waking him.

She hadn't woken him; she doubted even an earthquake could have. She stared at him unable to believe what she was seeing. He was lying on his back, eyes closed, body stiff and unresponsive. She laid a trembling hand on his chest but it lay still under her palm. His skin was waxy and cold.

"Logan?" she whispered softly, as if afraid to speak louder. He didn't respond, not that she really had expected him to. She tried again, getting louder and louder until she was almost screaming at him. Her mind was whirling like a washing machine. She didn't understand what had happened; he was healthy enough last night. Shit, had she done something to him? She wasn't thinking straight. She couldn't lose him, she had only just found him.

She had to save him, she had to try, she just hoped she wasn't too late. She knelt over him and placed both hands, one on top of the other, on his chest over his heart. She racked her brains, trying to remember what she had learned from the first aid course she had taken when she started at Athena's.

Vague memories came back to her and she began to press down on his chest in short bursts, counting under her breath. When she had done this the required thirty times, each compression seeming to take an age, she leant forward to open his mouth, ready to breathe life into his lungs. She tipped his head back and slipped her finger into his mouth, to pry open his lips. A sharp pain shot through the tip of her finger. She pulled back, startled and looked at her abused digit. A drop of blood hung there. She looked down at Logan's face; his fangs glinting in the light.

His *fangs*? It hit her like a ton of bricks. He was a Vampire. She turned away from him, couldn't look at him. It was all making sense now. Him owning the club, the feeling she had that he was holding something back from her. This was his secret.

Why didn't he tell her? Didn't he trust her? Her mind went back over all the times they had spoken about Vampires, her work, everything. She felt betrayed, like he didn't like or trust her enough to tell her. Was she just an easy conquest to him? Just one of the many women he picked up at his club and seduced, bringing them back to his place for a little nocturnal nookie?

She turned and looked at him in disgust. He was lying in exactly the same position he had been in before. He really was dead to the world. She felt an insane giggle bubble up in her throat at the same time as the tears began to fall. He was so beautiful, even in death. His skin was flawless, his body the same sculpted paradise she had explored the night before. His lips still the same soft ones she had melted against.

She reached out and ran her fingers down his face. That was the moment her heart shattered. She knew there and then that she had hastily, stupidly, fallen helplessly in love with this man. It didn't seem to matter that she had only known him a few days; her heart knew what it knew. She'd thought he was different, that he liked her for who she was. That he was being honest with her as she had with him.

She took a few deep breaths to try to calm herself but she could feel panic bubbling up inside her. She suddenly felt dizzy and claustrophobic. The room felt much smaller, like the walls were closing in on her. She had to get out of there. She scrambled off the bed and looked around wildly for her clothes. Her panties were on the floor, exactly where Logan had dropped them. She closed her eyes, trying to force away the memory of what had come next. She yanked them on and grabbed her dress. She didn't care about being quiet; it wasn't like it was going to make a difference to Logan's sleep. She banged about, dragging on her dress and shoving her feet into her shoes, not bothering with the stockings.

She risked one quick glance at Logan and wished she hadn't. Great Goddess, she still wanted him. Her body was urging her, begging her to lie back down with him, to wrap herself around him and cuddle up. She was so tired, her dream still haunting her. The thought of Logan as her husband felt so right, like they belonged together. Her body wanted to sleep. It remembered how nice it had been to fall asleep in his arms.

She told her body to shut up and opened the bedroom door, slamming it closed behind her. She hurried to the living area and picked up her bag from where it sat on the sofa. She draped her wrap around her shoulders and threw open the front door. She slammed that door too, a nice, loud, satisfying bang that took the edge off her frustration, just a tad.

She practically ran down the stairs, desperate now to get out into the fresh air. She needed to clear her head, she needed to think through all the thoughts that were buzzing around in her brain. She threw open the back door they had come through the night before, luckily for her it was also a fire escape.

She squinted in the bright sunlight, looking around, trying to decide what to do next. Dramatic exits are great (even when no one was awake to appreciate them) but it helped to have a place to go after you storm out. The fact that she didn't kinda took the wind out of her sails. But never one to wallow in self-pity (not for very long anyway) she started walking, almost automatically, in the only direction she knew.

As Topaz walked she weighted up her options, of which there were very few. She didn't have a hotel to go back to, she didn't have any of her possessions, no clothes, no laptop, nothing but the clothes she was wearing and the few items she had managed to stuff into her handbag. She had none of her friends to turn to and due to her recent splurging on outfits she also didn't have much in the way of funds left. The train to despair town was about to depart the station and she didn't want to be on it when it left.

She forced herself to calm down, taking deep breaths, trying to kick her brain into gear. She looked about, taking in her surroundings for the first time during her walk. Somehow, be it conscious or not, she had wandered all the way to the street that High Vampage was on.

Suddenly she wanted nothing more than to pour her heart out to someone and Ronnie seemed like the perfect person for the job. She knew about Vampires, she would understand. Topaz quickened her pace, hurrying down the street.

She burst into the shop, the bell dinging loudly, eyes searching out Ronnie. She didn't see her immediately, as she was hidden behind a rack of clothes. At the sound of the bell she looked up.

"Hey, girl, how you doing?" Ronnie looked pleased to see her, flashing a wide smile that slowly slipped away as she took in the look on her face.

Ronnie rushed over to her and threw her arms around Topaz. "Oh, honey, what's wrong? Did something happen?"

In response to her concern, Topaz was unable to hold back the tears that had been threatening to spill forth since she had left Logan's. She collapsed into her arms and sobbed her heart out. She didn't quite know why she was feeling so shaken up, so emotional. She had a horrible sicky feeling deep down in her stomach that just would not go away. She felt wrung out, weak, depressed. A headache was squeezing at her temples like a vice. She didn't understand it, she had been lied to by men before, and she had been dumped, unappreciated, used before. Hell, she was used to it, she almost expected it and now shook it off with very little effort. So why did she feel like her whole world had just collapsed?

Ronnie hugged her tighter for a moment before leading her over to the back room. She let go of her to open the door and dragged out two chairs. She placed one down in front of Topaz and eased her into it.

Leaving her sniffing and snorting, she disappeared behind the door. She was soon back, two steaming coffee cups in her hands. She handed Topaz one and plonked herself down in the other chair. Tope took a shaky sip and felt a little better.

"So," Ronnie began, her hands on her knees as she leaned forward towards her, "do you want to tell me what happened?"

Topaz took another sip of her coffee and sighed, gathering her scattered thoughts, before diving in mouth first

108

and letting it all spill out. She told her about how great their date was, about coming home and finding her room ransacked, about Logan taking charge and letting her stay with him. She told her (without going in to huge amounts of detail) about falling asleep in his arms, about her strange dream and waking up. She explained about finding Logan passed out and trying to save him. She sobbed her way through how she saw his fangs and finally about running out of the door and ending up there.

"Damn," Ronnie blew out the huge breath she had been holding, "a lot happened to you since we had lunch." Topaz nodded, that was the understatement of the year.

"So what do I do?" she pleaded, wanting her to help, to tell her what to do. In truth she wanted someone to tell her that everything was going to work out and to tell her how to make it happen. Unfortunately, she was an adult and this was something only she could deal with.

Ronnie sighed. "Oh, honey, only you can know what to do. I can't tell you what's right for you." She leaned forward and gave her knee a comforting squeeze. "But, tell me what you are the most upset about?"

Topaz thought about it while she sipped some more of her coffee. What was bothering her the most? It wasn't the fact that he was a Vampire, it was a shock, sure it was, but it also didn't put her off him. She had been singing their praises for years, trying to get people to understand them better, trying to prove to people that they were not the monsters that they were portrayed as. No, what had upset her the most was the fact that he hadn't told her. Here she was, having all sorts of feelings for him that, by rights, she shouldn't be having this early on and now she was feeling betrayed by him, like she was untrustworthy, like she was just another body in his bed.

Finally, she answered Ronnie, who was patiently sipping her own drink, letting Topaz think things through, waiting for the right time to impart some pearl of wisdom, which she really hoped she had, to make her feel better.

"I'm annoyed. I feel betrayed, worthless. I feel like I'm just another woman to warm his bed, like I'm not special enough to tell the truth to. I feel like he lied to me. I thought we were getting on so well, I told him almost everything about myself. I guess now I just don't know where I stand." She sighed deeply, unable to see past her own problems with the situation. Ronnie jumped straight in telling her exactly where she was wrong.

"Well first off, Logan didn't really lie to you did he?" Topaz looked at her in disbelief; it sure felt that way to her. "Well you didn't ask him if he was life challenged."

Tope chuckled a little at her description of Vampires.

"So it's not like he lied and said he wasn't one." Ronnie looked at her sharply until she nodded her agreement, seeing the truth in her statement. She ploughed on.

"And it's not like you've told him every little thing about you is it?" Reluctantly Topaz shook her head, she guessed that he knew she was a Witch, thanks in part, to her altar bits, but she certainly hadn't told him outright. She also hadn't told him anything about her past, nothing about ex's or how people treated her like a kook for believing in what she did. All the hard stuff to talk about she had left out, not wanting him to see her in a negative light.

"No, I didn't think so. Well you can't complain too much if he does the same to you. Anyway, you have to appreciate that most vamps never tell anyone what they are, it's dangerous. Really, you should be honoured that he invited you into his home and let you stay in his bed. That to me shows more trust and respect than anything." She nodded once in a there-see-I'm-right way.

Topaz thought about what she said and began to feel like a real insensitive bitch.

Ronnie got up and put her arm around her shoulders and Topaz laid her head on her arm and blotted away a few remaining tears.

"Don't worry honey, you can stay with me if you want. My last roommate just moved out, so I have a spare room. You can borrow some of my clothes until you get yours back, that shouldn't take much more than a day or so. Use my phone when we get home and call the police, tell them where you are and don't worry, everything has a way of working out for the best."

Topaz sniffed, her tears finally drying up and nodded her head.

"Thanks Ronnie, I'll take you up on your offer if that's OK, just for a night or two until I get myself sorted. What time do you finish here? I'm want to nip out and buy a few essentials."

"I get off at three."

"I'll be back then," Topaz waved goodbye as she headed out the door.

Chapter 9

"Thank you so much for letting me stay here, Ron, I really appreciate it." Topaz patted the bed on which she sat, and looked around the almost bare room. All personal touches of the person who had occupied it before, were gone, leaving only the bed, the dresser and wardrobe. She had already put her meagre purchases, a couple of pairs of knickers, a bra, two t-shirts, a pair of jeans and cheap trainers, away. Her cheap new jacket was hung up in the hallway.

"No problem, to tell you the truth, I'll be glad of the company," Ronnie smiled.

Topaz nodded, she could understand that, especially if she was used to having a roommate. Tope lived on her own and sometimes she got lonely. Maybe she should think about getting that cat she was always joking about; she didn't have the time and patience to devote to a dog, but a cat, yeah she could do that.

Ronnie slapped her knees with her hands and jumped up from the bed.

"Right, dinner. I propose we spring for a take-out to celebrate you moving in and then watch some girly movies."

Topaz could tell she was trying to cheer her up and, much as she wanted to crawl into bed and wallow in self-pity for about a week, she knew it wouldn't be fair on Ronnie, she didn't deserve to have Mrs Miserable camped out in her spare room. She slapped a smile on her face and nodded.

"Sounds great, what do you fancy?"

"Chinese?"

"Yeah, I could really go for some sweet and sour chicken and rice."

"And pork balls," Ronnie added. She pulled her mobile out of her back pocket and hit speed dial.

An hour later they were sprawled out on the sofa; plates piled high with delicious Chinese food, their eyes glued to the T.V. screen. They had decided on 'Practical Magic', always a winner for Topaz. Surprisingly enough, the sickly feeling in the pit of her stomach that had been plaguing her all day had eased a little in the past few minutes and she found she was actually enjoying the food. Her headache had almost gone too and her mood felt lighter.

She had just lifted another heaped fork full up to her mouth; her eyes firmly on the action on the screen, watching the two main characters try to bring a boyfriend back from the dead, when some inconsiderate git began to pound on the front door, shattering their peaceful night.

She looked at Ronnie in surprise, was she interrupting something?

"You expecting company?"

"Nope," she put her plate down on the small coffee table and got up to the answer the door.

Topaz continued with her food, determined not to be nosy and turned back to the T.V. Her head snapped back round to the door when Ronnie's gasped with surprise and a hint

113

of fear. Well anyone would be worried if they opened the door to find a tall, glaring Vampire standing there.

"I want to see her." His rich, velvety voice was rough with emotion but it was unmistakably Logan's. "I know she's here, I can sense her."

"Well, I don't think she wants to see you right now," Ronnie argued, blocking his view of the living room with her body. Stubborn arse that he is, Logan simply looked over her head. His eyes locked onto Topaz's and her heart started to sing out to her, begging her to let him in, to hold him, to kiss him. She told it to shut up and pulled her gaze from his and concentrated on her food. She forked up a mouthful of rice, but it seemed to stick in her throat, tasting like cardboard.

She could feel waves of anguish rolling across the room from Logan's direction and her resolve crumbled. She closed her eyes, praying she wouldn't regret her decision and put her plate down next to hers.

"Let him in, Ron."

Ronnie raised one eyebrow but dutifully stepped aside.

Logan entered slowly, as if gauging Topaz's reaction. At the moment she was torn between wanting to cut and run and the almost over whelming urge to throw herself into his arms. He looked terrible, his hair was un-brushed, falling in tangles around his head, she tried not to wonder how those tangles had got there but suspected her fingers had something to do with it. He looked like he had fallen out of bed and yanked on the things closest to hand. He was wearing the same clothes that he had worn last night but didn't look anywhere near as impeccable. The jeans were rumpled from being dumped on the floor, he hadn't bothered with his belt and his shirt was creased and buttoned up wrong. His leather jacket completed the look.

"Do you need me to stay?" Ronnie asked, bless her.

114

"No, we won't be staying, I'm taking Topaz out," Logan answered for her. Anger flashed through her, how bloody dare he?

"Oi, no," she jumped up and stabbed her finger in his direction, one hand on her hip. "You don't get to talk for me. I am not your property, I decided for myself." She pulled her head back in and looked at Ronnie. "It's OK, Ron, I'll be back later. Save my Chinese for me?"

She nodded, staying quiet.

She gathered her bag and yanked on her jacket, glad it was a warm night, as it was made of rather thin material. Logan held his hand out to her but she pointedly ignored it and breezed out of the door without a backwards glance.

She hurried down the street working up a good stomping strut, leaving Logan to trail behind her, but Mr Tall and Leggy soon caught up. She carried on ignoring him until they reached the quiet little pub at the end of Ronnie's road. He held the door open for her and she ducked under his arm without bothering to thank him.

She managed to maintain her stony silence until they found cosy seats in the back room and ordered their drinks.

Finally, she couldn't stay quiet any longer. She turned to Logan and fixed him with 'the look'.

"You wanted to talk, so talk." Oh, that came out harsher than she had intended but she wasn't going to back down. She crossed her arms and glared at him, almost daring him to try to bullshit her.

Logan looked up sharply from the table, at which he had been staring intently.

"I'm sorry," his first words knocked the wind right out of her sails and she felt her glare fade and her arms relax. She met his eyes and was blown away by what she saw there. Despair and anxiety clouded the warmth of his eyes but (maybe it was wishful thinking) she also detected something else. Something that made her heart skip a beat. He looked at her with so much affection (she didn't want to risk the L word) that she melted. He was watching her, searching her face for some clue as to what she was thinking. He was obviously content with what his search revealed.

"I should have told you. I know you, of all people would understand." She nodded her agreement. Damn straight she would, but she held her tongue, a minor miracle for a blabber mouth like her.

"I didn't want you to find out like that. I was going to tell you but everything happened so fast."

She cocked an eyebrow at this, things had seemed rather too slow for her liking, but waved him to continue. He sighed deeply.

"I was so scared when I heard you scream. I had to get to you. And later when I saw you standing there, in my bedroom, looking so beautiful, I couldn't think straight."

He reached out his hand again and this time she took it, placing her hand in his. His fingers curled around hers and he squeezed lightly. It felt so good to be touching him again, the last of her sicky feeling melted away, leaving her feeling better than she had all day.

"I guess I'm sorry too," she was a big girl, she could admit when she was wrong, on the very rare occasions it happened. She guessed that she had overreacted just a tad; talking with Ronnie had shown her that. "I shouldn't have run out on you like that, but you have to appreciate that it was a very big shock. I woke up to find you dead, Logan, *dead.* That is not something a person, even one as unusual as I am, can overlook. I admit it, I panicked. You're bloody lucky you didn't wake up to find yourself on an autopsy table, I almost called an ambulance. I did CPR and everything…" her words trailed off, the shock of seeing him up and about, holding her hand finally sank in and was almost too much to handle. The feeling of having almost lost him had been overwhelming.

Logan wrapped his arms around her and hauled her up to his side, and she let him. She leaned against him and

116

inhaled his wonderful Logan scent, pulling it deep into her lungs. It calmed her down almost instantly as he held her tight and stroked her back with long slow passes of his hand.

"I'm so sorry I scared you, darling, that was the last thing I ever wanted to do. I didn't mean for it to happen. I was going to tuck you into your bed before the sun rose."

She looked up at him.

"Why didn't you?"

"Because you felt so wonderful in my arms." He rested his head against hers and stroked his fingers down her arm. "Whenever I'm near you I forget myself. You were cuddled up against me and your skin was so soft and warm, and you smelt so good."

He shook his head, and she looked at him. "I just wanted to hold you all night, like a normal couple. I wanted to wake up with you still safe in me arms. I wanted to wake you with a kiss. I was stupid, I know that, I should never have allowed it to happen. It's my fault." He ducked his head, avoiding her gaze.

Her heart bled for him. When she thought about all that he would have been through in all the years he must have lived, never being able to get close to someone through fear of them finding out his true nature and running away, made her experiences pale in comparison.

She lifted her hand to his face and stroked her fingers down his cheek, down until she cupped his chin and urged him to look at her. He slowly raised his head and their eyes met. She was determined to show him the only way she could that she forgave him.

She leaned over and pressed her lips against his, giving him a soft kiss.

"You were not stupid. Sure, I would have liked to have known before we did the nasty, but I didn't. We can't change it now, what's done is done."

"I know I should have warned you, but," he paused.

117

"But what?" She urged.

"But I didn't want to lose you. And if I was going to, at least I had one night to know what it was like to have you with me."

She gaped at him. He was officially the sweetest man ever. She leaned over and kissed him again, harder this time, trying to show him with actions, rather than words, exactly how she felt about him.

Her hands crept around over his shoulders and she turned in his arms, climbing onto his lap as she had wanted to last night, fitting herself against him more snugly. Once you had made love to someone and woke up next to them, even if they were 'life challenged' at the time, it kind of took away any residual shyness you might have.

He groaned deep in his throat and wrapped his arms around her, one hand stroking her back while the other tangled in her hair to pull her closer.

"I can't believe you're mine," he whispered in her ear. "I have dreamt about you for so long." His tongue parted her lips and the kiss deepened, seeming like an age before they parted.

"Come home with me." He looked at her, but she shook her head.

"I can't, not tonight. I have to tell Ronnie I'm alright. She might be worried." She slid off his lap and took a sip of her drink, trying to calm her raging hormones.

Logan scowled. "I would never harm you, nor allow anyone else to."

Topaz smiled and patted his hand reassuringly.

"I know that, baby, I really do. But I'm talking more about emotional hurt," she sighed and picked up a drinks mat to fiddle with, needing something to occupy her hands. She didn't want to get all self-pitying but she wanted to be honest. No more secrets. "I was really upset earlier. I was afraid that you didn't trust me." She looked down at her hands shredding the mat she held and continued in a small

118

voice. "I was afraid that I was just another woman to you."
She looked up at him. "I couldn't bear that, Logan. I like you
a lot, I don't want to lose you either. I think we could have
something very special." She dropped the cardboard
confetti that was the mat back onto the table.

Logan sighed and pulled her close again and kissed the
top of her head.

"You silly darling, is that really what you thought?" She
nodded, hiding her face against his chest, but Logan was
having none of it. He cupped her face exactly as she had
done to his and forced her to look at him. "I don't *think* we
could have something special, I *know* we do. How could you
not know that I worship you? That you are the most
beautiful woman in the world to me? I would give anything
to have you with me forever."

He tenderly stroked her face and she finally met his eyes.
They were back to their usual warm brown, the gold
highlights shining bright.

She knew right then and there that she wanted the same.
She would do anything to keep him. She wanted so much to
tell him how much she loved him, how much he meant to
her, but her lips wouldn't form the words. It was too soon.
Every man she had ever been with had left her. Logan was
saying all the right things at the moment, but for how long.
How long until the novelty wore off? Until he dumped her
like Bradley had? She wanted to be completely honest with
him but just couldn't find the right words. She didn't want
him thinking about how the other men in her life had treated
her, what if he started noticing the same things they had?
She needed more thinking time.

"I have to get home," she repeated. He nodded.

"When can I see you again?"

"Tomorrow night?" His face broke out into a wide grin.

"That's perfect." He took her hand and helped her up.
"Come on I'll walk you home."

119

Chapter 10

Topaz stepped into the shower, the hot water poured over her, washing away her tiredness. She stuck her head under the stream and wet her hair before vigorously rubbing in some shampoo. She rinsed, then smoothed in some conditioner, stepping back, avoiding rinsing her hair too soon and lathered up her body with soap.

Warm hands crept over her shoulders and smoothed down along her chest. They swept over her breasts with smooth, sure, strokes. Strokes designed to excite. She leaned back against his chest, letting him support her, whilst his hands wandered over every inch of her body, exploring and caressing.

She moaned in pleasure and leaned her head back onto his shoulder. He took advantage of this and lowered his head for a kiss.

His tongue slid along the crease of her lips, licking softly, parting her lips to gain access. His tongue explored her mouth, delving inside, tasting her. His hands glided down her body and slid down between her legs. His fingers, slick with soap, parted her soft flesh and began to mimic the actions of his tongue.

She gasped into his mouth and reached behind her to catch his erection in her hand, cupping his sac gently with the other. She explored him with her fingertips, sliding them over him in a long caress, shaping his thick shaft and slid up over the engorged head. She heard him moan low in his throat as he slid one finger deep inside her. She moved her head so she could look at him. His head was thrown back, his eyes closed in pleasure.

She increased the pressure, wrapping her whole hand around his shaft and squeezing gently. He groaned and his spine bowed. He grabbed her arms and hauled her up against him, lowering his head to take one eager nipple in his mouth.

Topaz gasped and arched against him, one hand still stroking him while the other reached up to tangle in his hair, holding his head to her chest. Her breathing turned ragged as he used his tongue to wring more gasps of pleasure from her.

He suddenly grabbed her hips and lifted her slightly, tipping her forward so she had to catch herself on her hands, palms flat against the tiled wall of the shower. He used his leg to nudge hers further apart, positioning himself at her entrance. She closed her eyes as he invaded her, pushing through her tight folds, until he was buried in her right up to the hilt.

She braced herself more firmly against the wall as he began to move inside her, long, slow strokes, designed to arouse. One hand slid up her body to cup her breast while the other resumed its caressing. He rubbed her clit in slow tingling circles, heightening the pleasure that was building inside her. He increased his pace, thrusting into her hard and fast, his fingers seeming to dance across her flesh.

She could feel that delicious weight of orgasm beginning to build inside her. It built and built, as if waiting for that one stroke that would finish her off. It came and it pushed her over the edge. It brought her screaming his name; it bucked her body against his as he thrust deep inside her, as hard and fast as he could. He brought her again, a different kind of orgasm that seemed to build on the foundation of the first one, pleasure radiating out from her clit. As her muscles clenched around him, he dropped his hands to her hips and held her still, pulling her close as he thrust into her, his growl of completion mingling with her own cries of pleasure.

He wrapped his arms around her and held her to his chest as she panted, trying to catch her breath as aftershocks rippled through her. He slowly slid out, the feeling making her writhe against him.

"Don't do that, baby, please," he begged with a rough chuckle, kissing her neck. "You'll kill me."

"You're already dead," she teased and wiggled her butt against his crotch. He growled and nipped at her neck, licking the sting away with his tongue.

"True," he agreed, "but if I could die, I would die happy." He swiped at her butt with his open palm. "Now finish your shower." He let go of her and stepped out of the cubicle and disappeared.

He disappeared?

She sat bolt upright in bed, her body still humming from the dream. She had just had one of the most incredible sexual experiences of her life and it had been a bloody dream? Life was so not fair. Her body ached for Logan's, feeling wound up tight. The covers were tangled around her body and the t-shirt that she had worn in lieu of a night gown, had ridden up almost to her shoulders.

Someone knocked lightly on her door.

122

"Tope, you OK? You were moaning really loudly. Are you hurt?" Ronnie's concerned voice floated through the closed door.

Topaz quickly ran her fingers through her hair and tried to wake up enough to form a coherent answer.

"I'm fine, Ron. I was just dreaming. I'm sorry if I woke you up."

"That's OK. Can I come in?"

"Yeah, sure, babe," Topaz scrambled around, pulling her t-shirt down and fixing the covers before she burst in.

The door opened and Ronnie popped her head in.

"Are you decent?"

Topaz giggled. "Yeah, it's safe. No Topaz parts on display in here."

She scooted over so Ronnie could sit down next to her on the bed.

Ronnie leaned back on her arms and looked at Topaz, a cheeky smirk on her face.

"So," she began, "what kind of dream were you having that made you groan like that?"

Tope blushed a little under the scrutiny.

"That good huh?"

She nodded, embarrassed.

"I take it that Logan also played a starring role?"

She nodded again.

"Well, I wish I had dreams like yours." Ronnie bumped her shoulder against Topaz's leg, who couldn't help but giggle.

"I'm glad you and Logan made up last night, I didn't like seeing you so sad. I really like you Topaz."

Topaz smiled at her. "I really like you too, Ronnie, you're a good friend. I don't know what I would have done without you these past few days. Everything has just been so strange, I can't quite get my head around it all."

Ronnie raised her eyebrows. "What else has been going on that I don't know about?"

123

Topaz explained everything to her. She told her about feeling a connection with Logan, about the strange dreams she had been having, she reminded her about the burglary and Mason's absence.

When she was done she looked at Ronnie.

"Well, what do you think? Something just doesn't add up, I'm sure of it."

Ronnie sighed, and rubbed her eyes.

"To be honest, Tope, I think you have a very active imagination. You're taking stuff too much to heart." Topaz opened her mouth to protest but Ronnie held up her hand to keep her quiet. "I agree that this has been a hard few days but that's all. Mase has always been like this, he disappears for a few weeks then turns up again. I get that the burglary was hard on you, but you remember what the police said, it was probably someone that targets tourists, the lap top was all you really brought with you. And as for the dreams…" she looked at Topaz in triumph, knowing she had made her point, "well, I had a dream the other night that I was on a beach, the sun beaming down and a dog rubbing in the suntan lotion."

Topaz stared at her in amazement for a few seconds before laughed bubbled up inside her. Ronnie joined in and they both howled, rolling around the bed like loonies.

Thirty minutes later found them sitting on the sofa, sipping coffee. Their giggles had finally subsided enough for them to go their separate ways and get dressed, with only a minor wrestling match over who got to use the bathroom first, Ronnie won (that girl might be small but she can tackle like a line-backer). Topaz's butt still ached for its sudden contact with the floor.

Topaz was scoffing down a round of toast and Ronnie was tucking into a bowl of muesli, Tope couldn't stand the stuff herself, it reminded her too much of the stuff she used to feed her rabbit.

124

"You got any plans for today?" she asked Ronnie.

"Not really. It's Sunday so the shop is shut. I normally just hang around the house, do a bit of cleaning and catch up on my celebrity gossip." She patted the stack of crisp new magazines that sat on the coffee table. "What about you? I mean, you're welcome to stay in with me but you are visiting here, why not go out and see the sights?"

Topaz nodded.

"I took a bus tour the other day but I did want to check out one of the museums. Do you wanna come with me?"

Ron made a face and shook her head.

"No, thank you. I saw enough of them when I was at school. No, you go off and have a good time. Are you seeing Logan later?"

"Yeah, we're meeting later. He didn't say where, so I assume I'm meeting him at the club again." She took another bite of toast.

"You do know it's closed today too?"

Topaz shook her head, her mouth too full to answer. She chewed furiously for a few seconds before swallowing.

"Nope, I didn't know that." She shrugged. "Well I guess it doesn't matter too much," she paused, not knowing how much to tell Ronnie about Logan's involvement with the club, finally she settled on her old faithful half-truth. "Logan lives above the club, so I guess I'll just head over there anyway."

Ronnie nodded and stood up to take her bowl into the kitchen.

"That's cool." She smirked at Topaz. "So I take it you might not be coming back tonight?"

Topaz blushed a little at what she was, not so subtly, implying.

"I guess not."

Ron dropped the bowl into the sink and sat back down next to her.

125

"Are you OK with the whole waking up next to him dead thing? I mean, I know how hot Vampire sex can be, but is it a price you're willing to pay?" She looked at Topaz intently.

Tope thought about it for a minute and decided she was OK with it. Logan was the man she loved, he would never hurt her. She wasn't afraid of Vampires and, now she had gotten over her initial shock, she could deal.

"Yeah, I'm OK with it. It was a weird way to find out, but we talked about it and I'm over my little hissy fit now."

Ron patted her leg affectionately.

"Good, I'm glad. Logan is a good guy. The Vampires I donate to always speak very highly of him."

That took Topaz by surprise, she had completely forgotten about her donations. Ron just didn't seem the type. She recalled how she had talked about her reasons for doing it. The fact that it felt so good and seemed to be highly sexual was the top reason on her list. She felt a spurt of jealousy rush over her. Did Logan have a Donor? Ronnie made it out to be quite an intimate experience and she didn't like the idea of anyone else getting hot with her man. She realised that she didn't really know much about Vampires after all.

Sure, she knew about them in theory, from a mythological point of view. She knew that they were dead, and reanimated by magic. She knew that they died at dawn and arose at sunset (she had found that out the hard way) and she knew that sunlight was bad for them, unless of course they were glittery movie Vampires. She knew that they had to drink blood to survive, but she had always thought of it as purely a functional thing, like how the living ate food to survive, they didn't date the cow their steak came from. She decided that she and Logan would have to have a talk later. If they were going to work out, she had to know these things.

"Topaz, are you alright? Topaz?"

126

Ronnie's voice yanked her out of her musings. She shook her head to clear her thoughts.

"Yeah, I'm fine."

"Good, it's just that you had this faraway look on your face. Whatever you were thinking of sure didn't look pleasant." Topaz looked at Ronnie, her friend, who was also a Donor. The thought slipped into her head and out of her mouth before she could stop it.

"Ronnie, have you ever fed Logan?" She slapped her hand over her mouth, in astonishment. Where the fuck had that come from? Ronnie looked as shocked as she was.

"Oh hell, Ron, I'm sorry. I didn't mean to say that." Ronnie swallowed.

"No, it's OK, if I was in your situation I would probably be thinking the same thing." She looked her dead in the eyes. "I promise you, hand on heart, that Logan has never fed from me." Topaz didn't want to disbelieve her but she couldn't help herself, she looked deep into her eyes, searching for the truth, then relaxed a little as she saw the truth in her eyes but then immediately tensed again when she detected something else. Just a flash, there and then gone, but she could have sworn she saw disgust in her eyes. Topaz blinked as Ronnie. She must have imagined it.

"Thanks, Ron," she grimaced. "I'm sorry, I know I'm being stupid, but I just don't think I could stand the thought of sharing him." She didn't really know what else to say but Ronnie knew what she meant. She leaned across the sofa and gave Topaz a hug.

"You are not being stupid. It's perfectly understandable. You're a one man woman so he has to be a one woman man."

Topaz nodded, glad she understood.

She finished her toast and washed up her plate, along with Ronnie's bowl and their coffee cups. When she had dried everything and put it away, she gathered her bag and shrugged on her jacket. She didn't have any makeup with

127

her so she did without, just pulling her hair back into a pony tail. She was wearing her new jeans and a t-shirt. Not very glamorous but the club was closed, she had no reason to dress up. Logan would just have to get used to her as she was, dressed in comfortable clothes and bare faced. She paused at the front door.

"I'm off now, Ron, I'll see you later." Ronnie looked up from where she was curled up on the sofa, a box of chocolates next to her and a magazine on her lap. She waved her free hand.

"See ya later, babes. Have a good time. Don't do anything I wouldn't do."

Topaz pretended to be stern and mock glared at her. "You would do everything, so I think I'm safe."

She nodded and winked broadly. "Damn straight."

Topaz giggled and waved goodbye, shutting the door behind her.

Chapter 11

Topaz had had a fantastic day. She had wandered around
again, looking at all the shops and the buildings (even
though she had seen them all before) the whole place just
fascinated her. She felt like she belonged there, it was
familiar and comforting.

She had planned on going to the Museum of Edinburgh,
as without her laptop to look up other places, it seemed like
the obvious choice. She sat down on a bench to rest her
feet, she was knackered, having walked for over an hour
and was debating taking a taxi to the Museum. She sipped
from her bottle of water and looked around her, taking in the
people and the atmosphere. The building in front of her
caught her eye and she meandered across the road to have
a look.

It turned out to be the best thing she could have done.
The building she had stumbled across was The Scottish
Storytelling Centre. She watched a live story performance,
wandered around their Library, stuffed herself with

homemade cakes in their Café, and spent an hour deciding what to buy her friends from the gift shop. By the time she left it was almost dark. The sun was setting, the day traffic was winding down and all around her the night life was starting to emerge. The shops that were still open were lit up, their windows enticing her to browse. Music was trickling out of bars and clubs as the daytime tourists made way for the partiers.

A small thrill went through her at the thought of seeing Logan. She realised that subconsciously she had been waiting for the sun to set. Everything else was just filling time until she could be with him again. With a smile firmly fixed on her face she set off down the road at a quick pace, desperate now to get to Night Walkers.

The sun had set fully by the time she neared the road where the club was situated. There were less people around now; the streets were almost deserted, everyone having migrated to the more popular areas where the bars were open. The club was in darkness, the absence of the waiting crowd of goths making it seem slightly sinister.

A shiver skittered down her spine and goose bumps prickled her skin, a feeling of apprehension settled over her. She felt like someone was watching her. She spun her head around, this way and that, searching for the source of her unease.

She unconsciously sped up, needing to get away, needing to get to Logan.

With one last quick glance over her shoulder, and yet again seeing nothing untoward, she slipped down the alleyway that led to the back door of the club. The door was about ten feet away when she felt it.

All she could describe it as was a kind of psychic jolt. It made her pause, her steps faltering. She stood there like a prize ninny as a huge, dark, hairy shape dropped down from the sky to land in front of her.

The smell was the first thing she noticed about the creature, it smelt like a dumpster, the stench of rotting meat and sour milk clung to it. It was big, maybe 8 feet tall, and covered in fur. It stood on its hind legs, its knees bent as if ready to pounce. It resembled a human and reminded her of the classic wolf man from the old black and white movies. Its arms were raised in front of its face; wicked looking claws were nails should have been. Its face was elongated, its nose more of a snout.

She wanted to scream, but her throat had closed up completely in shock and all she managed was a pathetic little squeak. It took a step towards her, and she took two back, trying to back away slowly without alerting it to her intentions. Its head tipped to the side, its beady eyes watching her intently.

Oh Shit! What the fuck was she going to do? She was so scared she was quaking in her boots. Her eyes darted from side to side, trying to find a way out of this situation, but also trying to keep the creature in sight. She failed and looked away for a split second, but that was all it needed.

It pounced on her, driving her backwards. Her body smashed into the wall behind her, the back of her head making contact with the bricks with a resounding crack. White hot pain bloomed across her skull, dimming the aches coming from the rest of her body.

The creature's arms had landed either side of her torso, pinning her to the wall with its body. The pain was making her feel dizzy and unable to concentrate. It leaned into her body, its face so close to hers she could practically count its teeth, all of which seemed to be on display as it snarled at her, all pointy and sharp. Its breath was rancid, and it made her gag, her stomach rolling.

It snapped at her neck with its teeth, close but not touching. She let out a piercing scream guaranteed to wake up the whole neighbourhood.

131

The monster grabbed her by the throat, wrapping both of its huge, hairy hands around her neck and began to squeeze, silencing her almost instantly. She lifted her arms and grabbed its hands, digging her nails into its flesh, trying to loosen its grip, but it had little effect, the thick fur preventing her from doing any serious damage.

It squeezed and squeezed, she wheezed and coughed, trying to catch her breath, trying to pull some air into her lungs. Her chest burned and her vision began to grow a little fuzzy around the edges.

This was it. Her time was up. Her eyelashes fluttered as her eyes closed. If she was going to die now, she was thankful that she had met Logan and had one night with him. If Logan was here he would save her, she knew he would. She wished with all her heart that he was here. But she knew she would never see him again.

A tear slid down her cheek as she opened up her heart and sent out to the heavens her love for him. *Logan*, she thought, *I love you.*

Distantly she heard a bang, but her mind was too fuzzy to pay much attention.

"Now you will die," Stinky Breath hissed in her ear, a low sound deep in its throat, like an animal growl.

"Not tonight she won't."

She heard a sickening crack and the beast was yanked away from her, its grip broken. Topaz sank to the floor, gasping and choking, trying to catch her breath, dragging in a deep lungful of air. Sweet, sweet oxygen. She leaned her head back against the wall and closed her eyes, trying to gain some control over her shaking limbs. That had been too damn close for her liking.

Gentle arms scooped her up and cradled her close, stroking her back.

"Topaz, sweetheart. Are you alright? Speak to me."
She opened her eyes and blinked, trying to focus. Logan held her close. She managed to nod her head and raised a

132

shaking hand to give him a thumbs up; her throat hurt too much to talk yet.

"Oh, thank the gods." He dragged her closer and dropped his head to hers, capturing her lips. He kissed her with a desperate passion, which she more than equalled, wrapping her arms around him and holding him tight. Her hands met bare skin and she sank her fingers into his muscles, clinging to him, never wanting to let him go again.

Logan pulled back and looked at her, framing her face with his hands. In his hurry to get to her, he must have rushed out of the door in the middle of changing; he was wearing nothing but a pair of jeans. His chest was deliciously bare, as were his feet. She itched to stroke his soft skin. A feeling of warmth spread through her body, easing her aching head and seeming to caress her abused throat. Logan tipped her head up so she was facing him, cutting off her mental imaginings.

"I thought I had lost you."

She looked deep into his eyes, a mixture of fear, relief, anger and passion greeted her. She leaned into his touch, savouring the connection and the tingling of connection where their flesh met. She sucked all that lovely healing warmth down into her body and coughed, clearing her throat, trying to form words.

"It would have had to do a lot more than that to get rid of me," she joked, trying to dispel some of the tension that hung in the air. She sounded a little croaky, even to her ears, but she managed it.

Logan said nothing, instead he used his mouth for better things, trailing his lips down her neck, kissing softly over her abused skin, the pain dimming more with every touch of his lips. She risked a quick glance over his shoulder, looking for the creature. She suppressed a shudder of revulsion when she spotted it lying on the floor, slumped against the wall, its neck twisted at an odd angle. She closed her eyes, blocking out the sight.

133

"Don't scare me like that again," he whispered against her skin. *Like I did it on purpose,* she thought, but wisely kept her mouth shut, instead she gave herself over to the sensations his lips were producing. The last shivers of fear were replaced with something else, almost a primal need, a need to reaffirm life. She had heard about near death experiences and, while hers was a little less conventional than most, she felt the almost overwhelming need to feel alive.

She clung to Logan and dragged his face back up to hers, kissing him with every ounce of passion she possessed.

"I want you," she managed to gasp out. Logan pulled back and looked at her intently for a second, as if weighing up her mental state, before he grabbed her hand and practically dragged her through the still open door.

She managed to pull the door closed behind her before Logan propelled her forward. The door to the stairs that lead up to his apartment hung from its hinges, a sure sign that Logan hadn't come down at a leisurely pace.

They practically ran up the stairs. At the top they paused, Logan looked at her, a silent question on his face. In answer she stepped closer.

He picked her up in his arms, his hands cupping her buttocks, she wrapped her legs around his waist and wriggled her hips, grinding herself against his hardness. She shuddered in his arms and cried out, the sensation of him pressing against her, even through their jeans, was amazing.

His mouth descended on hers and he feasted, like a man who had been starved and was now faced with an all you could eat buffet. She met his passion with her own, sucking his tongue fiercely into her mouth.

He groaned and took two steps forward into his apartment but they didn't make it any further. She was pressed so tightly to his chest that he rubbed against her with every step. She groaned and wriggled, trying to get a

134

more satisfying touch, she was aching for him so badly she thought she might explode. He took another step and her back connected with the wall.

Using the wall and her own arms around his neck to keep her in place he released his hold on her butt and yanked at her top, but when it didn't come up fast, or far, enough for his liking, she unhooked her arms from his neck and leaned back against the wall (which tipped her hips up to meet his) reaching down to help. He held her up as she yanked the top up over her head and tossed it over his shoulder, uncaring as to where it landed. She locked her lips back onto his and swept her tongue into his mouth.

She wrapped one arm back around his neck for support as his fingers traced the lacy cups of her bra. With one deft flick of his fingers he undid the front hooks and her breasts spilled out into his waiting hands.

His mouth left hers to claim her breasts, he fed on them, suckling, caressing and licking, his tongue painting wet lines across her skin. She heard him moan softly just before he began to lift his head, but she was having none of it. Her breasts ached for his touch. She fisted her fingers in his hair and held his head against her flesh.

"Topaz," he groaned. She felt his tongue sweep over her nipple in one long, lingering stroke. She shuddered in his arms and pressed her breast closer to his mouth. She felt the gentle scrape of his teeth, his suddenly pointier, sharper teeth, against her skin, but rather than fear, desire rushed through her. She suddenly understood how feeding a Vampire could be erotic. The feel of his fangs on her skin, him being so gentle, holding back all that primal need in him was too much for her. She pushed her flesh deeper into his mouth and his fangs pricked her skin just a little. He stiffened for a second before pulling harder on her flesh, sucking, trying to get a more satisfying taste.

The sensation threw her head back and she moaned, grinding her body against his again. She wanted him

135

desperately, at this moment she didn't care what he was, all she knew was that she loved him and wanted him so much it hurt.

"You taste so good," he moaned around the mound of flesh that filled his mouth.

"I need you inside me," she groaned and forced her hand down between their joined bodies to rub him through his jeans. He growled deep in his throat, whether it was in response to her words, her blood or her touch, she didn't know, nor did she care.

She unwrapped her legs from around his waist and dropped to the floor. He grabbed hold of her jeans and ripped them off her, tearing them apart at the seams, taking her panties with them. She jerked at the sudden action and a small whimper escaped her throat, damn that was hot, he was hot. He picked her back up and she encircled his body with her legs and arms once again pulling him tight to her. Her nipples scraped against his bare chest, the fine hairs tickling her skin, tingles following in their wake.

She leaned forward and kissed his neck, licking softly.

"Now," she panted, desperate to feel him inside her, filling her. "I can't wait."

He began to work at his jeans, fighting with the belt and button. But he was so hard and she was pressed so tightly against him, he could not unzip.

"I need you higher," he growled but didn't wait for her response or help, he cupped her butt and lifted her up with one hand, the other finally freeing himself. His jeans dropped to pool around his ankles, leaving him to spring free, standing to glorious attention.

The tip of him brushed against her skin as he lowered her back down those few inches needed so he could guide himself to her opening.

She was more than willing but they had done little in the way of foreplay and she was tight, so tight he had to work his way into her, inch by delicious inch, pulling out almost all

136

the way before thrusting, just that little bit more back into her. She cried out with each thrust, lifting her hips up to meet him, begging him with her body to end his sweet torture and fill her.

With one last thrust he entered her fully. When they were pressed together as tight as they could make it, she twinned her fingers in his hair and pulled his head down to hers, swivelling her hips to grind her clit against his hard body.

"Please fuck me," she groaned into his ear, "I need you." She wriggled against him, begging him with her body. With her last words he stopped being careful, he lifted her into his arms and drove his body deep inside her, hard and fast. It was just what she needed, what she craved and she screamed out loud, then locked her lips onto his, kissing him madly as he drove into her, over and over again. Long deep thrusts that hit every spot she had, making her shudder in his arms.

Her hips moved restlessly against him, meeting his and trying to drive him in even deeper.

That wonderful sensation of growing orgasm began to build inside her and her breath came out in little gasps of pleasure that he swallowed with his kisses. She nipped at his mouth with her teeth, pulling his bottom lip into her mouth and biting down gently. He growled deep in his throat, the vibrations rumbling through his chest.

He leant her back against the wall again, tipping her hips back and changing the angle slightly. She closed her eyes at the sensation as he thrust back into her.

His hands found her breasts as she clung to him, holding herself up so that his hands could explore. And explore they did, one hand squeezed her flesh and flicked her nipple, rolling it between his fingers and pinching lightly.

Her hips bucked in pleasure as his other hand slid lower and caressed her heated centre, spreading her juices over her sensitive nub, rubbing her gently, never ceasing his exquisite thrusting.

137

Her whole body was trembling and shaking, the pleasure building until she felt like she would explode.

He leaned forward and began to kiss her neck, nibbling lightly at her skin with his fangs before sucking gently.

That did her in, the orgasm crashed through her and she came, screaming his name. His pace faltered slightly as he pulled her closer and thrust a little harder, speeding up.

She gasped and moaned as the pleasure continued to pour over her, like a cup that had overflowed.

He stilled in her arms and closed his eyes, clutching her tightly to his chest as he spilled himself inside her hot, wet sheath, his shout of completion mingling with her own cries of pleasure, his body spasming deep inside her caused little ripples of pleasure to jolt through her.

She leaned her head against his shoulder and tried to slow her breathing, her heart fluttering inside her chest like a caged bird. Logan rested his chin on the top of her head and held her, stroking her back in light circles as they regained their composure.

"You, are amazing," she said when she finally managed to form a coherent thought.

He chuckled, the sound rumbling in his chest.

"Not as amazing as you," he retorted.

"Fine, we're amazing together, that do you?" she sighed, too satisfied to move. She looked down at their still joined bodies and groaned.

"My bones feel like jelly," she moaned. "I can't move yet."

"I can," the beast of a man said, moving his hips against hers to prove it. She gasped as he moved over her still tingling flesh and whapped him on the arm. He pulled a face of mock pain and grinned at her, a sexy grin that almost melted her bones and she couldn't help but grin back.

"Just take me inside," she commanded. Still grinning he cupped her butt in his hands and moved away from the wall, kicking the front door closed and carried her down the hall to his bedroom.

138

Chapter 12

"So, what the hell happened down in that alley?" Topaz was snuggled up in Logan's arms, her head pillowed on his chest. He lay there with his eyes closed, a satisfied, very manly smile on his face, playing with the curls of her hair, wrapping them round his fingers. In response to her question he opened his eyes and looked at her.

"I don't really know."

"Well, what was that thing that attacked me? What did it want? It was trying to kill me right? I didn't imagine it?" A slight panic was beginning to build inside her yet she shivered and shrugged it off as best she could. She was safe now, that was all that mattered.

"Yes, I think he was. I don't know why but I do know what it was. It was a Werewolf."

She looked at him sharply. "Are you telling me that werewolves are real?"

He nodded.

"Wow, I mean, I always believed they were, I've written many papers on them, but despite all my research trips, I

139

have never been able to prove it." She was getting excited now, the possibilities unfolding in her mind. But something was niggling at her and she voiced her concerns.

"Why was he like that? All the literature I have read on them state that they turn into full wolves. He was more like a half wolf half man." She shivered. "He reminded me of a horror movie creature," she cuddled closer to Logan and wrapped her arms around him. Logan held her close and kissed the top of her head, just a quick little peck but it meant the world to her.

"I know a few Shifters, they are good people but that creature was not."

"How did he get like that?" She asked again. Logan was quiet for a moment before answering.

"I don't know how much you know about real Shifters so forgive me if I tell you what you already know." She nodded for him to continue and laid her head on his shoulder, fitting her face into the curve of his neck, giving the skin there a quick kiss.

"True Shifters are born, not made, they are born of two full Shifter parents, they can shift fully to become a wolf. A strong Shifter can hover between forms, shifting just the parts he wants to. Made Shifters are weaker than their full blood cousins."

Topaz closed her eyes and listened to his deep voice, with that sexy Scottish accent, letting it flow over her, soothing her jangling nerves. "Made Shifters are a result of an attack by a full Shifter. They can only shift in to that half man, half wolf creature. Unfortunately some don't survive the turn, and others will survive physically but mentally they become the animal, savage and cruel. Most Shifter groups will put the creature out of its misery, but some like to keep them, they seem to make good soldiers, they follow orders very well and never seem to question."

He looked down at her to see if she was following him. She understood it all perfectly. While she already knew

140

most of what he had told her about full Shifters she was completely in the dark about made ones.

"I knew about full Shifters but I didn't know that they could be made. I didn't find anything about it in any of the texts I had read on the subject." She stopped and turned the thought over in her head for a moment or two, Logan waiting patiently for her to finish speaking.

"So," she continued, "it seems that I got one of the made ones. If they follow orders, why was he here?"

Logan sighed and held her tighter, as if afraid to say what was on his mind. Finally, he spoke.

"I don't think it was an accident, I think he were sent here."

Tope sprang up out of his arms like a jack-in-a-box and whirled around to face him.

"What the hell do you mean he was sent here? Why would he be?" She pulled her legs up to her chest, uncaring that she was still naked, and wrapped her arms around her knees. She was scared and she wasn't afraid to show it. She didn't like the idea that some loony creature was out to get her, and worse yet some even bigger loony had ordered him to do it.

Logan sat up and pulled one of her stiff hands away from where it was wrapped around her leg and took it in his, playing his fingers softly over her palm, dancing over her skin.

"I'm beginning to think that your burglary was not a random act."

She glanced at him sharply. She had thought the same thing earlier but Ronnie had convinced her she was just being paranoid, but maybe she wasn't.

"Well what do you think it's all about? I haven't done anything to anyone, I haven't rubbed any wolves up the wrong way, I don't even bloody know any." She jumped up suddenly and began to pace back and forth next to the bed.

141

"What did you do to the beast downstairs? What if he comes looking for me?"

Logan leapt off the bed and swept her into his arms, halting her panicked pacing, and she sank gratefully against his chest, holding him close, needing the comfort he offered. He stroked her hair softly which helped her calm down.

"Don't worry, sweetheart, he's dead, I killed him. He won't harm you every again." She leaned her head against his shoulder and sighed allowing his words to sink in. She was safe, the monster was dead. "I don't know why they targeted you but I intend to find out." He said this with such conviction that she relaxed.

"I'm so glad you were there, Logan, another minute and I might not have been alive to save." A thought suddenly occurred to her and she lifted her head to look up at him. "How *did* you know I was in trouble? I hadn't called to say I was coming, so how did you know I was there?"

Logan looked uncomfortable and ignored her question. She poked him with her finger, she wanted to know, she needed to know. He unwrapped his arms from around her and took her hand, leading her back on to the bed. She sat down and he followed, still holding her hand.

"I knew you were near, I could feel you. I was changing me shirt when I heard you calling out to me."

She looked at him, now she was officially confused.

"But I didn't call you, I couldn't. It all happened so quickly, he jumped me and I managed a scream before he began to choke me."

"I know, but I heard you." He tapped his temple with his finger. "I heard you in my head."

"In your head?" she screeched. "How is that possible? I mean I know about telepaths but I'm not one of them."

"I don't know, lass, I've heard stories over the years but never meet anyone who has found theirs." He seemed to be talking more to himself than her.

142

"Their what? What have you heard? Is it bad? Am I a freak?" She didn't want to be any more unusual than she already was, her street cred wouldn't take it.

He stared at her, almost in wonder, like she was a priceless piece of art he had only seen in books. She squirmed, slightly uncomfortable with his scrutiny.

"That they had found their Soul Mate."

"Their Soul Mate? But there's no such thing. It's just a cute story that people make up, soppy lovey dovey stuff. I mean, I like you, Logan, I like you a lot but Soul Mates? Maybe it's just something to do with my witchcraft, maybe I was projecting." She desperately wanted to believe it, it couldn't be true, they couldn't be Soul Mates.

Logan looked a little sad but nodded in agreement.

"I know. I like you a lot too," he sighed. "Dawn is coming, I need to call someone to take care of the body in the alley. If you want to go home, I understand but I would love for you to stay with me tonight."

She thought about it for a moment or two but realised that the last thing she wanted was to be alone tonight. If some big nasty was after her she wanted to be with the one person that she trusted to protect her, even if logically she knew he would be dead to the world and unable to help, just the thought of having him near her soothed her in a way she didn't understand, but it was late, very late and she would have to ponder over that after some sleep.

"I don't want to be alone, I know it's stupid but I'm still scared. It seems that someone is out to get me and I don't like it one bit."

"Neither do I, darling." He squeezed her hand. "I'll make that phone call while you get settled, I'll be right back." He gave her a light kiss and headed out of the door. A moment later the sound of his talking on the phone floated into her.

She pulled back the covers and slipped in between the sheets, already half asleep when Logan crawled in beside her. She turned on her side and he wrapped his arms

143

around her, pulling her in close to his body. They fitted together perfectly; the curve of her buttocks cradled in his lap, Mr Happy snuggled against her flesh. She turned her head for a kiss.

"Everything sorted?" She mumbled.

"Aye, sweetheart, don't you worry." He kissed her again. "You go to sleep, we'll talk more when we wake up."

She nodded and snuggled up closer. She felt safe and secure in his arms and there was nowhere else she wanted to be.

She puzzled over what he had said about Soul Mates as she drifted off, but it just didn't make any sense to her. Maybe Soul Mates meant something different to his kind, but the cynic in her was scoffing. Nobody had a Soul Mate, life just wasn't like that. If you were lucky you might meet someone that you could love with all your heart and live happily ever after, but unfortunately she lived in the real world.

She did love Logan, she didn't know if it was an ever after kind of love, but she cared for him deeply. He was sweet and kind and loving, he was perfect. She didn't know how he felt about her, she sensed that she was not the love of his life, but she hadn't expected to be. The man was who knew how old and she would be incredibly stupid if she believed that he had never loved anyone else. She wasn't about to kid herself that she was any more special than anyone else to him, she was just going to enjoy what they had together while it lasted and try to protect her heart, preparing herself for the inevitable ending. He had been affectionate to her, loving almost, but until he told her he loved her, she was keeping her feelings to herself, it was safer that way.

Tiredness was weighing her down, it had been a long day and an even longer night, and she was more than ready for some sleep. Logan was cuddled up close to her back, holding her tight in his arms. She was just drifting off when she felt Logan's arms go limp and heavy around her and his soft breathing, which had been tickling her ear for the past few minutes, abruptly stopped.

She pulled away slightly and twisted her head, peering over her shoulder to look at him. His face was slack, his eyes closed. She studied his face closely but any signs of life had been extinguished by the coming of the dawn. She knew that he died, she had seen it herself, but actually witnessing it happening was a little strange. But weirdly enough it wasn't a bad strange, she still felt an incredible sense of peace, the headache that had been niggling at the back of her eyes all day had gone and her stomach felt calmer than it had in days.

She pulled his arm back around her more snugly and closed her eyes. Sleep came quickly after that.

Chapter 13

She was standing in her dream house, throwing herbs into her cooking pot and chanting softly under her breath. She didn't know what she was saying but the words flowed freely, familiar and comforting. She stirred the bubbling brew one last time before dipping a ladle in the mixture and pouring it out into a wooden jug. She glanced quickly at her sleeping children before heading out the door.

She began to walk the perimeter of the house, slowly dribbling the mixture onto the ground. The night felt weird, like trouble was brewing. She felt something watching her and was scared. She desperately wanted Logan to get home so she could finish dripping out the mixture and shut the door, to lock the evil of the world out and keep their family safe. A sudden noise made her glance up. A shadowy figure was standing by the garden gate, staring at her intently. She wasn't safe out there, she hurried over her work, more scared now, and just prayed that it would work…

Topaz awoke to the sound of running water. She stretched and rolled over. Logan's side of the bed was empty. Abruptly the water turned off and almost immediately the bathroom door opened and Logan appeared. He had a towel wrapped around his waist and nothing else. His chest was still wet, beads of water clinging to his skin, practically begging her to lick them away. His hair hung in wet strands around his face. He looked amazing. This was by far the best sight she had ever woken up to.

"Evening, sweetheart," he flashed her the kind of smile that could drop a girl at twenty paces and she smiled back at him dumbly for a moment before she remembered herself.

"Hi," she didn't know what else to say, she hadn't had much practice in waking up with a bloke, especially not him. "Did you sleep well?" she asked. *Way to go, Tope, that's just the thing to say*, she smacked herself on the forehead, but, far from being annoyed Logan just looked amused.

Ignoring her guff, Logan came and sat down next to her on the bed. She suddenly felt rather shy; all the talk last night about Soul Mates had left her feeling out of sorts. She didn't know how to act around him anymore.

She ran her hand through her hair, buying herself a little time. Her fingers stuck in her curls, her hair a wild mass of tangles, no doubt caused by Logan and their I-almost-died sex. She must have looked a right state and the realisation of this made her feel worse. She meeped and wrapped her arms around her head, trying to hide the birds nest that was her crowning glory.

Right at that moment in time she wanted nothing more than to escape into the bathroom, sort out her hair and get dressed. She needed some space, some time to make sense of all the thoughts running around in her brain. As if sensing her unease Logan backed off a little.

147

"Why don't you go and have a shower, and then we can go out and get you something to eat?" he suggested, making no move to touch her.

She nodded, smiling in relief. He was giving her time, not pushing for anything she wasn't ready to give, trying to make her feel comfortable in his company. She appreciated that more than she could say.

"That sounds like a plan. But I do need to check in with Ronnie later. I doubt she will be too worried but things have been so strange recently, I think she worries about me."

"No problem, darling, you go get ready and we can stop by Ronnie's on the way, maybe see if she wants to come out too." he smiled at her. Bless his heart, he was trying so hard to make her feel better. She was getting warm fuzzies.

"That sounds perfect." She stood up, dragging the sheet she had wrapped around her body with her. "I'll go get washed up." Without thinking she leaned down and gave him a quick kiss. Logan looked stunned for a second, but almost immediately hooked his fingers in the hair at the nape of her neck, drawing her a little closer to deepen the kiss.

She was a little breathless when they parted and shocked at how natural it had become to kiss him, even after so short a time. It wasn't something she even thought about, she just did it. She shook her head, trying to clear her thoughts and hurried into the bathroom, closing the door behind her.

Logan walked into the living room and flopped down onto the sofa. Groaning, he cupped his head in his hands.

Way to go, Logan, he chastised himself, *now you've scared her off.*

He knew that he probably should have waited before telling her about Soul Mates, but after the whole, her waking up to him dead, debacle, he didn't want to keep anything else from her.

148

He felt it, deep down in his heart, that she was his Soul Mate. It was just too much of a coincidence, how much she looked like his beloved wife, how she reacted to him, everything.

They were also showing all the classic signs of a bonding. From the first time he had touched her sparks had flown, literally if you count the tingles they felt, a sure sign of Soul Mates.

He had begun to feel her emotions, making it easier to know when to push his luck a little and when to back off, always helpful when dealing with a woman. He had been waiting for the other signs, such as shared dreams and mental communication before getting his hopes up, but it seemed to be true.

He had hardly dared believe it when he had dreamed for the first time since he had turned, and what a dream it had been.

He had dreamt that she was in the shower, all that vibrant red hair streaming down her back, water running down her luscious body in rivulets.

He had wanted to touch her and with a thought, he was behind her, his hand sculpting her curves, pulling her against his chest, his body already hard with need. She had instantly relaxed back against him, accepting that he was there without a word.

Things had progressed very nicely, cumulating in some of the best sex he had ever had.

He had awoken with his erection tenting the sheets, desperate to touch her again. He had felt her coming nearer and had leapt into the shower and dried his hair in record time.

He had felt her almost at his door, just outside in the alley when a rush of fear shot through him. He had known she was in trouble and had paused only to yank on some jeans, her voice ringing through his head, begging for him to help her. He had rushed out his door, taking full advantage of his

Vampire speed and strength, and down the stairs, crashing through the door at the bottom and out into the alley.

His heart was back in his throat as he recalled the rage, shock and fear that had rolled over him upon seeing the creature, with its hands around her delicate throat, squeezing the life out of his love.

He had reacted almost instantly, launching himself onto its back and snapping its neck in one easy move, his fear coupled with his extra strength and abilities had made it almost instinctive. He had thrown the creature carelessly behind him, taking a little satisfaction from the heavy thud of its limp body hitting the wall opposite.

He had immediately scooped her up into his arms, desperate to know that she was alive and safe after he had almost lost her.

He had wanted to kiss her and love her, hold her to him and protect her. He felt like he had failed her, letting her get hurt right outside his home. He had worried that she would hate him, blame him, that he would lose her another way.

But that had not happened, she had clung to him like he was the last solid thing in her world and he had loved it. He had felt an almost primal need to take her, kiss her, make love to her. It had been amazing when she had reacted the same way, kissing him hungrily and grinding her body against his, telling him with her words and actions what she wanted, needed.

If only she hadn't wanted to do the thing that all women insisted on after great sex, talking. It was natural that she would ask about the creature that had attacked her, but she was too smart for her own good, wanting to know the how's and why's of the situation.

He didn't like the conclusion he had reached, the realisation that someone wanted his precious Topaz dead was not something he had wanted to think about. But think about it he had to, he needed to be on the ball, he needed to be prepared, he needed to protect her, because next time he might be too late.

He had felt her withdrawal at the mention of Soul Mates and he had mentally kicked himself over how he had blurted it out. She had freaked out a little but calmed down enough to sleep, curled up against him where he could keep her safe.

He was glad she had slept right through, another sign of Soul Mates for Vampires, their other half needing to be with them all the time, even needing to sleep when they did. He wanted to ask her if she had been feeling sick and headachy like some did when they were separated, but didn't want her asking anymore questions. He needed her to come to terms with it in her own time.

Knowing what he did of her, he knew that until she worked things out, thinking them through completely until she had reached a satisfactory conclusion, she would feel odd around him, not knowing how to act, worried about what it would mean.

And hopefully that was exactly what she was doing in the shower, thinking things through. He had sensed her confusion and backed off, giving her space. She had seemed grateful for that. He had been a little shocked when she had kissed him but he had gotten over it quickly and kissed her back.

He had relaxed back onto the sofa and closed his eyes as he mused over everything that had happened. His head snapped up at the sound of his name.

Topaz took quite a long time in the shower, taking her time shampooing her hair, working out all the tangles, soaping her body and rinsing away all the suds. All the while she thought about what had happened last night. Obviously somebody had a major problem with her, or something she had done. She didn't have a clue what it was but it must have been serious to send a monster like that after her. She felt rather sorry for the creature; it wasn't his fault that he had turned into a raging beast.

She began to mentally run through everything she had done, everyone she had met or spoken to since her arrival in Edinburgh, ticking them off on her fingers. It was a very short list. Apart from Logan, Ronnie and a few shop assistants, Mr and Mrs Baker and staff at the club, she was drawing a blank.

She put it aside to puzzle over later as her mind kept drifting back to what was happening between her and Logan. What she had first thought of as just a harmless holiday fling was turning into something much, much more. The feelings she had for Logan went way beyond anything she was supposed to feel for someone she had known less than a week. She was so confused, wished that she knew what Logan was thinking, how he felt about her and how much further he wanted their relationship to grow.

She turned off the shower and wrapped a big bath towel around her body, tucking it in over her breasts, toga style. After she wrapped her hair up in a towel turban, she sat down on the toilet and prepared herself for a long hard think.

She decided to be completely honest with herself. She was going to ask herself a question and say the first thing that popped into her head.

Ok girl, here goes, she asked herself what she felt for Logan, but didn't need to say the first thing that came to mind. She already knew. She loved him, completely and utterly. She didn't care that they had only known each other for a few days, it felt right. She believed in fate, she believed that Deity had a plan for her, and she believed that Logan was a part of that plan. She didn't believe in coincidences, the fact that Mason had not been there that first night and Logan had, was meant to be, she felt that they were destined to meet and be together.

152

She thought about what Logan had said about Soul Mates and tried to think about it logically. Vampires, she knew from her studies, were a very old species. Maybe they originate from a time when Soul Mates were believed in, searched for, accepted and even counted on. Maybe to them Soul Mates were a partner, someone you loved and made love to, someone you counted on and who counted on you, someone you could believe in. If so, then she could handle that. She knew she could count on Logan, in the past few days he had proved that over and over again by rushing in to help her, giving her a place to stay and even saving her life.

They had a connection, one that went more than skin deep. It wasn't just a mutual attraction that they were acting on, she had never experienced anything like it before and she had worked with some of her very dearest friends for years. They all connected while working in a magic circle but, out of it, nothing like this. She had heard stories from Andy and Clarissa about how they were connected. They felt each other's emotions and knew when the other was in trouble. She had always felt that to have that connection with someone was a blessing from Deity, and if that was what she had with Logan, then she was more than alright with it. She could feel how he was feeling and she hoped that it would develop further. They had that weird tingle thing going on, but that too had become normal, another special little thing that was just between them.

He was gorgeous, he listened to her, he found her attractive (well he certainly seemed to anyway) and he cared for her, cared about her welfare, her comfort and her safety. What more could a girl want? What more indeed, the answer to that was nothing. Logan was perfect. She was just trying to talk herself out of what could be a wonderful relationship, and she didn't know why. She thought about it a bit more but could only conclude that, with her lack of

153

relationship experience and her past experiences with other men, she was just scared.

Well not anymore. She slapped her hands down on her knees and jumped up, her mind made up. The powers that be obviously wanted them to meet, it was fate and who was she to argue with fate? She was going to be with Logan, nothing was going to stop her and they were going to live happily ever after, Dammit.

She dried herself off and patted her hair dry with the towel. She brushed her teeth with his tooth-brush, well; it wasn't like they hadn't swapped more than spit. Who knew that Vampires brushed their teeth, what could they get stuck in them? Were blood clots a problem? She shook her head at her ridiculous and somewhat gross thoughts.

She turned and reached automatically for her clothes, only to realise that she had none. As she cast her mind back, she recalled yanking her top off and throwing it away in the hall last night and that Logan had ripped her jeans off in a fit of passion.

Damn, she thought to herself, she would have to run about naked. Obviously Logan wouldn't have a problem with that but the rest of the world might, and honestly, she didn't have a bad body but she really wasn't comfortable flashing her assets to the whole city.

She opened the bathroom door a crack and stuck her head out.

"Logan," she called. Within seconds he appeared in the bedroom, looking worried.

"I can't get dressed," she continued. "I don't have any clothes." He looked confused.

"Why not, where are they…" comprehension dawned on his face and a slow, sexy, very male smile came into existence.

"Don't look so proud about it," she grumbled.

"Never, darling," he teased in that yes-dear way men got when they were just humouring you.

154

"Just find me something to wear," she snapped, holding the towel firmly in place when she noticed his eyes beginning to cloud over, going from brown to golden, something she noticed happened when he was feeling particularly horny. "And get your mind out of the gutter." He chuckled, holding his hands up in surrender.

"I'll go and look in my wardrobe, I might have something that will do." He crossed over to the cupboards on the other side of the room and began to flick through the clothes on the rails. She couldn't help but smile. He came back with a pair of faded blue jeans, a belt and a t-shirt.

Topaz thanked him and disappeared back into the bathroom, quickly pulling on the clothes. The jeans were too big and, while the belt helped keep them up, she had to roll the cuffs to keep them from dragging on the floor. It felt weird to be wearing jeans without any underwear but unfortunately they too had been ripped off her. Her bra would be salvageable but it felt kinda wrong to be wearing it with no panties, so she decided to forgo that too, let Logan think about her sitting next to him, wearing his clothes but naked underneath. The thought made her smile wickedly. She pulled on the t-shirt and lifted it to her nose. It smelt like Logan, even though it was clean, like his scent permeated everything he owned. She liked that it did.

155

Chapter 14

They had walked all the way to Ronnie's holding hands, it had been lovely. Since Topaz had had the little inner pep talk with herself, she was feeling calmer, more relaxed. She knew that he was feeling happy and contented, the emotions rolling off him in waves, she squeezed his hand and smiled up at him as they turned into Ronnie's street.

She practically ran up the steps to Ronnie's front door and happily banged the knocker, jiggling up and down impatiently waiting for her to open up and let them in, wanting to tell her everything that had happened and invite her to dinner.

Logan put his arm around Topaz and she snuggled into him, sliding her arm around his back and leaning her head against his chest, while they waited.

After waiting for a minute, she knocked again. When it became obvious that she wasn't in they decided to try the shop.

Logan waited outside while Topaz spoke to the girl behind the counter.

She was as tall as Ronnie was short. The floaty black dress she wore clung to her almost non-existent curves, showing off her willowy frame to perfection. She had very blond hair, cut in a shoulder length, shaggy style, with pink streaks contrasting nicely.

The girl gave Topaz a dazzling smile as she entered, looking up from the book she was reading.

"Hi there, can I help with anything?"

Topaz couldn't help but beam back.

"Yeah I hope so, I'm a friend of Ronnie's, I'm staying with her at the moment. Have you seen her today? I stayed at my boyfriend's last night and when I came home she wasn't in."

The girl nodded slowly.

"Yeah, I know Ron. She was supposed to be working this shift as I was on early, but she never showed. I tried calling both her home and her mobile but got no answer."

Tope frowned, it didn't seem like Ronnie to miss work and not call.

"That doesn't seem like her. Has she even done anything like this before? You know, missing work and not calling or answering her phone."

The girl shook her head.

"Nope, not that I know of."

Topaz didn't really know what else to say.

"OK, thanks for your help. I'll keep looking for her, I'm sure she'll turn up," she turned back to the door. "Thanks again."

"No problem, but if you see her, tell her that Shelly is pissed. I had plans tonight and had to cancel."

Topaz nodded. "Will do."

Logan was leaning against the wall outside, watching the people milling around. He turned as Topaz opened the door.

"She in?"

She shook her head.

"Nope. She missed her shift and the girl in there, Shelly, said that she tried calling and got no answer. I'm getting worried. What if something has happened to her?"

Logan frowned.

"Like what?"

She had a quick glance around them but there were far too many people for her liking. She suddenly felt very vulnerable.

"Let's go eat, somewhere quiet. We can talk then."

He nodded and, wrapping his arm around her shoulders, led her to the café that she and Ronnie had gone to. It reminded her that she was effectively missing, and she began to worry even more.

Topaz ordered a cheeseburger and chips, nothing exciting, but good old comfort food. Logan ordered a coffee, nothing more.

"So, it's true that you lot don't eat?" she asked, making conversation, though her choice of openers had a lot to be desired. Logan nodded.

"Aye, but we can drink anything we like. Alcohol only affects us when mixed though."

"Mixed, what like a cocktail?"

He leaned forward and whispered in her ear.

"Mixed with blood."

"So, the cocktail list at Night Walkers is real?" she gaped, her mouth hanging open in shock.

He nodded again.

It suddenly hit her then, he drank blood to survive. She knew that Vampires drank blood, hell she'd had a whole conversation about it with Ronnie, but Logan seemed so normal, and she had never seen him drink any, and he most certainly had never tried to bite her. Ronnie had promised her that she had never fed him but she had to ask who did, she couldn't not ask, the question would roll around and around in her head driving her crazy with all sorts of

158

scenarios, most that would probably make her so jealous she could spit, she had to know.

"Where do you get yours, do you use Donors?" she tried to ask casually, not wanting him to hear the jealousy in her voice.

He looked at her steadily, searching her face before answering.

"No, not anymore." The breath that she hadn't realised she had been holding rushed out of her. "I only drink at the club." Topaz raised an eyebrow in question. "It all comes from a blood bank."

She nodded, that made sense. People donated to save lives; technically they needed blood to survive so why not get it from a blood bank, save a starving Vampires from extinction. Now that might not be the kind of tag line that would entice people to tap a vein but the idea made her smile, just a little.

"Don't you like feeding from people anymore?" she asked him, "I mean Ronnie, you do know she is a Donor right?" He nodded and she continued. "She said that it is very nice, that the Vampires enjoy it as do the Donors," she blushed slightly, "she said it's almost sexual and very pleasurable for all concerned." There, she had asked him.

Logan looked down at his hands, currently wrapped around his coffee mug.

"I do like feeding from a live Donor, but after a few hundred years," Topaz raised her eyebrows at this; damn she was dating an old guy. "They become kind of faceless, there is no connection. Aye, it feels good while you're doing it, but after there is nothing, kinda like a one night stand. With the right person it can be amazing, it makes you feel connected and aye, Ronnie is right, it's very sexual, it can make the act of sex a hundred times more intense. When you're with someone you like and are engaging in the sex act, it's completely natural for us to want to bite them, feed from them, deepen the connection. Sex is linked very closely with feeding, when we get aroused our fangs come out automatically, unless we try very hard to stop them."

Topaz looked at him, letting his words sink in. He had never made a move to bite her. Did that mean that he didn't find her as attractive as he said? He certainly seemed to be willing but maybe he just liked sex. Not really wanting to ask but feeling she had to she leaned forward, closing the distance between them and lowed her voice.

"Do you not like me then? Do you not want to bite me?" She hated to sound so whiney and needy but she just couldn't help it.

He took her hands in his and looked deep into her eyes, his own eyes changing from their usual brown to the deep gold.

He leaned closer to whisper in her ear.

"I could not think of anything better than holding you in me arms, sliding myself deep inside you and making love to you. Then, just when our pleasure reaches its peak and you scream out my name, sinking my fangs in to your luscious neck to sup your delectable blood, making your pleasure more than you could ever imagine." He pulled back and kissed her neck, running his tongue lightly along her skin. "Just give me permission."

She had closed her eyes at his words, images of what he proposed formed in her mind and lust shot through her, pooling low in her womb. She shuddered at the feel of his lips on her skin. Maybe this whole biting thing might be worth a go after all.

Logan leaned back in his seat and smirked at her, obviously proud of the effect he had on her, the ratfink. She pulled herself together, shot him a quick squinty-eyed look and asked the other question that had been bugging her.

"Do you think Ronnie's disappearance could have anything to do with her donating?"

He shook his head, all seductiveness gone from his tone in response to her lets-be-serious question. "I doubt it, most

160

Donors only donate at the club, and if they donate outside It's only with a person they know very well. We have rules we stick to so she would not come to any harm from us."

"Yeah, Ronnie mentioned some rules." Topaz broke off when the waitress delivered her food. She thanked her and took a big bite of her burger, chewing thoroughly while she pondered over Ronnie's disappearance.

"Do you think someone might have taken her to get at me?" She finally asked, voicing the question that had been swimming around in her brain, percolating most of the day so far.

Logan looked at her, the skin between his eyes crinkling in concentration as he thought about what she had just said.

"I don't know," he answered honestly. She was glad he hadn't pussy footed around but in some ways she wished he would have just lied to her.

"All we can do at the moment is keep looking for her. I'll make some calls and alert the head of the Donors Guild."

Topaz must have looked confused because he elaborated. "They keep tabs on all their Donors and the feeders, they can help look. Some of my staff might even know her, I'll get them to ask around too. In the meantime, I'm going to talk to some Shifters that I know, I want to see if I can get some information about the turned one that attacked you last night." He took her hand. "I promise you, my heart, I will do everything in my power to keep you from harm."

She smiled at him, feeling all girly and squiggly inside, he called her his heart. She wanted to leap up onto the table top and do a little happy jig chanting 'he's mine, he's mine' but she stomped on the urge.

"I know you will. I trust you, I know you will always be there for me."

He smiled back and took her hand in his, bestowing a soft kiss on her knuckle, rubbing her fingers between his.

161

Topaz finished her meal in silence, not bothering with conversation, she was too worried, for Ronnie, for herself and strangely for Logan. She didn't know why but she felt danger was coming their way and she had no idea how to stop it.

As Logan paid the bill her mobile rang, Ozzy's Crazy Train, blasting out, it took her a second to realise that it was hers, she hadn't had any calls the whole time she had been away. She glanced at the display before answering, NUMBER WITHELD flashed up. All her friends' numbers were programmed in. Who the bloody…?

"Hello?" she answered, trying to keep the suspicion from her voice.

"Miss Thompson?"

"Yes?" She didn't recognise the smartly clipped English accent, it sounded slightly strange after almost a week of mostly Scottish.

"This is Inspector Jackson. I just wanted to inform you that we have finished with your room, and all your belongings. I'm sorry to report that it is just as we expected. We found no prints and no evidence. It looks like they got away. We will of course keep an eye out for your computer but we don't hold out much hope of its return."

She sighed, just what she had expected.

"Well, thank you. Does that mean that I can go back and pick up my stuff? I'm kinda lost without all my clothes."

"Yes, of course. Mr and Mrs Baker are expecting you."

Topaz thanked him again, though for what she really didn't know and turned to Logan, who had been listening in.

"Can we go back to the hotel? I can pick up my stuff now and could do with it." She gestured to his too-big clothes she was currently wearing.

"Sure, sweetheart," he smiled indulgently. "Let's head over there now." He took her hand as they walked out the door.

162

Chapter 15

Mr Baker met them at the door, there was no sign of Mrs Baker, she was no doubt upstairs somewhere, praying for Topaz's eternal soul or some such thing, she tried not to take it personally.

"Inspector Jackson called and said that they had finished with my belongings and that I could pick them up. Is now convenient?" she asked, keeping her tone as respectful as possible.

Mr B nodded. "Aye, now would be good. The missus wants to go in and clean as soon as possible. She has been complaining nonstop about the state of it, what with all the dirty shoes that have traipsed through. Go on up." He stepped aside and allowed them entry.

Topaz started up the stairs, Logan following close behind her. She glanced over her shoulder at him and found his eyes firmly fixed on her behind. She smiled to herself and turned away but not before giving her hips an extra little wiggle to show that she had caught him staring.

When they reached the top Logan was grinning unashamedly, obviously having enjoyed his front row seat. He smoothed his hand over her left buttock as she opened the door, squeezing gently before giving it a light pat.

"Hey," Topaz mock scolded, turning round to face him. "Hands off the merchandise, you don't touch what you can't afford."

He wrapped his arms around her waist and cupped both of her cheeks in his hands. "Name your price."

She pretended to think about it, putting on a serious expression, while rocking her butt against his palms.

"Twenty kisses," she answered.

"So cheap for such a quality product," he mused, squeezing as if testing their ripeness. "I would gladly pay a million, but I accept your offer." He pulled her close so she was squashed up against his chest, his groin pressed against hers. He leaned his head down for the first kiss of many.

"Ahem." Someone coughed loudly behind them. Topaz jumped about a mile in the air as they hurriedly broke apart and turned to look. Mrs B stood there, hands on hips, one foot tapping in irritation. "This is a respectable abode, I don't tolerate such vulgar displays."

Topaz blushed and hid her face in Logan's shirt. Logan, cool as a cucumber, gave her a dazzling smile.

"Mrs Baker, so nice to see you again." He held his hand out for her to shake but took it back when he saw the look of disgust on her face, undeterred he carried on. "We beg your pardon, we didn't realise that anyone else was on this floor. We shall endeavour to keep our affections to ourselves in future." He was oozing his old-world charm effortlessly.

Not fooled for a second she scowled at him. Topaz bit her lip, trying to hold in the manic giggles that were bubbling up inside her. Now was certainly not the time to laugh but unfortunately such times always bought out the worst in her.

164

"What are you doing here, didn't we tell you that you were no longer welcome?"

Logan's face dropped, all attempts at a smile gone. Topaz put her hand on his arm, silently urging him to keep his temper.

"We are here to collect Miss Thompson's belongings," Logan all but growled, clearly he had had enough of making nice with the grumpy old woman. "Much as we would love to spend all day in bed together, we can't, therefore Topaz needs her clothes." He pushed Topaz swiftly through the open door and closed it behind him, locking it, blocking their view of Mrs B's startled face.

Topaz cracked up laughing and flopped onto the bed, recalling the old woman's expression.

"I cannot believe you just said that to her. What must she think of us?" She wiped away the tears of laughter from her eyes and tried to sit up. "She must think we're in here soiling her sheets right this minute."

"Then why not?" Logan flashed her a wolfish grin and leapt on top of her, catching his weight on his hands and knees, pinning her beneath him. She wriggled around helplessly, trapped against his hard body and the soft bed. He bent his head and kissed her thoroughly, exploring her mouth and neck with his lips and tongue.

She batted at him rather ineffectually, whapping him on his shoulders, trying to get him to stop before she lost her resolve and let him have his wicked, but oh so pleasurable way with her.

"Logan, No. We can't do this now, not here." Logan ignored her to concentrate on lifting the hem of her t-shirt, nuzzling the neckline back from her throat, trying to expose more flesh. He found quite a lot due to the fact that it was his shirt and practically drowned her.

She moaned at his touch, the feel of his tongue running over her skin was almost too much to bear.

"You have to stop, baby," she snaked her fingers into his hair and pulled his head up. "It's not that I don't want to but I would much rather be at your house. Imagine it," she dropped her voice to what she hoped was a sexy purr and pressed herself against him, lifting her hips to rub against his groin. "You and me... your huge bed... no clothes... lots of skin to nibble." She kissed his neck and bit down, just a little, drawing a moan from him. "Much better than a quickie in a messy hotel room, don't you think?" She looked up at him, raising one eyebrow.

He swallowed loudly before answering. "Much better, but I warn you now," he dropped down on top of her and let her feel just how happy he was to be with her, "I won't wait too long."

She nodded dumbly, enjoying the feel of him pressed so tightly against her.

"OK," he agreed and bounced upright, leaving her panting on the bed. "Let's get you packed up."

He grabbed her suitcase from the open wardrobe and dumped it on the bed, then bent down and scooped up a handful of her clothes and chucking them into the open case.

"Aren't you going to help?" he asked, his tone mildly teasing.

Topaz jumped up and began to hurriedly gather her scattered belongings, dumping them unceremoniously into the case. All she wanted to do was get back to his and finish what they had almost started.

As they worked rude images kept popping into her head and she was pretty sure they weren't all hers (well, one or two might have been her doing, but definitely not the rest), not that she was complaining. Some of them looked very interesting. She glanced at Logan but he was ignoring her, humming innocently, still filling the suitcase.

She allowed her mind to wander as she worked, alighting upon and remembering the last time she had helped someone clear up after a burglary. Her good friend, co-worker and fellow coven member, Imogen, had been burgled last year and the police had found no leads.

They were convinced that it was someone she knew, as they had broken in when they were away on holiday in Spain. They had all gotten together and cast a spell to reveal who the culprit was. It has turned out to be Imogen's ex-boyfriend. They had never been able to prove it to the police but had called upon the God and Goddess the next full moon, asking them to send him some just deserts (they read later in the local newspaper that he was currently serving a nice long prison sentence for assault and robbery).

Maybe she could try to do the same thing, try to find out who had stolen her laptop; maybe it would give them some clue as to why monsters were being sent to kill her and why her friend was missing. She really wanted to know the reason behind it.

"Logan," Topaz called. He looked up from where he had been happily studying her lingerie collection.

"I want to try something." He raised an eyebrow and gave her a hopeful, cheeky grin, no doubt think very un-innocent thoughts.

"Get your mind out of your pants," she groused good naturedly. "I want to try to figure out who did all this." She swept her hand out, gesturing to the still strew contents of her suitcase.

"What do you need me to do?" he asked all teasing gone, you gotta love a man who gets down to business fast.

"Nothing at the moment. I'm going to sit on the bed and meditate for a bit, and then I'm going to try and pick up an image or an energy signature from whoever broke in here. I'm guessing it might be someone I've met while here. It's not much but it might give us a clue."

He nodded and picked up the upturned chair. He placed it in the corner of the room, in front of the door, no doubt in

167

case Mrs B decided to force her way in to catch them up to no good. Smart man.

She settled herself down on the bed, sitting up with her back straight and her legs crossed. She rested her hands palm up, on her knees, closing her eyes.

Topaz took several deep breaths and let her mind empty of all thoughts except those of the burglary. She opened her mind and her third eye to the room, taking in the atmosphere, letting it soak into her, immersing herself in its energy. She inhaled deeply, taking in the aroma of her magic (everyone's magic has a signature smell), the scent of lilac, a favourite of hers, and allowed it to sink into her body, relaxing her further.

She worked her way through the underlying sexual tension left over from their romp on the bed and pushed deeper.

She began to feel vulnerable again and shivered. The room had a bad feeling to it now, one that she couldn't quite explain.

She opened her eyes and 'looked' with her psychic sight. The room looked fuzzy around the edges, like it was slightly out of focus. She scanned the room slowly, her gaze landed on Logan, she noticed that he had the same 'non-aura' that Avery, the bartender had, except that Logan's body was edged with gold the same colour as his eyes. Interesting. She mentally pushed it aside to pick over later.

She could have sat and stared at him all day but she forced herself to move on and saw a pulsing energy that reminded her of Inspector Jackson, it felt authoritative and business-like. Next she caught disapproval, two lots in fact, they must be the Bakers. Ronnie's energy was there, twitching away on the bed next to her, just how she was in life, impatient and bouncy. Other wisps of left over auras were scattered here and there, mainly around the door area and her wardrobe, fading even as she watched. She put that down to the police team that had examined the room.

168

She scanned the room again, slowly and carefully, but found nothing else, no energy, no aura patterns, no residue anything.

She slowly closed down her extra senses and took a few deep breaths to centre herself before moving. The scent of lilac began to fade.

"What did you find?" Logan asked when she opened her eyes.

"Nothing."

"It didn't work?"

She shook her head. He looked slightly disappointed, she knew he was desperate to get his hands on the person responsible.

"Oh, it worked. I found the residual energy of the Inspector, the Bakers and Ronnie. There was also a little residual energy that I guess is from the police team."

"Anything else?"

"Nothing," she confirmed. "No other living thing has been in this room."

"What do you mean living thing?" His voice held a hint of suspicion, like he knew exactly where she was going with her theory.

"Just that, no one alive has entered this room." She looked at him. "My guess would be a Vampire."

"Are you sure?"

She sighed before answering.

"No, I'm not sure. But that's my best guess."

Topaz shrugged, unfolded herself from the bed and moved towards the suitcase, ready to begin packing again but the energy drain from using her powers must have been greater than she thought. She wobbled as her legs gave out and almost dropped. Logan was there in an instant, catching her before she fell.

"Whoa there, sweetheart, take it easy." He sat her back down on the bed. "You rest, I'll finish the packing and then we can go home. We're due to meet some people at the club later."

She nodded, grateful he was here and willing to take charge. She didn't like this one bit. If the lack of energy residue did indicate a Vampire, then she was all but screwed, and Ronnie, who she was now sure had been kidnapped or some other kind of horror, wasn't much better off than she was.

Chapter 16

Two hours later found Topaz camped out in Logan's office, in a comfy chair next to his desk, surrounded by people she only knew by sight. The club had yet to open so everyone who was anyone was now staring at her like she had just sprouted a second head. Thankfully, she had taken the time to change into her own clothes before she left the hotel, though she had generously let Logan choose for her.

She was now wearing a short-ish, tight, dark purple skirt and her lilac silk blouse, and yes he got his way with her underwear too. Knee-high black boots completed the look, she had even slapped on a bit of make-up for the occasion.

The two bouncers from the front doors were there, leaning against the door frame, one on either side, like they were propping it up, that casual, slouch thing that men do. Logan had told her that they were wolf Shifters. She took another quick peak at their aura's trying to imprint the image in her brain; you never knew when it might come in handy.

Dane, the one she had spoken to with Ronnie had grinned cheerily at her but the other, his twin brother Drake was as surly as Dane was friendly, he had graced her with a grunt of acknowledgement but that was it.

Logan had introduced her to Damian, his manager and second in command. Damian had bestowed on her a winning smile and kiss on the cheek, murmuring something about how glad he was that Logan had finally found her. She hadn't been aware she was lost, but had returned the kiss. His cheek had been cool to the touch, just like Logan's and she guessed that he too, was a Vampire. She was surrounded. If she didn't trust Logan so much she would have been just a teensy bit nervous.

Damian was amazing to look at. He was tall, about 6ft 2" at her guess and lean, you wouldn't call him skinny, because even through his shirt you could see the definition of his muscles. His skin was as white and flawless as the finest porcelain, shown off to perfection by his hair, which was as black and glossy as a raven's wing. It was long and straight, flowing down his back in an almost endless wave, stopping just above his knees. All that luscious hair surrounded an almost perfect face, which had a delicate shape to it with rounded curves as opposed to Logan's hard lines, only the strong line of his jaw stopped him from looking feminine. His eyes were a startling shade of green, an amazing contrast to his dark hair, so bright they reminded Topaz of a cat's.

She felt like she was at a male models house party, there were so many hot guys in the room. She felt very plain in comparison, it's never nice to know your man is better looking than you are, you always kinda hope it's about equal. With this lot she had no chance.

At least she wasn't the only one. A lady who at first glance looked middle aged but was actually no more than early 30's, sat quietly in an armchair in the corner of the room, just off to the side of Logan's desk. She had short, straight brown hair, cut in a no-nonsense bob, with conker brown eyes that were looking straight at her. Her face was kind of plain, nothing really stood out on its own but the whole package was pleasant none the less. She wore a grey skirt suit, with a peach coloured blouse underneath, which looked rather like silk. She had a briefcase on her lap, which she was gripping like a comfort blanket. She had an up-tight air about her and radiated annoyance at being made to wait. She turned her head to talk to Dane and it was then that Topaz noticed that her neck sported twin puncture marks, two on the left side and one on right. She guessed that she must be a Donor.

Avery, Topaz's old friend the bartender, was also there, lounging on a sofa in the corner, his limbs arranged in what she assumed was his version of a relaxed and seductive pose, one arm hanging over the back of the sofa and his body stretched out, displaying all that muscled perfection, one leg propped up on the other, which immediately drew the eye to his crotch, not that she was looking, she only had eyes for one man.

Don't get her wrong, Avery was drop dead gorgeous -no pun intended- he had blonde hair, with a slight wave to it, which hung down his back to just under his shoulder blades, and beautiful blue eyes. His face looked like it had been sculpted by a Greek master, all straight nose and strong, almost cocky jaw. His cheeks were sprinkled with stubble, just enough to draw attention to his full mouth. He was wearing black, very tight jeans and another piratey shirt, one that had big, loose sleeves and laced up the front, though he had left it unlaced to reveal a good portion of his smooth chest. He had another bandanna wrapped around his head, this time bright red. In short the guy was H.O.T.T hot, but he wasn't a 6ft plus hunk of man meat with a sexy Scottish accent.

The Scot in question finished tapping on his computer and shifted his desk chair back a few inches so he could

173

lean back and prop his feet up on the desk. Topaz smiled to herself, recalling how she had done the exact same thing last week at Athena's.

He cleared his throat and everyone stopped talking amongst themselves and turned to give him their undivided attention, all except Avery, who was resting his head back on the couch, eyes shut. Once Logan was happy that everyone was listening he put his feet down and sat up straight in his chair.

"First we would like to thank all of you for either coming in early," he nodded to Avery and the twins, "or taking the time out of your busy schedule to meet with us," nod to Miss Up-Tight, who inclined her head graciously in return.

Everyone except Avery looked at Topaz, surprised that she had been included in the introduction. *Yay, I'm special*, she thought and beamed at them.

"I would like to remind you all, before we continue, that by agreeing to come here and offer your assistance to my Chosen One," everyone gaped in open surprise -Miss Prissy in the suit even gasped- at Logan's words, he ignored them and smoothly continued, "and myself, you are agreeing to complete and utter discretion. No one else shall know about what we discuss. Is that so?"

All around Topaz, heads nodded in agreement, Avery gave a lazy thumbs up. Logan nodded too, apparently satisfied that their secrets would not be blabbed to the entire preternatural community of Scotland.

"We need information." He proceeded to tell them everything that had happened to her over the last week. Starting with why she was here, then the burglary, what she had discovered about that, the attack by the creature in the alley and lastly Ronnie's disappearance.

"Oh, so that's how the body we disposed of ended up in the alley," Dane said when Logan had finished. "We did wonder."

174

"Yes," Logan admitted. "Now we need to figure out why Topaz was burgled and attacked. We also need to locate the Donor, Miss Veronica Simms." He turned to Miss Never-crack-a-smile. "Miss Jennifer, can you tell us anything about Miss Veronica's donating? Did she have specific bleeders and if so did they only feed here or did she partake in private house calls?"

Miss Jennifer sniffed. "You know very well, Mr McGregor, that I cannot reveal the personal, out of club hours, actions of Miss Veronica. I can however check my database for any relevant information and check with her bleeders myself. I will also put an alert out on our forum for information regarding Miss Veronica's whereabouts." Logan nodded, apparently satisfied with her answer.

Topaz sat there quietly -a very hard thing for her to do- and listened, taking it all in. Look at what she had learnt so far, she hadn't even known Logan's last name was McGregor for God's sake. She had also learnt that Little Miss Jennifer talked like she had a plum in her mouth and a stick up her butt, but Topaz didn't voice that opinion out loud.

Logan snorted and coughed into his hand. She looked up at him sharply, if she didn't know better, she'd have thought he was covering up a laugh, not that this was the time. She scowled at him but he just smiled innocently back, ignoring her look that was intended to drop someone at ten paces. Irritating man, she grumbled under her breath.

"Avery, Damian, can you ask around, see if anyone knows anything? You're good at getting people to talk."

Avery saluted from his position on the couch not bothering to lift his head or open his eyes. Damian merely nodded.

"Dane, Drake, did either of you recognise the attacker?" They both shook their heads, confirming what Topaz already feared. Nobody had a clue what was going on or why.

175

"Nope, never seen him before," Dane answered. "But we can ask around in the Pack, someone might know something. We would hate to see Topaz hurt again," he glanced at his watch. "Listen, it's almost opening time, we have to get back to the door but call if you need anything." Drake turned almost instantly to the door and opened it, a man of few words. Dane on the other hand gave Topaz a friendly wave before leaving.

"If that will be all," Miss Jennifer stood up, clutching her briefcase, "I shall take my leave."

Logan stood to shake her hand.

"We thank you for your help." He shook her hand briefly, before waving towards the door. "Damian will show you out."

She nodded graciously and swept through the door Damian held open without a backwards glance.

As soon as the door shut behind her, Avery opened one eye.

"Is she gone?"

"Aye, my friend," Logan chuckled.

"Thank fuck for that," Avery bounced upright and re-arranged his body into more of a relaxed position.

Topaz raised one eyebrow, curious. Miss Jennifer didn't strike her as the most fun person in the world but she didn't seem all that bad either.

"Miss Jennifer is a bleeder feeder," he began.

"A what?" It was a new one to her.

"A Donor," Logan corrected.

"Oh, I see. I did kind of figure that out seeing as her neck is covered in some major hickies."

Avery chuckled.

"Bleeder feeders is kind of a derogatory term, they don't like it." Logan explained, looking pointedly at Avery, who blatantly ignored him.

Topaz turned back to Avery, trying to cover up her slight smile of amusement.

176

"So what did you do to Miss Pissy Knickers, that you felt the need to hide from, and ignore, her?"

"Well," Avery began, preening slightly, and settling back against the couch, getting into story telling mode. "It was about ten years ago. Jenny was my Donor, and a sweet little thing she was too." Topaz snorted in disbelief at this and heard Logan chuckle quietly behind her. "We had a sexual relationship alongside the feeding, but she wanted more. She wanted to be my Chosen One. I had to let her down gently." He grinned unashamedly.

"Like you could do gently," Topaz teased.

"Well, I tried. Anyway, we broke up, in all ways we could. I thought that was the last of it, you know, after the tears and the begging and the threats finally stopped." He waved his hand, as if brushing it under the carpet. "Years later she becomes head of the Donors Guild for this area. She has been making my life miserable for the last few years."

"How so?"

"Mucking with my Donors, cancelling appointments, sending me the wrong gender or blood type. Everything you could think of," he sighed. "I've almost given up trying."

Topaz felt so sorry for him that she went and sat next to him on the sofa and put her arm around him. For all his bravado, she could tell that this woman had hurt him deeply. He was such a fun-loving guy, always chatting and laughing, a hit with the customers. She could easily tell how someone could fall for him, especially if being bitten was as sexual as Logan and Ronnie had said. She felt a small thrill of anticipating run through her at the thought of experiencing it with Logan.

As if her eyes were pulled automatically in his direction she glanced at Logan and he smiled at her, a sexy smile, flashing just a hint of fang, as if, again, he had read her mind. She was beginning to think that there might be more to this Soul Mate thing than she had originally thought. She pulled her thoughts back to Avery as quickly as she could.

177

"So, what is a Chosen One anyway? Why did she want to be yours so badly?" And more importantly, what had she let herself in for? She hadn't spoken about it with Logan and he hadn't asked her to be his, yet he had introduced her as his tonight. Damn, these vamps were gonna take some serious getting used to.

"A Chosen One is a partner, someone you choose to be with exclusively. Many Vampires and other beings pick a Chosen One after being alone for many years, it's someone you can share your life with. They are very special, they are protected by you and yours, no one would dare harm another's Chosen One. It's not something that is taken lightly, they are almost as special as a Soul Mate." He looked at Topaz and then at Logan.

"Of course," he continued. "Most of us are never lucky enough to find our Soul Mate." He shot a pointed look at Logan, who returned with a we'll-talk-about-this-later-don't-make-a-scene look, Topaz knew that look well having been on the receiving end of it many times herself.

"Why?" she asked, curious. It looked like she was going to get more information out of Avery than she had Logan.

Avery took her hand in his and pulled her around to face him, Topaz risked a glance at Logan, wanting to see his reaction. He was looking at her too, his face blank, as if he didn't want to show his true emotions.

"Soul Mates are a rare and precious thing. They are the other half of our soul, they complete us. They compliment us in every way. They are our perfect match. They are made just for us."

She looked at him, the raw longing in his voice was clear. He wanted to find his Soul Mate.

"How can you tell if you have found your Soul Mate?" she asked quietly, her voice barely above a whisper, but he heard her, they both did.

Avery put his arm around her and pulled her close, giving her a hug, there was nothing sexual there, just two people

178

taking comfort from each other. He was saddened by the treatment he had received from Miss Jennifer, and Topaz was just plain done in, she was fed up with feeling uncertain and scared. She needed this hug, snuggling closer. Avery continued in a dreamy kind of voice.

"They say that your bodies can instantly recognise your other half from the first time you meet. Your bodies will react, sometimes in the form of sparks or tingles. You will be uncontrollably attracted to each other, taking it slow is not part of the equation." Well, that was certainly true, she thought ruefully.

"Your minds connect next, normally starting with the ability to sense each other's emotions, then a telepathic link will begin to emerge, getting stronger the more you physically... erm..." He looked at Topaz and wiggled his eyebrows, "... connect." She got the meaning crystal clear.

"What happens then?" she asked, desperate to hear the rest.

"Well, then you would probably bond."

"Bonding, what's that?"

"Well, there are five steps to a bonding. The first is recognition. This is the tingles. Then 'knowing' that's the telepathy, sharing thoughts and emotions, sometimes even dreams too." She looked at Logan sharply when she heard this, had they done that? She thought of the dream had had involving him, her and a shower and blushed, just a little.

"What else?"

"Then comes the claiming, this is when the two of you verbally tell the other that you want them for your own. Sometimes it's done in front of other people, kind of like a marriage ceremony."

Marriage, Shit!

"They will lay their hands on each other and kind of 'brand' them with their mark. This is normally something that is special or of significance to the person, like a family crest. Then comes the mating or joining, they go off alone for that

179

and, well, you don't need a diagram there." Cue another eyebrow wiggle.

"They then share blood and it's done. But it's not something to be taken lightly, it means that they are joined for life, and that normally means the immortal's life. The other becomes immortal too." He shrugged, and then said casually. "Like I said it's a big commitment. The stages can be done in any order, but they all have to be completed." He finished with a sigh. "I don't know why I know all this, it's not like I'll ever need it."

"Don't say that," Topaz begged him, laying her head on his shoulder. "You are fabulous, the right girl for you is out there somewhere, you just have to find her. I'll help, I promise, we both will. Maybe I can do a spell or something."

He smiled and kissed the top of her head. "You're so sweet, T, I'll hold you to that. Logan is a lucky guy." He pulled away from her and bounced up, his previous mood forgotten. "I have to get to work, drinks don't make themselves you know."

"Is Mason not in again?"

"Nope, the rat. He knows I don't like to work every night. I'm only filling in to help out Logan."

Logan crossed the room and took the seat next to her that Avery had vacated, putting his arm around her, urging her close. Avery watched them with barely concealed longing, Topaz felt so sorry for him.

"Well, that's very nice of you," she commented to Avery.

"He's my best mate, I'd do anything for him."

A thought crossed her mind.

"Hey, you don't think that Mason could be involved in all this do you?" She looked first at Avery then at Logan.

Logan picked up a lock of her hair and began to play with it, pulling the curl straight before letting it go, as if to watch it bounce back into place. She could tell he was stalling, thinking it over carefully before talking.

180

"Aye, it is possible," he mused, still fiddling. "I must admit the thought had not crossed my mind. Mason is well known for taking off for weeks on end."

"Why do you put up with it?"

Logan sighed. "He is the child of an old friend of mine, when he was turned I was asked to watch over him. I have tried to live up to my responsibility."

She impulsively kissed him on the nose. "That's very sweet of you. He's lucky to have someone who cares."

"That's it I'm outta here," Avery moaned, good naturedly. "I'll pop round and check out Mase's place later, just to make sure everything is in order."

"Good idea," Logan agreed. "Let us know if you find anything."

Topaz smiled, she loved the way he said us, instead of me, automatically including her. She snuggled a little closer.

"See ya," Avery gave them a sarcastic wave, exiting as quickly as possible. Music floated out from the club beyond proving just how late it had gotten.

"What now?" she asked when the door shut behind him.

"Now, I take you upstairs and we finish what we started back at the hotel." She gaped openly at him for a second, before treating him to -what she hoped- was a sultry smile.

"Well that's not quite the answer I was expecting but it sounds like a good plan." She leaned forward and gave him a quick, light kiss that he immediately tried to turn into something more substantial. She held him back with a restraining hand on his chest.

"Oh, no, you don't. Not here. I'm not making love in an office where anyone could walk in."

"They would not dare," Logan all but growled, his eyes going all possessive at the thought of someone else seeing her naked. She grinned, secretly pleased with his reaction.

"Come on, Stud, take me upstairs. You promised me a session in your bed, with lots of time to explore and I'm going to hold you to it."

181

"Can I hold you to me?" Logan asked, slipping his arm around her waist and trying to draw her onto his lap. She let him and settled herself down; wriggling her butt in what she hoped was a suitably seductive manner.

"Darling," she purred in his ear, wrapping her arms around his neck. "You can hold any part of me you want." She licked his ear lobe, pulling it gently into her mouth before giving it a little love nip. He moaned and she felt him grow under her, his impressive erection straining his jeans and pushing against some suddenly sensitive areas. She ground herself against him, just a little, letting her willingness be known.

He practically leapt off the couch, with her still clinging to him. She squeaked and wrapped her legs around his waist, hanging on for dear life.

With an amazing show of his increased speed, he raced out of the door, slamming it shut behind him and had her up the stairs and in his apartment before she could even blink.

Chapter 17

They took their time disrobing each other, running their hands and mouths over every bit of skin they exposed. Touching, kissing and exploring.

Topaz dropped to her knees to work on his jeans, undoing his belt and un-popping the button. She eased the denim down over his hips, letting his erection spring free. She stared at it, face to face as it were. She had never really enjoyed giving a man oral sex, but they had always seemed to appreciate it. Logan had driven her wild with his mouth the night before, she decided it was her turn to repay that favour.

He looked down at her, kneeling between his legs, his erection thick with need. He desperately wanted to make love to her and was just about to pull her into his arms and lay her down on the bed when her hands reached for his pulsing erection, wrapping her fingers around his shaft and squeezing lightly.

His breath left his lungs in a long rush when she suddenly bent her head and took him deep into her mouth. His hands came up to tangle in her hair, wrapping the silken strands around his fingers, pulling her closer.

Her mouth was hot, tight and moist, gliding over him with slow, seductive moves.

One hand cupped his tight sac while the other gripped his shaft, caressing where her mouth couldn't reach.

Her tongue did a swirly kind of dance that made his head spin. He moaned deep in his throat and she moaned with him, the sound vibrating up his shaft. She increased the suction and his hips began to move, thrusting in and out of her amazing mouth.

This was fantastic, how could she have ever not liked doing this before? Because you were never doing it with Logan, a voice in the back of her head stated.

Every time she tried something new, his pleasure seemed to flood through her, pulling an answering jolt of pleasure from deep inside her womb. She found she could tell what he liked most, what really did it for him, what made his eyes roll back in his head and his body shudder, his hips moving restlessly, thrusting in time with her mouth.

She started to make love to him with her mouth, her hands wrapping around him to grab his arse, and what an arse it was, smooth and hard, round and yummy. The sparks were making the experience very interesting, like she had a mouthful of the old-fashioned popping candy but Logan seemed to enjoy it.

She started to suck him harder, rolling her tongue over him and ever so lightly score her teeth down his shaft, adoring the smooth, hard length of him.

She moved her mouth, straining her neck to meet his every thrust, letting him set a pace that pleased him most.

She heard his breathing change, his hips thrusting harder the second before he came, pulling on her hair to keep her close, like she would ever want to stop and miss that.

She sucked hard as he thrust into her mouth, his cool seed pumping down her throat. She drank him down almost greedily, doing what had previously repulsed her. He groaned and his legs shook with the strain of holding himself upright.

She slowed down her sucking, licking him with soft, light strokes, bringing him back down slowly. His hands relaxed their death grip on her hair and he took a shakey step back. She let him slide out from between her lips, resisting the urge to pull him back towards her.

He flopped backwards onto the bed, his breathing ragged as she slowly stood up, crawling onto the bed. She was going to lie down next to him but Logan had other ideas. His arms darted out, wrapping around her waist, hauling her on top of him. Her breasts crushed against his chest as he captured her lips in a searing kiss. She swung one leg over his waist and straddled him, turning her head for easier access.

He kissed her as if he could breathe her in through his mouth and she kissed him right back, drinking him down and sucking on his tongue as if he were the last drop of water in a desert.

Her tongue brushed his fang and blood welled up, filling her mouth. He stiffened against her, as if afraid of her reaction, but when she didn't pull away he went wild, feasting on her mouth. He fell into the kiss, his hands on her body, pulling her closer.

She rubbed her body sensuously against his. He groaned into her mouth and she felt him harden in response, a hard bulge pressing against her sensitive flesh. The feel of him, so hard and ready pressing against her drew small, whimpering sounds from her mouth. He pulled back and looked into her eyes.

185

"What do you want, my love?" His hand trailed down her back to caress her behind.

"You," she all but groaned, "deep inside me. Make love to me Logan, please I need you."

"I thought you would never ask," he whispered and slid his hand down between their bodies to stroke her lightly, slipping his finger inside her as if testing her readiness.

"Shite, you're so wet," he moaned, licking her neck. She nodded and moved her hips restlessly, trying to get a more satisfying caress. He reached down between her legs and positioned himself at her entrance. She raised her hips accommodatingly, feeling his head pressing into her, penetrating just a little. His hands came up to grasp her hips as his own lifted to glide him into her. She gasped with pleasure at his invasion and kissed him hungrily.

He sat up so she was sitting on his lap facing him, buried deep inside her. She wrapped her legs around his waist and her arms around his neck, holding him tightly. They were staring into each other's eyes, so intimately, as his body began to slide in and out of her, her hips riding him.

She was so wet and willing that he moved easily inside her and he took full advantage, shoving himself deep, as if he knew exactly what her body wanted, needed, without words.

He used his hands to guide her, moving her, just a little, until he found the spot he wanted. Her breathing hitched as he plunged deep, as if he could fill her up so they would never be apart. She moaned for him, every time he slid over that sweet spot, her breathing changed and he noticed, changing his rhythm, so he was hitting that spot every time.

The pleasure built and built, more pleasure than ever before. The dam broke and she came hard, moaning deep in her throat, her breathing ragged, sawing in and out of her lungs. Her body trembled and shook as he continued to thrust into her, strong hands gripping her hips, holding her still as he worked himself in and out of her body.

186

"Come with me, please," she begged, almost incoherent with the pleasure that still assaulted her. Her head flopping forward onto his shoulder as he bent forward and wrapped one arm around her leaning her backwards. His other hand began to caress her breasts, drawing swirly patterns. With each tweak of her nipples, jolts of pleasure shot through her, directly to her womb, causing her muscles to clamp around him, holding him captive within her tight, wet sheath.

He thrust into her harder and began to kiss her neck, nibbling at her skin. She knew what he wanted and realised that she wanted it too, more than anything.

"Do it, please," she gasped, grinding herself against him. He thrust one more time and kissed her neck again before biting down.

His fangs sank into her, a sharp pin-prick of pain that immediately melted away to pleasure so bone deep that she came again, screaming his name. The feel of his mouth sucking her down and his body pounding into her was almost too much to bear. It was almost like there was a direct link to her clit, to the very centre of her pleasure, she could feel it pulse with each pull of his mouth on her vein. He was right, she had never felt anything like it, her body arching and twitching as he continued to thrust into her core, hard and fast. She couldn't take much more, the sensations racking her body were making her dizzy, a never ending flow of pure pleasure holding her in its grasp.

Then suddenly he stilled, his head whipped back, his spine bowing, his arms pulling her upright into his embrace as his roar of release filled her ears. She felt him pour into her, branding her with his essence. She wrapped her arms around his back and sank into his chest as he collapsed back on to the bed, his eyes closed.

She snuggled closer and pulled the duvet over them. Logan's hand began to move on her back, running his fingers up and down her flesh, caressing lightly. She shivered and wriggled against him.

187

"No, baby, not again," he groaned, wrapping his arms around her to hold her still. "I don't think my heart could take it."

She lifted her head to grin at him. "I don't think that is a problem for you. I'm sure that sex won't kill you. I mean, you're how old?" She looked at him in question.

Groaning he used his feet to push himself up into a sitting position, his back propped up against the pillows. He lifted his arm and she settled down beside him, her head pillowed on his chest.

"I was born in 1546."

Her mouth dropped open as she gaped at him.

"So you're..." She did some quick mental calculations, "464 years old?"

He nodded. Damn, he was old.

"And sex hasn't killed you in all those years, so I think you're safe now." She got back to her original point.

"Ah, but none of them were you," he pointed out.

"Aww, you're making me blush," she preened. But it had got her thinking.

"You must have had many lovers over the years, maybe many wives too?"

He looked at her sharply, his eyes narrowing.

"Why do you want to know?"

She nuzzled her head into the curve of his neck.

"Just curious, I guess. Maybe I want to know where you've been, I don't want just anyone's sloppy seconds." She said in a teasing voice.

"Sloppy seconds?" he mock growled, rolling over and pinning her legs with his, he began to tickle her. "How do I know you're not damaged goods?"

She screamed and laughed and begged for mercy, flopping about uselessly beneath him. She decided that distraction was the best form of retaliation and stretched her neck out to give him a kiss. She let him take over the kiss,

188

turning it into something more substantial and rubbed her body against his.

She broke the kiss to purr in his ear. "Do I feel damaged to you?"

He ran his hands appreciatively over her curves and shook his head, swallowing before answering.

"No, you feel amazing to me."

Topaz wrapped her arms around him and pulled him close, resting her chin on his shoulder. They lay like that for what seemed like an age, just holding each other.

She was running her fingers up and down his back, tracing protective symbols on his skin when his body went slack and heavy. She lifted his head up in her hands and instantly recognised his 'dead' face. His eyes were closed and his fangs had run out, his skin was growing cooler by the second.

She puffed and panted, wriggled and pushed and finally managed to heave his top half off her and onto his own side of the bed. She yanked her legs out from between his and rolled him onto his side.

"Nice way to get out of talking about your ex's Mister," she grouched. "You're not going to get away with it you know. I'm like an elephant, I never forget. You will answer my questions, so prepare yourself." She warned his inert form with a wag of her finger.

She curled herself around his back and flung her arm over his chest, pulling him closer and closed her eyes. Sleep came quickly.

Chapter 18

Topaz awoke to the sound of her phone ringing from the depths of the apartment. She tried to ignore it but you try ignoring Crazy Train, blaring out a full volume. Yeah, didn't think so.

After it kicked in for the third time and she could still hear it through the pillow she had smushed over her head, she sat up.

She glanced around half-heartedly for her phone but couldn't see it. She was too warm and comfortable to even contemplate getting up, hoping to catch some more shut eye after she spoke to the inconsiderate sod that would phone her at, she squinted at the clock, ten in the morning.

Groaning in frustration, she rolled over, hanging her arms and part of her upper body off the side of the bed, rummaging around in the pile of discarded clothing until she plucked out the offending phone.

She stabbed at the call answer before answering with a rather grumpy, "Topaz Thompson."

"Topaz? It's me." Her voice was weak and trembling, she sounded bunged up and nasally, like she had been crying for too long.

Topaz sat bolt upright in shock and relief at hearing her voice.

"Ronnie, honey? Thank the gods, we were so worried about you. Where are you? Where have you been?" She was babbling but couldn't seem to stop, she was just so relieved to hear her voice.

"They have me, Topaz." Topaz shut up instantly and started to pay attention.

"Who has you, Ron?"

"The monsters. I went out to get some milk while you were with Logan and they attacked me." She started crying again, great heaving sobs that racked her body and almost broke Topaz's heart. "They knocked me out and when I came round I was locked in a room."

Her voice dropped so low, she had to strain to hear her. "I'm scared, Tope. They said they'll kill me tonight."

"What can I do, Ron, where are you?" Topaz could hear her own voice raising, fear pressing down on her.

"You have to come get me." Her voice was rising too now, until she sounded almost hysterical. "Just you. No one else."

"But where are you? I can't come get you if I don't know where you are. What do they want? Why do they want us?" She jumped out of bed and began pacing up and down the side of the bed, trying to walk off some of the tension building inside her.

"I don't know, Tope, I really don't. I haven't seen anyone until today," she whimpered in fear. "They have guns. One is pointed at me right now through a hole in the door. They just threw in a phone and told me to call you."

"But how do I find you?" Topaz was getting desperate now.

She heard Ronnie squeak in terror, and a deep voice growled into the phone.

191

"We will text you directions when you leave the Vampires house. Go outside, get into a taxi and then we will send the text. Tell no one or the girl dies. We will be watching." The phone went dead as he hung up on her.

Topaz stood there like a ninny for a few moments, trying to digest everything and think of some kind of plan. But thoughts deserted her, she could see no way out, no other choice.

She bent over Logan, still curled up on his side, in exactly the same position he had fallen asleep in. Tenderly she brushed the hair back from his face and looked down at him. Even in his death sleep he was breath taking to behold.

The waxy, paleness of his skin and the slackness of his features only succeeded in enhancing the otherworld magic that seemed to cling to him. She didn't know what she was letting herself in for, though she did know that Logan would have tried to stop her if he had been awake. But as he was out for the count, she couldn't see any other way. Ronnie was her friend, she was scared, and she was being threatened. Topaz couldn't abandon her to her fate. Plus, guilt was nibbling at her conscious, she just knew that all this was somehow her fault.

She pressed a gentle kiss to Logan's lips, savouring the feel of them, the taste of him. Who knew if he even knew she was there, let alone able to hear her, but she whispered to him anyway.

"I promise that I will try to be careful, but I can't leave her there. I love you. I know I haven't said it to you, but it's true."

She brushed another quick kiss onto his forehead and turned away, her heart pounding, trying not to think about what she was about to do. She didn't want to acknowledge the fact that she might not see him again.

She rushed into the blue bedroom where she had unpacked her clothes and yanked on fresh underwear, socks and a pair of jeans. She pulled a t-shirt over her head, ran a brush through her hair, pulling it back into a pony tail

192

and called herself done. She quickly brushed her teeth, not bothering to wash her face and picked up her purse on the way out.

She was out on the street in less than five minutes. It was pouring with rain and she shivered, wishing she had pulled on a jumper or a coat. She looked about, trying to catch sight of anyone who might be watching her, but the street was practically deserted and the people who were around, were hurrying along, heads bowed against the rain, fighting with umbrellas and taking zero notice of her.

She thought it would take ages to hail a cab, sure that they would all be in use due to the weather, but almost immediately one sailed past, its 'for hire' light on. She stuck out her arm and it slowed to a stop beside the kerb, splashing her with gutter water. Great, just great. Not only was she on her way to certain doom, she was going to arrive looking like she'd taken a dip in Loch Ness.

She yanked open the back door and threw herself into the seat, slamming the door behind her.

"Where to, lass?" the driver swivelled round in his seat to look at her.

"I erm… I don't know yet. Can you hang on for a second?"

He looked at her like she was bat shit crazy but shrugged his shoulders in a what-the-hell-I'll-humour-her way.

Topaz jumped when her phone buzzed in her bag. She grabbed it with fumbling fingers and flipped it open to read the text.

She didn't recognise the address or the street so she simply handed her phone over to the driver.

"I need to go there, do you know it?"

He whistled, his eyes wide, his be-pleasant-to-the-customer smile growing wider by the second. He shook his head, as if to collect himself.

"That's a fair old way, you sure you wanna take a taxi?" he generously informed her, obviously thinking he was doing himself out of a big paying fare.

She gulped, that didn't sound good. But she had her instructions. She looked quickly out of the window, trying to look casual, her eyes scanning the street for the person who was supposedly watching her. Again she saw no one, not that she had really expected to.

She sighed and accepted her fate.

"Yeah, I'm sure. I need to go there."

The driver shrugged, flicked on his indicator and eased away from the pavement, looking very pleased with himself.

Topaz settled back into the seat and closed her eyes, calling upon the God and Goddess to protect her. Well, as they say, every little helps. And she had a feeling that she would need all the extra help she could get.

Chapter 19

A castle. They had dragged her to a shitting *castle.* What the actual fuck? Had she stumbled across a bad horror movie set?

Topaz handed over the cab fare, her eyes watering at the final total, and climbed out of the taxi. The driver waved goodbye and drove off, leaving her standing there like a lemon. She now had no clue as to what she was supposed to do next.

She looked up the long drive way and shuddered. The place was dark and depressing. There were no lights on anywhere inside, giving it an untouched air. It towered over her, dominating the sky line. Thunder boomed overhead and a streak of lightning flashed across the sky. She made a face, could this be anymore clichéd?

Next to it, a little way down the hill on which it stood, was an honest to Goddess cemetery. Normally she found them peaceful, almost beautiful, but not this time. Topaz lifted her head and scanned the sky, expecting to see a couple of

195

ravens circling overhead. She felt mildly disappointed, cheated even, when there were none. The weather wasn't helping the over-all feel of the place, gloom and doom seemed to radiate from the structure, sinking into her skin and making her shudder. She guessed she had answered her cliché question.

Taking a deep breath, she forced her legs to move, walking slowly up the driveway. She averted her eyes as she passed the graveyard and carried on to the front doors. The doors were huge, probably made of oak and looked very solid. She dreaded to think what could be lying in wait for her behind them.

About eye level was a big brass knocker, bigger than her head; it depicted a gargoyle that had a ring through its nose, its tongue sticking out like it wanted to lick her. Topaz lifted the ring and slammed it down onto the outstretched tongue, the noise booming out, echoing in the silence, so loud that, even though she was prepared for it, it made her jump.

She listened hard and caught the sound of footsteps coming from inside, gradually getting louder.

She tried to smooth out her face, clenching her fists to her sides, trying to pull herself together. She didn't want the bastards thinking she was scared. Didn't want to give them the satisfaction.

The footsteps stopped and she heard the sound of a bolt being drawn back. The door swung open and she prepared herself, ready to face whatever horror stood before her.

What she didn't expect to see was Ronnie standing there, holding up a candle stick, the glow from the flame illuminating her face.

Topaz's mouth dropped open and she gaped at her in surprise.

"Oh my gods, Ronnie. Are you OK?" She flung herself into her arms and hugged her tight. "I was so worried about you."

Ronnie gave her a wobbly little smile. "I'm OK, Tope, really. I'm so glad you came." She pulled back a little. "I'm sorry we had to do this."

Topaz looked at her, confused.

"Do what?"

"You're such a nice girl, I'll miss you."

"What do you mean, miss me?"

Out of the corner of her eye Topaz spotted movement as Ronnie raised her arm, but Ron was quicker than she was. The bitch slammed the base of the candle stick down onto her skull. Pain blossomed in her head and stars danced before her eyes.

Topaz felt her legs go and she dropped to the floor with a crash that shook her bones. She managed a grunting oath before blackness swept over her and she faded into unconsciousness.

Logan awoke to an empty bed. He looked around for Topaz but couldn't see her. He listened for a moment, waiting to hear some indication of her whereabouts, but none came. He opened his mind to her but felt nothing, not a trace. She was gone. He opened up a little more but sensed nothing.

He began to panic; knowing that something must have happened to her, the only way she would be off his radar would be if she was unconscious or dead. He didn't want to think about either possibility.

He swung his legs out of bed and raced through the apartment, not bothering to put on any clothes, searching for her, growing more frantic by the second. *Not again*, he chanted under his breath, *not again. I can't lose her again.*

Topaz came to, with a throbbing pain crushing her skull. She groaned and tried to lift her arms to cradle her head in her hands wanting to relieve some of the pain, only to have them jerked back. She heard the rattle of chains and forced her eyes open. She was chained to a wall, a freakin' wall.

197

"Oh, that bitch is gonna fry," she mumbled groggily, her mouth felt like it was stuffed with cotton wool. She rolled her tongue around her mouth a few times, trying to work up some saliva.

"Sounds like a plan," a deep voice responded.

Topaz jerked her head round and immediately closed her eyes against the sickening pain.

"Is my head still on my shoulders, not rolling around the floor?" she asked.

"Yes, love," the voice answered, amusement evident in the tone.

"How long was I out?"

"I don't know, I only just woke up myself, but as I'm awake I'd say a fair few hours, it's dark now."

She cautiously cracked one eye open and looked towards the sound.

A man was chained to the opposite wall. His clothes were ragged and filthy and his skin was grey, sunken in at the cheeks like he hadn't eaten in a week. He looked vaguely familiar but she couldn't place him.

"Do I know you?"

The man flashed his fangs in a smile before answering.

"Not officially, thought I wish we could meet under better circumstances. I'm Mason Barrett."

"My Vampire?"

He chuckled, his gaze raking up and down her body as gave her a slightly leering smirk.

"Sweetheart, I wish I could be your Vampire. But unfortunately you're taken."

She shook her head, still a little dazed.

"What do you mean, taken? How do you know?"

"You're a Soul Mate."

She shook her head.

"No, I'm not."

"Believe me, darling, you are. If you weren't, that blow would have damn near killed you."

198

Topaz sagged against the chains holding her up.

"I'm sorry, I'm being a little slow today, my friend just knocked me out. What are you talking about?"

"Yeah, I hear you. That bitch screwed me over too. Anyway, Soul Mates are a little harder to hurt, one of the perks of being linked to a Vampire, I guess."

"But I'm not linked to any Vampire."

He shook his head. "Not, all the way, no, or that blow wouldn't have knocked you out. But you have begun the binding process."

"Logan," she whispered, the truth finally dawning on her. Everything Avery had said was true. She *was* his Soul Mate. Shit, that was scary. But damn, was she glad she was, she very much doubted she would only have a headache if she wasn't.

A wide smile spilt Mason's face.

"Really, you're Logan's?" Topaz nodded wearily. "Damn, that's fantastic."

She scowled at him. "Why so fantastic?"

"Don't you get it? He's waited his entire Vampire life for you. I heard him talking to my Pappy one day, when he was visiting, before I was turned. Anyway, they were talking about Logan's wife-"

"His Wife?" she butted in. "He's married?"

"No, not anymore, he's widowed. She died the night he was turned, along with their two children." He sighed. "Logan doesn't know I overheard. He doesn't talk about them to anyone. He's been so lonely, no woman has ever matched up to her. He always said that he wasn't going to look for his Soul Mate, or even a Chosen One, because Alcina was his human Soul Mate and no one else would compare."

Alcina? Topaz had heard that name before, but she knew full well Logan had never told her. Where the hell had she heard it? She tried racking her brains but her head hurt too much to think that deeply.

199

She closed her eyes and turned away from Mason. She didn't want to know anymore, didn't want to think about it. Logan would never love her the way she loved him, he was still in love with his wife.

"Hey, Topaz?"

She opened her eyes and looked straight ahead, noticing for the first time that a mirror was propped against the far wall. She stared at her reflection, she was chained to a dirty, stone wall, her legs pulled slightly apart and her arms bound low to her sides. A chain was around her waist, keeping her upright.

"Topaz?" he called again.

She looked at Mason.

"What?"

"You're the special one now. You're his Soul Mate, his other half. He is so lucky to have found you." The sincerity in his tone made her relax a little, but she wasn't ready to talk about it yet.

"Where the hell are we?" she asked, needing to change the subject.

Mason looked around him. "Crypt I'd guess, judging by the tombs over there and the general smell of decay."

She squeaked and arched her back away from the wall, not wanting to touch it, whipping her head around in search of the tombs. Yep, there they were, against the far wall. All marble, and square and creepy looking. Cobwebs hung from the ceiling and down to drape over them. Luckily the looked like they hadn't been opened in years, but you never could tell with these damn Vampires, as she was finding out.

"A crypt?"

"Yep."

"Well shit," she tugged at the chains binding her, but they wouldn't give an inch. "We have to get out of here."

"Not going to happen I'm afraid," a voice commented from the shadows.

Topaz eeped in shock and spun round. A man melted out of the shadows, walking towards her.

He was a handsome devil, she'd give him that. His hair was pale brown, cut short and his face was one a Hollywood super star would be proud of. He was tall, about 6ft 3 at her guess and was clad in a dapper looking suit. All he needed was a cape to complete the look. He looked totally out of place in the dank surroundings.

He stopped before her and looked her up and down, a slight sneer on his face. She was beginning to get pig sick of people checking her out like she was a horse they wanted to buy and resisted the urge to open her mouth, presenting her teeth for inspection.

She pulled herself up to her full height and leaned back, lifting her chin and trying to look as casual and unafraid as possible. She met his eyes and stared at him, waiting for him to make the first move.

"So you're the one all the fuss is about? You're Logan's Soul Mate and the little Witch that is planning on exposing us?"

Topaz scowled at him, completely lost.

"What the fuck are you blabbering about? I haven't done anything. I'm not planning on exposing anyone."

He stepped closer to her, getting right up in her face, his fangs flashing dangerously as he snarled.

"We have your computer and your notes, we know what you have been working on."

He stepped back and leaned against the wall beside her, looking completely at ease. "That is just not acceptable to us. We had to stop you."

Topaz tossed her head in annoyance.

"What so you couldn't just ask me? You had to kidnap my friend, and lure me out here?" It suddenly dawned on her. "Are you the sick fucker who sent that monster after me? Oh, you're so dead when my boyfriend finds out, he'll kick your arse from here to London and back again. If I were you

I would start running now, maybe get a head start." She knew her eyes were flashing with anger, she had gone beyond scared and into right royally pissed off. How dare he?

In a move too quick for her eyes to register, he drew his hand back, slapping her full across the face. Her head snapped back, smashing her already abused head into the wall behind her, her cheek stung from the impact. Tears sprang up in her eyes but she refused to let them fall. She took a deep breath, trying to breathe through the pain. She slowly licked her lips and tasted blood, her lip already swelling.

"That's right, hit a harmless woman, you big, tough Vampire," she glared at him, almost daring him to hit her again. *Yeah, alright, maybe baiting the psycho was a bad thing,* she thought to herself, *so sue me.* His nostrils flared and he leant closer to her face, sniffing at the scent of blood. Mason groaned in the corner and she knew he had smelt it too; she could sense his hunger from across the room and knew the poor thing had been starved. Mason was yanking at his chains and straining to get closer.

"Humm," the Vampire murmured, "the smell of your blood is making me hungry." He turned towards the door of the crypt and yelled out. "Veronica, come."

The door opened almost immediately, Ronnie sauntered in. She wrapped her arms around his waist and snuggled close, resting her head on his chest so she could look at Topaz who just couldn't hold back.

She jerked at her chains as she lunged forward, trying to get at her. She wanted to do some serious damage.

"You bitch," she spat out. "I thought you were my friend. How could you do this to me?"

Ronnie yawned like she was bored.

"Yeah, yeah, just give it a rest will you? All I've heard from you is whine, whine, whine." She raised her voice and continued in a mocking tone, "oh, I'm scared, they're out to get me. Logan doesn't love me enough. He's a Vampire, what do I do?" Her eyes grew cold, and so did her voice. "You're pathetic. I'm so glad that I don't have to pretend to like you anymore you were driving me nuts."

She turned in the Vampire's arms and rested her hands on his shoulders, anchoring herself before leaning back, exposing her throat and a good deal of her breasts. She looked over her shoulder at Topaz. "Shall I show you how a real Vampire needs to be fed?"

The Vampire swept the hair back over her shoulder and grabbed a handful, stretching her neck back. He bared his teeth, showing that his fangs were well and truly out and struck, the sudden violence of the act startling Topaz.

Ronnie gasped as his fangs hit home and almost immediately began to writhe against him, wrapping one leg around his waist and grinding herself against his crotch. Topaz began to look away, not wanted to see the display. Mason was watching them with hungry eyes, his fangs had run out and he was straining at his chains.

"No, you will look," Ronnie ordered. Topaz looked back, startled by the command in her voice. Her fingers were twisted in his hair, a look of rapture on her face. Small noises spilled from her mouth as he drank, getting quicker and deeper as she rubbed against him like a cat.

He reached one hand up and exposed her breast, pulling it roughly from her top. He lifted his head from her neck, leaving her panting and groaning. He lowered his head to her breast and Topaz saw a flash of fang just before they sank into her soft flesh. Ronnie screamed in pleasure and bucked against him, her body convulsing.

Topaz closed her eyes, sickened by the display. It was nothing like what had happened between her and Logan during lovemaking. That had been pure and beautiful, loving and caring. With none of the violence and pain, she was witnessing.

203

Ronnie's body slowly calmed down as the Vampire withdrew his fangs and licked her flesh, sealing the puncture marks. He pulled her into his arms, turning her so she faced Topaz. She arched against him and kissed his neck, her left breast was still exposed showing the puncture marks that still oozed blood, but she didn't seem to care.

She laughed, a cruel sound coming from her throat.

"Look at your face, its priceless. I can tell that Logan has been gentle with you," she sneered, curling her lip in distaste. "That won't last, he's a Vampire. He'll grow bored of you. Not like my Seger." She ran her had possessively down his arm.

Seger's hands stroked her neck, causing her to shudder and arch into his touch. He leaned down to speak into her ear.

"Actually, my dear, I am rather bored of you." His arm snaked around her waist and held her tight against him as she looked at him in shock. "I'm afraid you have out lived your usefulness." His forearm came up around her neck and she began to struggle, thrashing around wildly, but the loss of blood was too much. He restrained her easily and cupped the sides of her head in his hands.

He licked his lips, as if savouring her taste. He looked thoughtful.

"You know, my darling, you need less fat in your diet." Ronnie's scream of outrage was the last thing she did. In one smooth move he twisted his hands, snapping her neck.

Ronnie's body flopped against his and he let go, dumping her lifeless form onto the floor. He stepped over her and looked down. "Pity. She was a good lay." He clapped his hands then rubbed them together like he was about to do a trick. "Anyway, let's get down to business. I need you and Mason dead, but I don't want the blame to fall at my feet. What to do?" He tapped his chin and pretended to think about it.

Without warning he walked over to Mason and punched him square in the face. Mason, weak as he was, stood no chance. He crumpled to the floor.

"What the fuck-" Topaz started but he ignored her, instead reaching into his pocket and pulling out a key.

"Oh, that's not good," she whispered to herself as the psycho proceeded to unlock the cuffs around Mason's wrists and ankles. Once Mason was free, Seger stood up and glided towards her. He grabbed hold of her wrist and pulled her arm towards him, stretching out her forearm. Topaz began to struggle, trying with all her might to pull her arm back, she threw her whole body weight backwards but it was like trying to reason with an elephant.

He stood there, two fingers circling her wrist, a bored expression on his face, like he could hold her there all day and not break a sweat. He waited for her to run out of energy, which she thought took a little longer than he expected. Eventually she sagged back against the wall, her arm going limp in his hand.

A flash of silver caught her eye and she watched in horror as he raised the knife in his other hand and brought it down, slashing her arm. Pain jolted through her and she hissed, gritting her teeth so as not to make a sound. She didn't want to give him the satisfaction. He roughly squeezed the jagged edges of the cut, making her wince. Blood welled up and began to drip down her arm onto the floor. He lifted his head and his nostrils flared, like a dog scenting the air, leaned closer, his face almost touching hers and she shrank away, not wanting him anywhere near her.

"If I were you," he hissed into her ear. "I would pray to whatever Gods you have that your death is quick. Do you know what a Vampire is like when they are hungry?" She shook her head, too scared to speak.

He shrugged and walked away. "You'll find out." He opened the door and slammed it behind him, the sound of a

205

key turning in the lock was the worst thing she had ever heard.

Topaz looked over at Mason but he was still out for the count. She wasn't stupid; she knew what Seger had planned. He was going to let Mason kill her and then blame her death, and probably Ronnie's, on him. No one would believe Mase, he would be as good as dead too.

She tugged on the chains around her ankles, not really expecting anything to happen, but not willing to stand idly by and wait for a hungry Vampire to wake up and have her for a midnight snack. That was so not part of her plan.

She closed her eyes, leaning her head back against the wall, taking deep breaths to try to calm her racing thoughts. She was a Witch, Gods damn it, not some weak, helpless individual. She was a Vampire's Soul Mate; she was not going to go down without a fight.

Wait a minute, she was a Soul Mate, could she use that? She racked her brains trying to recall everything Avery had told her. She remembered what he said about a special connection, about mental telepathy between Soul Mates. Logan had said that when she was attacked in his alley way, he had heard her in his head. Could she do it again? She didn't really know how, seeing as she hadn't done it deliberately the first time, but how hard could it be?

She tried to concentrate and open her mind, hard to do when Mason began to groan in the corner, obviously beginning to regain consciousness. She wriggled her toes then her legs, working up her body, trying to release all her tension.

She focused on Logan's image, just like she did when she was visualising during her ritual work. She focused on his face, picturing him as clearly as she could, recalling how he smelt, how he felt, all the emotions he invoked in her. She remembered how tenderly he made love to her and suddenly she felt him, as clearly as if he were standing right next to her.

206

Logan? She called out in her mind, imaging him hearing her.

Almost instantly he was there, in her mind. *Topaz, lass? Is that you? Where are you? Are you alright?* She could feel his worry, his fear, but also his determination to find her. She sighed, so happy to hear his voice.

Oh, Logan. Thank the Goddess. You have to come help us.

Us?

Yeah, Mason is here too.

Where's here?

She smacked herself on the forehead and almost lost the connection.

Duh, I'm so stupid. We're in a crypt.

A crypt? She could hear the disbelief in his voice.

Yes, a crypt. I think it's in the graveyard next to the castle.

Now there's a graveyard and a castle? Are you a fairy tale princess in disguise? She could hear that he was joking but she didn't have time to muck about. She could hear Mason moaning in his corner, he was waking up. Quickly she repeated the address that she had been text, thankful that she had such a good memory for details.

Logan we have to hurry. I'm in danger. Mason has been here for ages and he's starved. I know this sounds like a bad movie plotline but it's true. Seger has left me chained to the wall and unlocked Mase. He's coming round and I don't have much time.

Wait, wait. Did you say Seger?

Yeah, you know him?

Everyone does. I'll be there as quick as I can, I promise. Just try to hold them off. I'll come get you. I will not lose you again.

She smiled to herself.

I believe you.

She felt him withdraw a little, but he didn't leave her completely, he hovered at the back of her mind.

207

She had a think about what she could do to stay alive. She sighed. She was a Witch dammit, she had magic, she wasn't going to wait around for Logan to save her, even though she hoped that he hurried. She was going to help herself.

She opened herself up to the universe, to the magic of Deity and visualized Hecate, Goddess of witchcraft. She stood before her dressed in a flowing black gown, her raven hair billowing out behind her, blown by an invisible wind. She carried a sword in her hand. A lion sat by her feet and it roared silently, shaking its head, its mane rippling around its face.

She gave Topaz a regal bow of her head and raised one eyebrow in question.

Topaz bowed as much as she could in her position. "Great Goddess, I beg of you, bestow upon me your protection. I am your humble servant."

Hecate inclined her head, which Topaz took to be a yes.

Topaz started to intone her spell, imagining a bubble of protection growing around her.

"Bubble of protection, surround me, keep me safe. Protect me from harm, let none enter this space." Hecate raised her sword towards Topaz and she couldn't help but flinch. Light burst out of the tip of her sword and flowed around Tope, building upon the foundations of her own power. The protective bubble flared into life and then disappeared.

Hecate gave her one last, piercing look and vanished. Topaz hoped that her intervention would be enough.

"Thank you," she whispered.

Topaz pulled in her magical sight and looked back at Mason. Damn it, he was sitting up, she didn't have much time.

What was she to do? Did she stay quiet and hope he didn't notice her, at least until Logan got here? Or should she attempt to reason with him?

208

Mason's head jerked up suddenly and he sniffed the air, evidently catching her scent, the aroma of the blood that was trickling down her arm and dripping onto the floor. She flattened herself against the wall and tried to keep as still as possible, imagining herself as a tiny, invisible mouse. It didn't work. She was about as mouse like as a wolf.

Mason eased to his feet in one graceful move, making it look effortless. He turned and looked straight at her, his eyes locking on the gash on her forearm. His tongue darted out and he licked his lips, his fangs running out, glinting evilly in the dim light. He glided towards her, his body movements reminding her of that boneless grace a panther displays.

Her heart was pounding in her chest, all the breath leaving her lungs, as if somehow, by holding her breath, he would look past her. No such luck.

He stood before her, his head tipped to one side, as if he were evaluating her, like she was a juicy steak or a lobster in a tank.

"Pretty," he said at last. His eyes had bled to red and he looked so bloody scary, she almost cried.

He leapt forward without any warning, but her protective bubble obviously didn't need it. It flared into life, about a foot around her. Mason crashed into the bubble with such force that he bounced backwards and landed on his butt on the floor.

She held in a giggle as he rolled about like a turtle, trying to get up, his face a picture of shock.

He finally staggered to his feet, his face contorted with rage. Topaz braced herself as he took a running jump at her but her bubble held. But this time he was ready for it. He howled and snarled, clawing at the bubble. Out of the corner of her eye she caught a flash of Hecate, standing with her sword raised, feeding power into her protection bubble.

"Mason, honey. It's me, Topaz. Calm down. Logan will be here soon," she tried, pleading with him. He paused and seemed to listen for a second before attacking the bubble with renewed vigour, trying to get at her.

"Mason, No," she snapped, putting force behind her words, adding a little magical push of suggestion. "You cannot have me. I am not yours."

She glared at him to emphasis her point, hoping she looked and sounded braver than she felt. He looked like he was thinking about what she had said but it wasn't enough. He pushed experimentally against her shield, obviously trying the softly softly approach.

Topaz 'saw' Hecate reappear and raise her hand, pointing a finger at Mason. The bubble glowed for a second, as if waiting for him to make his move.

He didn't disappoint her. His teeth flashed as he lunged at the bubble, hands raised like claws, eyes glowing eerily red. The second his hand touched the bubbles surface, a light flashed across the perimeter of the bubble and a bolt of, what she can only describe as magical electricity, shot up his arm. Mason screamed and dropped to the floor like a stone, twitching and jerking. As he slowly stilled and quietened, Hecate bowed her head in her direction. Topaz bowed back as low and respectfully as she could, fixing her eyes on that of the goddess.

"I am your servant," Topaz repeated again. "If you have need of me, you have but to call." Hecate inclined her head in acknowledgement before turning to the door. To Topaz's surprise she heard the lock slide back and the door open. She braced herself, ready for Seger. But it wasn't Seger who burst in, it was Logan.

She sagged with relief and began to cry, she was just so glad to see him. She was safe.

"Topaz, sweetheart. Are you alright?" He rushed towards her but suddenly stopped dead. He lifted his head and sniffed the air. "You're hurt, you're bleeding." He stepped towards her and she stilled, ready to drop her bubble, but she didn't need to. He stepped straight through her shields

210

like they weren't even there and picked up her arm, turning it to look at the ugly gash. It was still bleeding but had slowed to a sluggish trickle.

He took hold of one of the chains that shackled her to the wall and gave it a hard yank. It parted company with the wall and her arm dropped to her side. He made quick work of the others and she dropped to the floor, grateful to be able to move.

He sat down next to her, gathering her up in his arms, she snuggled close and rested her head on his shoulder. But the sudden contact on her abused face made her quickly lift her head away hissing in pain.

"What did he do to you?" he asked, concerned. He gently cupped her face in his hands, turning her head to inspect the damage. He winced in sympathy.

"That bastard," he growled, "I'll kill him."

Topaz shook her head. "We don't have time." She nodded towards Mason's prone body and then towards Ronnie's still form. "Mase will wake up again soon and he's dangerous. We need to get help. Seger might be back soon. He's already killed Ronnie," she paused, tears prickling her eyes. "He killed her right in front of me."

Logan held her tighter as she sobbed, whispering sweet things into her hair.

"What a touching sight," a mocking voice crooned. They both spun round to face Seger. He was leaning against the door of the crypt, looking so casually relaxed, Topaz wanted to slap the smirk right off of his face.

As if sensing her thoughts, Logan placed a restraining hand on her arm before standing up, taking her with him.

He pushed her behind him and stood in front of her, shielding her body with his own.

"You will not touch her again, Seger," he snarled, the warning evident in his tone. "No one hurts my Soul Mate and gets away with it."

Seger stepped forward, his eyes flashing.

"And what do you plan on doing about it?" he asked, his head tipped to one side like he was seriously considering the question. "You couldn't stop me last time, and you won't stop me this time. Your Soul Mate will die and this time I won't take pity on the pathetic being that is you."

Logan stiffened in front of her and she realised what Seger had just admitted to. He was the one who had killed Logan's wife and children, turning Logan in the process. Oh, this fucker had to die. No one threatened her man and got away with it.

Rage began to build up inside her, and she pulled on it, savouring it. This was the man who had broken into her hotel and stolen from her, hired a deranged monster to kill her, worked against her with someone she thought was her friend and then killed said friend, lured her to her death, chained her up and injured her, left her with an unchained starving Vampire and now, now he had just admitted to killing her Soul Mate and his family. Oh, that was so not on.

Logan obviously thought so too. He changed his stance, adopting an aggressive pose, ready to strike.

Seger took one look at Logan then threw his head back and laughed an evil, manic laugh that chilled Topaz to the bone, making the hairs on the back of her neck stand up.

"What do you think you can do, kill me?" he asked, still chuckling to himself. "I am one of the Elders, you have no authority over me." He stepped closer to Logan, getting right up in his face. "I made you," he hissed in his face, baring his fangs, "I own you."

Logan lifted his chin and straightened his back.

"No one owns me." He suddenly swung his arm back and made a fist, punching Seger square on the jaw, in a move too quick for Topaz to register. She stepped back, out of the way, as Seger staggered slightly but kept his footing.

"You are a fool," he growled. "I will kill you both."

Logan nodded, is voice perfectly calm. "You are welcome to try."

Seger lunged, his fangs bared and for the first time Topaz noticed that his fingernails were long and curved, like cats claws. He tried to rake his fingers down Logan's face but was too slow. Logan spun away and again adopted that fighter's stance of his. His own fangs had descended, glinting wickedly in the light.

The two men circled each other, like a pair of jungle cats, waiting for the other to make the first move. Seger broke first and leapt on Logan, sending them both crashing to the floor. They rolled around, wrestling on the dirty ground, punching and attempting to kick, snarling and attacking with fangs, trying to do serious damage.

Topaz just stood there, backed against the wall, she felt powerless to do anything to help. Both men seemed equally matched, physically, thought Logan was a few inches taller than Seger. Logan landed a good blow, smacking Seger's head against the floor and she gave a spontaneous little whoop of delight.

Seger snarled and wrapped his legs around Logan's waist, flipping him over and landing on top of him, straddling him, so Logan was pinned to the floor by Seger's body.

Topaz looked around wildly for a weapon but found none. What sort of lousy crypt didn't have something a girl could use as a weapon? No old bones, no dusty candle sticks, thanks to Ronnie for that idea, nothing. Well that sucked.

You are a weapon. A female voice whispered in her head. She whirled around, trying to locate the source, but apart from Ronnie's body, Mason's still form and the two Vampires still rolling around, punching and biting every inch of flesh they could reach, the crypt was empty.

Use your powers, the voice urged. *They are strong within you.*

213

Yeah, use the force Luke, she muttered to herself, looking about again her gaze come to rest on the mirror in front of her.

She stopped and gaped. Instead of seeing her own, no doubt bruised and frazzled reflection, she was looking at someone who looked remarkably like her apart from the style of clothing she wore. She/Topaz was wearing a long brown dress and a white apron. Her hair fell wildly around her shoulders and she smiled at her. Topaz put her hand up to feel her own hair, still tied back in its pony tail and to her amazement the mirror image did the same. Topaz plucked at her jeans and the other lifted her skirt.

The world around Topaz seemed to fade away and she found herself standing in the kitchen that featured in her dreams. She was holding the old, hand bound book that she had seen before. She sat down on one of the little wooden stools and placed the book in her lap. Opening it she looked at the words, to her surprise it was written in Latin. She scanned through it, realizing quickly that it was no ordinary cook book, as she had first thought, but an Almanac. Topaz closed her eyes in shock.

Images began to flash before her eyes, like a sped up film, she saw herself as a young girl, growing up, marrying Logan, heavily pregnant, holding their children, watching them grow. She also saw herself performing what she now knew was a protection spell, exactly as she had in her dream. She saw herself step out of her house to fetch water, felt her panic as she saw a shadowy figure enter the house almost instantly she heard the screams of her children. She felt the pain as the monster, which had Seger's face, sank his fangs into her neck. And then nothing, the images ended and everything went dark.

Topaz opened her eyes and found herself staring at the mirror image of herself.

214

"Who are you?" She asked in a quiet voice, trying to ignore the fact that while she had been out of it, Seger had managed to get Logan off of the floor and had him pinned against the wall. Logan was kicking out at Seger, who had stepped back, just out of range.

I am you. We are one and the same. The voice answered in her head, the images lips moving as if she were talking.

"You what?" Topaz demanded, thoroughly confused.

I am you. We are one. She repeated. *Soul Mates.*

"You're my Soul Mate?"

OK, she thought, *I'm being thick, sue me; I've had a tough day.*

The image of her obviously thought the same; she groaned in frustration and tossed her head towards Logan and Seger. Logan had managed to get the upper hand again, executing a perfect round house kick, knocking Seger against the wall and had wrapped one of the chains that had held Mason around Seger's neck.

"Logan?" Topaz asked then promptly answered her own question, comprehension dawning. "I'm you? We're Logan's Soul Mate?"

The image nodded, looking slightly pissed off (a look Topaz had seen on her own face a number of times) glad Topaz had finally gotten the point. She lifted her arms and Topaz found herself doing the same. The image of Alcina, for that was who she was, drew a complicated pattern in the air with her hands which Topaz somehow mimicked perfectly, the actions coming like a long forgotten dance.

Power whizzed through Topaz, more power than she had ever felt before. But it wasn't scary, she felt empowered. This was hers of old. The power settled over her shoulders like a favourite jumper and she knew just what to do.

Picturing Hecate again, Topaz drew on the Goddess's power, asking her one last time for help. She responded instantly, forming before her. She raised the hand in which she carried her sword and offered it to Topaz. She reached

215

out and felt her hand close around hers. With a smile, Hecate faded away, leaving Topaz clutching her sword.

Topaz stared down at it. What the fuck was she supposed to do with it? She didn't have a clue how to use it. Her gaze fell upon Logan, still pinning Seger to the floor, the chain twisted in his fist, crushing the other Vampire's throat.

She didn't know how to wield a sword but she would bet her last pound that Logan did.

"Logan," she yelled.

Logan looked up, startled. He stared at the sight of her clutching the sword, in amazement.

"Catch," she tossed the sword over to him with as much strength as she could muster. Logan leapt to his feet and caught it deftly in his hand, twirling it around in his palm like it was the most natural thing in the world, getting a feel for it.

He was dishevelled and bloody, his clothes torn, ugly gashes marred his face and neck. Yet he grinned at her widely.

"You are the most amazing woman in the world." He blew her a kiss and spun back to face Seger, who had taken advantage of his moments reprieve to get free of the chain. He was on his feet; crouching low to the floor, ready to pounce.

Logan swung his arm back and slashed at Seger's chest. Seger leapt back but crashed into the wall. Logan calmly stepped forward and used the tip of the sword to pin Seger to the wall, the blade sliding into the flesh of his abdomen like a hot knife through butter. Seger howled in pain as the sword pierced his flesh, driving into his stomach and hitting the wall with a dull clunk.

"Now, I finish you," Logan growled. Topaz couldn't let him kill him, not right now. They needed answerers.

"Wait," she yelled, leaping over Mason and grabbing Logan's free arm.

Logan scowled at her. "We can't wait; he has to die."

But she shook her head. "Not yet." She turned to Seger. "First you have to reveal your diabolical plan, that's what they always do in the movies."

Logan rolled his eyes, leaning a little more onto the sword but she ignored him. "Why did you do all this? What did we do to you?"

Seger eyed Logan with distaste and coughed, blood welling up and spilling over his lips.

"I owe you nothing."

Topaz threw her hands up in disgust. "Death is too good for you," she spat at him, the answer already forming in her mind. She rolled she hands, drawing in all of her new powers.

She faced Seger, raising her arms into the air.

Looking him dead in the eyes she slowly began to intone her spell.

"I banish and bind thee, Seger, to the place between worlds." She drew the binding ward in the air with her hands. Golden threads sprang from her fingers and wrapped themselves around Seger's struggling form, but Logan held him pinned, leaning all his weight against the hilt of the sword.

"By the power of the four elements. North, East, South, West, Earth, Air, Fire, Water. You are trapped between worlds; no harm will you do to me or my own."

Seger began to yell and thrash as the last words left her lips but it did him little good. His form began to fade, the golden threads pulling tighter, binding, squeezing. There was a faint *plop* noise and Seger disappeared, the sword clattering to the floor before winking out of existence.

Topaz sagged to the ground, Logan catching her in his arms before she made contact with the floor and kissed her thoroughly.

217

Chapter 20

Topaz wrapped her arms around Logan's neck as he carried her, bride style, up the stairs to his apartment.

She unlocked the door with a wave of her hand. Logan raised his eyebrows, but said nothing. He kicked the door shut behind them and preceded down the hall to his bedroom. But instead of dropping her on the bed like she expected he put her down gently onto her feet and turned to go into the bathroom.

She was puzzled for a second before she heard the sound of the bath running.

Logan popped his head back round the door frame.

"Well, don't just stand there, get undressed," he demanded before disappearing back into the bathroom. Topaz stood there like a lemon for a moment before she shrugged her shoulders and began to strip. When she was completely naked she entered the bathroom to be greeted with the wonderful sight of Logan, completely starkers, bending over the tub testing the water, his fabulous butt presented for inspection.

"Mmm," she purred, giving it a loving caress with her palm.

Logan chuckled, reaching back to catch her hand in his. "Wait until we've had our bath, sweetheart."

Topaz pulled on his hand, urging him to turn around. Ever since she had banished Seger and Logan had taken her in his arms, before pulling out his mobile phone and calling for back up, she could hardly bare to be parted from him, feeling the almost overwhelming need to be touching him all the time. They had left Mason in Avery and Damian's capable hands and allowed Miss Jennifer to remove Ronnie's body from the crypt, apparently they had resources for that sort of thing, Tope didn't want to know the details. She hadn't stayed around to watch, begging Logan to take her home.

Logan turned around to face her. Now that he was out of his clothes she could see the full extent of the damage that Seger had inflicted. Logan's beautiful chest was cut to ribbons, shallow slash marks, obviously from Seger's claws, criss-crossed his previously flawless skin. Jagged flaps of flesh indicated the places that Seger's teeth had managed to take hold. Blood was still oozing out here and there, mingling with that which had already dried. She hissed in sympathy and reached out a tentative hand, wanting to caress him but afraid of inflicting more pain. Seeing her indecision, Logan grabbed her hand and pressed it to his chest, closing his eyes as the feel of her skin on his.

"Poor baby, what can I do to help?"

"You could kiss me better," he suggested with a little leer.

Tope pulled a slight face at the sight of all the dried blood and crypt grime. "Maybe we could take that bath first?"

Chuckling, Logan stepped into the tub, settling back into the warm water, still holding her hand he pulled her down in

219

to his lap. She sighed in bliss as the warm water washed over her tired, aching muscles.

After relaxing for a few minutes she slid from his lap and turned around so they were facing each other, their legs wrapped around each other's waists.

She reached for a flannel and wet it, before gently washing away all the blood and grime from Logan's skin. Logan repaid the favour, running the cloth over her skin until she was squeaky clean.

When they were done, Logan turned her around, urging her to lean back against his chest, cradling her in his arms.

"You were wonderful tonight," he whispered into her ear. "You reminded me of," he stopped, a slightly guilty don't-talk-about-the-ex look on his face. She turned her head to look at him fully.

"Of Alcina," she finished for him.

"How did you...?" Logan stuttered.

She leant her head back against his shoulder, closed her eyes and sighed. "It's a long story."

She began to tell him everything, about her strange dreams, describing the house and the children in perfect detail. She told him all about the things she was feeling for him. She left nothing out, no matter how embarrassing it was.

When she had finally finished, she opened her eyes and looked at Logan. Thin, red lines of blood were dripping down his cheeks, the Vampire equivalent of tears.

"Oh, darling," he whispered. "I thought I had lost you forever."

He couldn't believe that it was really her, that his wife had come back to him. They were two totally different people, Alcina having been quieter and more solemn, while Topaz was louder, more fun loving, but when he actually thought about it, he realised that one of the reasons he had fallen so quickly for her was that there was so many similarities between the two women.

He loved Topaz just the way she was, but he needed to know more, he had to know what she recalled of their life together, their home, their children. He found that his voice trembled as he asked, "What do you remember?"

Topaz was crying too, now. "I remembered everything. I remember Thomas and Mary. I remember our wedding day," she trailed off, the pain of their loss was almost too much to bear. She cupped Logan's face in her hands, wiping away his tears with her thumb. "I love you, Logan McGregor. You are my Soul Mate."

Logan grinned widely and pulled her closer to his chest.

"I love you too, Topaz Thompson. You are my Soul Mate," he looked her in the eyes. "I never want to risk losing you again." He clutched both of her hands in his and pulled them into his chest. "Bind with me?"

She nodded, tears streaming down her face now. "Yes, I will gladly bond with you. I never want to live without you again. We were parted once, I couldn't stand it again."

Logan beamed, hugging her close, but her brain was whirling away. Now that they were about to Bind she was suddenly nervous, it was alright thinking about something but doing it was another matter.

"What do we have to do?" she asked him in a small voice.

Logan swept her wet hair back from her face and placed a small kiss on the curve of her neck. She shivered at his touch and leaned back against him, fitting her body into the curve of his. His skin was already beginning to heal, the flesh knitting together to become the perfect, flawless skin she knew so well.

"As Avery told you, there are five parts to a bonding," he sat up a little, leaning his back against the side of the bath, Topaz went with him, sliding under his arm to rest her head on his shoulder, glad that the tub was so huge. "The first is recognition," he held up one finger.

221

She nodded. "We've got that one covered, I certainly notice you." She ran her hand lightly down his chest, coming to a stop on his stomach, just before things got interesting.

Logan cocked an eyebrow in warning and she smirked at him, not even bothering to appear innocent.

Shaking his head in that the-things-I-have-to-put-up-with way, he continued. "Next, stage two, is what some call the 'knowing', this starts by being able to pick up the others emotions and progressed to thoughts and dreams."

"Well we know we can communicate telepathically but I don't know about sharing dreams. I think I would know if we had done that."

A sly grin worked its way onto his face, one that she had come to recognise as trouble. "Fancy sharing a shower some time?" he asked, innocently.

She blushed slightly as she realised her suspicions were right, they had shared the shower dream. "What's the third stage again?" she asked, ignoring his pleasure at making her blush.

Logan sighed dramatically, which was slightly more impressive on him than on her, as he didn't have to breathe.

"The third stage is the claiming or the marking." Seeing the look on her face, and obviously picking up on her mental image of her, bending over, butt in the air, while Logan advanced with a branding iron, Logan reassured her at once. "It's nothing like that. When the time comes you will know instinctively what to do, I promise."

She nodded, secretly relieved and waved him to continue.

"Well normally the claiming is followed by the mating." She pulled a face at the wording, but like the idea. Any time spent 'mating' with Logan was time well spent, in her opinion.

"Then last but by no means least, is the blood sharing," he looked down at her like he expected her to freak out.

"Well, we've done that already. You've fed from me before." She pointed out, shrugging, to show that she didn't see it as a big deal.

Logan shook his head. "No, darling, we haven't." He cut her off as she was about to argue. "We both have to share blood, it will complete our bond, and it will connect us," he looked deep into her eyes, "forever. It will make you immortal."

She gulped. "Forever? Immortal?"

"Well, for as long as I live, which is forever if no one cuts of my head, stakes me or," he looked at her, "banishes me."

She gave him a squinty eyed look that said, don't-push-me-or-it-might-happen, but they both knew she didn't mean it.

"What if I don't want to take your blood?"

He sighed, a small sad sound and hugged her closer.

"Then we will be together until the end of your natural life. I love you Topaz, I always will." He lay there, holding her but not looking at her face, allowing her to think things through and make up her own mind. She loved him and she wanted to be with him, and yes, she wanted it to be forever. One lifetime with Logan would never be enough.

"Wait, this won't make me into a Vampire will it? I'll still be able to go out in the daylight? I won't have to drink blood? Or give up food? I'm sorry, but giving up cheese, I'm not sure I'm ready for that."

Logan couldn't help but laugh, she looked so very serious.

"No, it won't make you a Vampire, you'll be just as you are, human, but with a little added extra, you will heal quicker, be harder to hurt and, as I said before, you'll be immortal. Do you think you want to do this?"

"I'll try," she promised. "I can't say more than that. I want to be with you forever, but I'm not sure I can bring myself to drink blood."

223

He nodded, apparently satisfied with her answer, understanding her completely.

"So what now?"

Instead of answering, Logan slipped his arm under her legs and scooped her up against his chest, standing up out of the bath, taking her with him. She squeaked in surprise and shivered as the cold air hit her skin.

"Don't worry, sweetheart," he grinned, "I'll warm you up."

Chapter 21

Logan laid her gently down on the bed and, true to his word, proceeded to warm her up beautifully.

He covered her with his body while lowering his head for a kiss. The kiss started out sweet, little loving nips and licks. Soft kisses fluttered over her lips his tongue ghosting out. She opened her mouth obligingly and he immediately took advantage, stoking the fire and building the passion.

Topaz clutched at his shoulders, pulling him down closer, wanting to wrap herself around him, lose herself in him, revelling in the feel of the ever present sparks.

Suddenly he sat up, taking her with him, so she was sitting in his lap, facing each other. The look on his face was very serious and for a second she wondered what she had done wrong.

Without a word he placed his hand on the small of her back and held it there, taking her hand in his other he placed it on his chest, over his heart.

Looking deep into her eyes he finally spoke.

"I, Logan McGregor, claim thee, Topaz Thompson, as my Soul Mate. I promise to love you for the rest of our days. Nothing shall part us." Topaz felt a warm, tingling sensation crawl over her skin where his hand rested on her back and, instinctively, she knew what to do.

She kept her hand where it was, over his heart, and placed her other on top. She looked into his eyes, almost overwhelmed by the love shining out of them, his eyes were solid gold now, glowing like a beacon in the dark of night. That's what he was, her beacon of hope, always there to guide and protect her. She said the first things that came to mind, saying what was in her heart.

"I, Topaz Thompson, claim thee, Logan McGregor, as my Soul Mate. I promise to love you for the rest of our days. I promise to show you that love, every day, to be your best friend, your lover, your partner. We shall laugh together, cry together, live together and love together. So mote it be."

Her hand tingled against his skin, and she felt the same warmth as she had from him. She lifted her hand slowly, staring at his chest. There, on his skin, almost like a tattoo, was a pentagram, a five-pointed star that is commonly used to represent her religion. She lowered her head and placed a kiss over it, as if sealing the deal.

Logan reached up and untied the leather thong around his neck that held the two gold rings. He selected the smaller one and picked up her left hand, sliding the ring slowly down onto her second finger. She looked down at it and realisation dawned on her, they were our wedding rings, from when she had been Alcina. He had kept them all these years.

"My beloved wife," he whispered.

Tears sprang up as she took the other from his palm and repeated his move, slipping it onto his finger.

"My darling husband," she whispered back.

Logan tenderly wiped away her tears, mindful of her bruised cheek.

"Why are you crying, sweetheart? Did I do something wrong?"

She shook her head. "No, baby, you did everything right." Logan looked slightly baffled, in that women-are-crazy way that men have perfected. "I'm crying because I'm happy," she explained. "I love you more than anything in the world."

"Good," Logan declared, tipping her backwards so she flopped down onto the bed. "Now can I make love to my wife?" Topaz shivered in delight at the combination of his words, he called her his wife, and the feral look in his eyes that promised many good things to come.

"Oh, yes," she groaned as he dropped down on top of her, his arousal pressing tight against hers. She was already wet and aching for him, that ever present need she had for him burning her up inside. "I want you, now, baby, please." She ground herself against him, gasping at the feel of his cock sliding against her flesh, just stroking over her clit sending a little burst of pleasure through her.

He did it again, rocking his hips and using the tip to spread her juices, leaving her slick and ready.

He positioned his head at her entrance, sliding in barely an inch. She growled in frustration and tried to lift her hips, wanting him in deeper.

"Is this what you want?" he purred in her ear, thrusting slightly. She moaned in response, showing him with her body just how much she wanted him.

With a groan that seemed to come from deep, down inside him, he flexed his hips, thrusting inside her right up to the hilt in one smooth glide. She gasped in pleasure and wrapped her arms and legs around him pulling him tight against her.

She lifted her head and kissed him hard as he began to move, gliding in and out in slow, smooth thrusts. He pulled back from the kiss and, lifted himself up on his arms, changing the angle of penetration.

227

She lifted her head and looked down the length of her body, watching him sliding in and out of her. The sight was too much and it threw her head back, her back arching in pleasure.

She fought her body and lifted her head again to watch his face. She wanted to watch him orgasm, wanted to see the pleasure of their joining etched on his face.

An orgasm tightened her body and she reached out to pull him down over her, she cradled his face in her hands looking deep into his eyes.

The love shining out of them was enough to bring her. Waves of pleasure spread through her, through her body, causing her muscles to spasm around him, as she gasped for breath.

His eyes grew wide and his rhythm changed and he thrust deeper, quick and hard.

She knew what she wanted, she wanted him to come buried in her every way he could be, she realised how much she craved his bite, knowing the pleasure it gave him.

She directed his head down to her neck, shivering as his lips caressed her skin, his teeth nipping lightly.

His movements grew more frantic, like he was unable to control himself. She pulled him close, her body calling out for her to make him hers completely. She eyed the soft flesh of his neck and her body reacted for her. She lifted her head and kissed his skin mimicking what he was doing to her.

She opened her mouth and bit down, sinking her teeth into his soft flesh, he jerked against her and groaned. She felt his fangs pierce her own skin as she tasted the first salty tang of his blood on her tongue.

She sucked hard on his flesh, and felt his body spasm inside her, she came again, lifting her mouth from his skin to scream his name.

He writhed on top of her, thrusting deep one more time before going still.

She felt something shift inside her just as his cool seed spilled into her. It felt like something detached itself from her soul and called out to him. She felt an answering pressure from Logan and moaned in ecstasy as his essence poured over her, their souls merging, joining, completing each other.

It felt like nothing else, it was out of this world. The sensations that slid through her, as if caressing her from the inside out, hitting every possible pleasure spot she had. Her nipples tingled, her clit pulsed, her inner walls rippled around his shaft. But it wasn't just her own pleasure she felt, it was his too. Just like when she had taken his cock in her mouth and sucked him to completion, she felt the same, his pleasure echoing through her, making her own deeper, more intense.

Powerful shock waves danced across her skin as she held him tight, his body shuddering, his eyes closing with a groan, in response to their shared pleasure.

He collapsed on top of her and held her tight, kissing her neck and lips in turn.

She lovingly licked at the spot on his neck where she had bitten him, revelling in the feeling of being so close to him. He lifted himself up on his arms to smile down at her. As she watched the last of the gashes on his chest closed, leaving his skin smooth and unmarked, not even a scar to be seen. She kissed him deeply, showing him with her kiss how much she loved him, adored him, worshipped him.

When they finally broke the kiss, he pulled out slowly and rolled onto his side, taking her with him so he was snuggled up behind her, her butt resting against his crotch. She was still panting, trying to catch her breath, her body shivering with little aftershocks.

"That was amazing," she finally commented, when she regained the power to form words. "What the hell was that anyway?"

229

"That, my love, was the finally step of the binding. You took my blood, now you're stuck with me." He smiled a self satisfied, extremely male smile and kissed her neck, licking over the small puncture holes.

She ignored his comment, instead snuggling down into his arms and closing her eyes, dawn was coming. She started, her eyes jerking open, how the hell did she know that? Must be something to do with being bound to a Vampire.

She stroked her fingers up and down his arm where it lay over her, playing with the little hairs. A thought struck her.

"Hey, where are our tingles?"

Logan looked down at his arm where her fingers were still caressing his skin.

"The tingles often fade after the joining, we don't need them anymore." She nodded to show that she understood.

"I'm gonna miss them though," she mused.

"Aye, me too, but we have something even better now." She felt a wave of remembered pleasure flow from him and smiled in agreement as she lay back down and snuggled closer to his chest.

Logan's fingers were drawing lazy circles on her hip, his touch light as a feather. It was relaxing and she felt herself drift off to sleep, safely cuddled up in Logan's arms.

Chapter 22

Topaz woke up after Logan did. The wonderful man had ordered her breakfast, if you could call it breakfast at 7:30 at night. They had slept the whole day away.

Logan had placed the tray on the bedside table and now she could hear him humming away in the shower. He had obviously just ordered a little of everything. There were pancakes on one plate, fruit salad in a bowl. Another plate contained scrambled eggs, bacon, sausage and toast. A cup of coffee and a glass of orange juice were there also. A small red rose completed the tray.

As she inhaled the wonderful smell, her belly rumbled, reminding has that she had not eaten in almost two days, she was famished.

By the time Logan came out of the shower, she had eaten the bacon, eggs and sausage, demolished the toast and managed to find room for two of the pancakes. The orange juice was gone and she was sipping the coffee when he emerged from the bathroom, nothing but a small towel around his waist.

She looked at him and felt hungry all over again, but not for food.

He grinned at the look on her face but shook his head.

"Sorry, darling, but we don't have time. Avery has planned a welcome back party for Mason and our presence has been requested."

Topaz pouted a little before giving in and getting up, heading for the bathroom. She glanced at herself in the mirror and stared in wonder. The bruises on her face had faded completely, her skin was completely unmarked and the gash on her arm was healed, leaving only a faint pink scar. The only marks she could see were the slight bruises left from Logan's bite.

She turned to look at herself fully, catching sight of the small of her back. There just like Logan had, was a kind of tattoo on her skin, as far as she could see it was the image of a sword, a Claymore, she thought they were called. The point of the blade stopped just above her butt, while the hilt rested just above where her waistband would sit. It was about six centimetres long and had what looked to be the McGregor clan emblem on the hilt. *I'm branded for life*, she thought, mock sighing, as she turned on the water. Oh, she didn't really mind the mark, in fact, she loved it. Rings and jewellery could get lost, this was a permeant symbol of their love and commitment.

She had a quick shower, not bothering to wash her hair as Logan had done it the night before. She was out and dry within ten minutes.

Logan had helpfully laid out an outfit for her on the bed. He had chosen her favourite bra and panties set, a deep purple plunge bra and matching lacy french knickers. A short black skirt, a purple vest top and black high heels completed the outfit. She smiled at his cheekiness but donned the clothes anyway, might as well give him a treat.

She brushed out her hair and left it hanging down almost to her waist. She swept on a little makeup, just some eye shadow and a little lipstick. It was all she needed, her skin was now pale and flawless, no powder needed here.

Logan was sitting on the sofa in the living room wearing faded blue jeans and a plain black t-shirt. His damp hair was slicked back from his face but unbound, just how she liked it.

He smiled when he saw her, his eyes lighting up and his fangs running out. She knew that look, she licked her lips and allowed her hips to sway a little as she walked to the door.

She looked back over her shoulder at him.

"You coming then, we don't want to be late?"

He was behind her in a second, his arms around her waist, pulling her into his body.

"You're a tease," he growled in her ear, his tongue flicking out to lick her neck. She shuddered and leaned closer.

"Yeah, but you love me anyway," she answered.

"I will make you pay later," he threatened, though it sounded more like a promise.

"I'll hold you to that," she responded, turning her head to nip at his nose.

"Little Witch," he groused good naturedly, patting her butt. "Let's get going." He reached around her to open the door and she slipped under his arm, catching his hand in hers as he locked up and lead her down to the club.

The party was in full swing by the time they made it down to the club, they had stopped several times to have a little kiss and grope session on the stairs and she had had to bribe Logan not to drag her into his office.

The club was not as busy as it usual was, there were far less people. Three tables that had previously been scattered around the edges of the dance floor had now been pushed together, near to the bar.

A bartender that she didn't know was pouring drinks left, right and centre, trying to keep up with demand. Avery was

233

sitting at one of the tables, between Mason -who was looking much healthier than the last time she had seen him, his face had filled out and he had lost the hungry look from his eyes, he was dressed in fresh clothes and his hair had been washed- and a beautiful female vamp, his arm around them both, laughing uproariously. If she didn't know better she would say they were drunk. Dane and Drake were also there, and she took a moment to wonder who was manning the doors. As if reading her mind, and he probably was, Logan answered her.

"The club is closed tonight, this is a private party." She nodded to show that she understood. Logan took her hand and steered her towards the nearest table, pulling out a seat and helping her to sit down.

A cheer, accompanied with wolf whistles, rang out as they sat down, but she blatantly ignored them, lifting her chin and sniffing with mock distain.

Logan chuckled and received a scowl for his troubles.

"Can I get you a drink, my love?" he asked.

"Yes please, I'll try a Vampires Kiss."

"Good choice," he agreed with a wink and got up, heading for the bar.

Avery immediately slid into his vacated chair and flung his arm around her shoulders, planting a smacker of a kiss on her cheek. She smiled at him indulgently, because damn, she really had grown to like the flamboyant Vampire.

"Hey, gorgeous, what's a nice girl like you doing in a place like this?" he waggled his eyebrows.

She played along and sighed dramatically, as if the weight of the world was on her shoulders. "Waiting for a man to sweep me off my feet," she answered in her best southern belle accent.

Avery jumped up immediately and swept his hat off his head and into a courtly bow, bending at the waist. He straightened up and dropped the hat onto the table in front of her.

"Well ma'am, can I have the pleasure of this dance?" He held out his hand.

"Why certainly, good Sir," she inclined her head and took his hand, allowing him to pull her to her feet.

The song playing was by no means suitable to dance to, thanks to the heavy rock beat of Def Leppard's Let's get Rocked, none the less she put her arms around his shoulders and held on. Avery was an enthusiastic dancer, bouncing on the spot and throwing his hair around. By the time the song was over they were both laughing hysterically, leaning on each other for support.

Logan, who had been standing at the bar watching them with amusement, came over.

"Avery," he said in a mock stern voice. "What do you mean by wearing out my woman?" He gave her a small wink and whispered ,"that's my job," in her ear. She blushed a little at his obvious suggestion.

Avery tried to look contrite but failed miserably.

"Come on," she tugged on Logan's arm. "I really need that drink now." She dragged both men back over to the table and sat down, taking an appreciative sip of the cool cocktail.

As the party rolled on around them, she began to feel a little weirded out. They hadn't really spoken about what had happened to them last night. She had just been so grateful to be out of that pace that she hadn't stopped to wonder why she had ended up there in the first place, or how Mason had got there either.

She felt a gentle hand on her shoulder and turned to see Logan watching her, concern evident on his face.

"What's wrong, darling?" he asked. "You've been sitting there staring into your drink for over twenty minutes."

She sighed and rotated her neck, trying to work out some of the tension kinks. Logan's other hand come up and he began to massage her neck and shoulders, gently but

235

firmly. She moaned in pleasure and leaned into his touch, feeling the knots ease under his skilled fingers.

"Well?"

She shook her head. "Nothing's wrong," his eyebrow lifted, she could tell he didn't believe her, "well not really."

She paused, her nose screwing up in concentration as she thought about it. "I have just been going over everything that happened in my head, trying to make some sense out of it, but I can't. I just don't understand it. Why did they do it? What did we ever do to them?"

Logan sighed. "I think that maybe something that Mason can shed some light on."

She looked across the table at Mase, who was laughing uproariously at something someone had said, his arms firmly around the waist of a good looking bleeder feeder, who was draped across his lap.

"Hey, Mase," he called across the table. "Can I have a wee word?"

Mason looked up and immediately extracted himself from the over enthusiastic Donor. He strolled over to them, a definite swagger in his step. He threw himself down in an empty chair next to Topaz.

"Yes, boss. What can I do for you?"

Logan put his arm round Topaz's waist and pulled her onto his lap, turning her around so he could see Mason clearly.

"We were wondering if you were up to talking to us about what happened. We're a wee bit puzzled about the series of events."

Mason appeared to think about this for a moment, before nodding.

"Yeah, I'm up for that. To be honest, I do want to talk about it."

"Do you want to come to my office? It's a bit noisy out here." Laughter broke out near Avery's end of the table, his deep booming chuckle overpowering everyone else's.

236

"Might be an idea," Mason agreed, smiling himself.

Logan stood up, taking her with him and gently set her on her feet. Taking her hand, he led the way towards his office, nodding at Dane and Drake as he passed. Both men silently stood up and followed them wordlessly towards the employee door.

Topaz settled down in the chair she had occupied during their previous meeting, sinking into it gratefully and slipping off her shoes so she could curl her legs up underneath her, mindful of her short skirt. Dane and Drake took up their positions by the door and Mason made himself comfortable on the sofa Avery had lounged on.

A knock on the door had them all looking up.

"It's Avery," a disembodied voice called out. Dane looked at Logan, waiting for permission to open the door. Logan nodded and waved his hand, indicating that they should let him in.

Avery sauntered in, his hat now firmly back on his head, and flopped down next to Mason.

Logan lent forward, resting his elbows on the desktop and looked at Mase.

"Are you ready to talk?" he asked, his voice low and soothing.

Mason nodded, but he didn't look happy about it and Topaz suddenly began to worry about what he had to tell them.

"It's alright, mate," Avery said, his hand on Mason's shoulder, "You don't have to tell us if you don't want to."

"No," Mason stated, shaking his head, his voice firm. "I have to tell this. I have to apologize to Topaz and make things good."

"What do you mean by that?" Logan all but growled, his fangs peeking out from between his lips. Topaz jumped up from her chair and plonked herself down onto Logan's lap, winding her arm around his neck, placing a small kiss on his cheek. She felt him relax a little as his arm snaked round

237

her waist and held her close. She wriggled a little to get comfortable, she didn't know how long they were going to be sitting here.

She turned to look at Mase and smiled at him, showing him that everything was going to be ok.

"Please tell us, Mason, I need to know. Someone I thought was my friend died there and I was attacked and beaten," Logan's arm tightened around her and she patted his hand, urging him to ease up. "I'm scared, I have to know that no more monsters are going to emerge from the woodwork and that the people I care about are safe." Her voice had taken on a pleading tone that she wasn't proud off but needs must. Mason looked at her for a long moment before he finally spoke.

"I didn't mean for this to happen," he finally blurted out. "I didn't know it was so serious." He stopped and looked down at his hands, which were resting on his knees.

"What was serious?" Topaz asked gently.

He looked up. "Our secret."

"What secret?" she asked, confused.

"The secret of our existence."

She was still confused and looked at Logan, who now had a look of growing understanding on his face.

"Our existence has been kept a secret for many years, as much as it could be," Logan began, "not just ours but that of all supernatural creatures." She nodded, understanding so far.

"Some of us, Mase, Avery and myself included, feel that the time is right for the world to know about us, to learn that we really do exist. But others, normally the elders of our species, believe we should stay hidden." His fingers began to draw little patterns on her thigh where she was cuddled up on his lap, making it a little harder to concentrate, but she knew it was an unconscious gesture on his part, a need to touch and be touched, so she focused very hard on what he was saying.

238

"As we have talked about, now would be the best time to reveal ourselves, humans are less afraid of us now than they were say, a hundred years ago. But it has been forbidden. We have had meetings with other beings who also agree." He frowned at Mason. "But it seems that Mason here took it upon himself to take the first step towards revelation."

Mason jumped up and began pacing, running his hands through his hair, agitated.

"I didn't mean for this to happen. I thought I was helping," he threw himself back down onto the couch, bouncing Avery. "I thought that if the human's magical community knew of our existence and accepted us, as others have done in the past, then we would have proof that the time is right."

Comprehension was dawning on Topaz.

"So, let me get this straight. You contacted my organisation because you wanted me to conduct an interview with you, and you wanted to use us as a kind of sound board?"

Mason looked uncomfortable. "Well, it wasn't quite like that," he admitted. "I knew you were looking for proof of our existence, I've been keeping up to date on your discoveries for some time, and I knew that you would be the perfect person to help us. I'm afraid I used your enthusiasm against you." Mason looked so sorry for himself that she melted.

Topaz got up from Logan's lap and went over to Mason, plopping her butt down on the edge of the sofa, she gave him a hug which he gratefully accepted.

"I don't blame you," she assured him. "You were only doing what you thought was best, I can understand that. You didn't know how it was going to turn out." She patted his shoulder and got up, wriggling her butt into the gap between Avery and Mason. Avery immediately put his arm around her and she leant back into his embrace. Logan gave her a small smile and she smiled back, it was so

239

refreshing to have a man so comfortable with himself that he didn't get jealous of her having male friends, though she was sure he would soon see off anyone who had serious intentions.

"Please tell us the rest of your story, Mason," Logan said, waving him to continue.

As Mase nodded to himself, Topaz took his hand in hers and gave it a comforting squeeze.

"Tell us how you came to be at Seger's home," Logan suggested.

Mason leant back against the sofa and held her hand a little tighter.

"I was getting ready for work, it was about 9 o'clock. The doorbell rang and I went to answer it," Mason began. "It was that Veronica girl. I had arranged for the Donors guild to send over a Donor for me as I knew it was going to be a long night. I was supposed to meet up with Topaz, here at the bar. I had seen Miss Veronica around so I let her in. She was acting a little strange, sort of giggly and was a little unsteady on her feet. But, I'm ashamed to say, I didn't pay much attention, I didn't want to be late. I just invited her in and fed from her."

"Almost immediately after she left I began to feel weird, I suppose you could say faint, but it's been so long since I've experienced any human ailments, I shrugged it off and left for work. I couldn't have gotten more than a few yards when I must have passed out, the next thing I know I'm awake and chained up in that crypt. Veronica must have taken something that was in her blood stream, I don't know what it was but it knocked me out real good."

Mason was griping Topaz's hand tightly by this point but he seemed more angry than upset.

"Seger was there. I think he had gone quite mad. He kept ranting at me, saying that he knew what I had done and that I would pay. I didn't know what he was on about but Veronica was more of a talker. She would come in every

240

night and talk for about an hour, gloating." He shuddered a little, as if the memory was too much.

"She would tell me things that they had done, like hiring turned Shifters that had gone mad to kill Topaz, about stealing her belongings, that sort of thing. She was very annoyed when Topaz met Logan and all their plans were foiled. Then one night she skipped in and happily told me that Topaz had moved in with her." He closed his eyes and sighed.

"Seger was one of the older generation that didn't want us to reveal ourselves," Avery supplied for Topaz. "He's very old and was on the Immortal Council."

"What's that?" she asked, the researcher in her was dying to know.

"The Immortal Council is like our governing body," Logan informed her. "They make our rules and make any major decisions regarding our fate. Each supernatural species has elders on the Council, that way it's fair. They have two representatives for each species, a male and a female. This has worked well for hundreds, if not thousands of years, but lately we have begun to change."

Avery took up the explanation.

"We of the younger generation, the young guns, as the Elders like to call us, want to come out of hiding. We are tired of lurking in the shadows, we want to be able to live with humans, not dominate them. The older generation want to stay hidden, they have refused to change with the times. They want to stick to the old ways, feeding from humans and glamouring them so they don't remember anything. They want us to move every fifteen or twenty years so no one will notice, but we don't want to, we want to settle down. We build lives, communities, businesses, we don't want to keep packing up and starting again."

Topaz nodded, she could understand that, the need for a place to call home.

241

"So why don't they want to do it, why don't they want to go public?"

"They are stuck in their ways. They don't think the world can handle the knowledge of our existence. They aren't as savvy to the world as we are, they don't care about the media, or the tolerance people have nowadays. They make the rules, and they expect us to follow them without question."

"I get that, but why did Seger take it upon himself to try to kill us rather than just stopping us?"

"He's mad, sweetheart, he had no logic," Avery said, hugging her.

"And poor Ronnie got dragged into it all," Topaz sighed. "She thought he loved her," She began to sniffle, fearing that the tears were about to start flowing again. "And he killed her."

Logan rushed over and gathered her into his arms, rubbing her back and whispering soothing nonsense, until her tears eased away. She snorted and snuffled accepting the hanky that Drake handed her with a little smile of thanks.

"I'm sorry to be such a wimp," she apologized when she had pulled herself together. "I'm not usually like this, but it's been a tough week."

"Are we done here?" Avery asked.

Topaz looked at Logan, who nodded. Apparently they were.

"Yes," he answered Avery. "Get back to the party. And thank you, Mason, for talking to us."

Avery gave them a theatrical bow and headed out the door.

"Thank you for understanding," Mason said, his face showing his relief. "And again, I apologize for putting Topaz in danger. I'm so glad you found each other."

Logan wrapped his arms around her, pulling her up against his front.

"So are we. Go on, get back to your party."

Mason smiled before exiting, shutting the door quietly behind him.

"Do you want to go back to the party?" Logan asked her.

She shook her head. "No, I want to go to bed. I'm tired and need to sleep."

Logan turned her round so she was facing him and gave her a long, slow kiss.

"Are you sure I can't tempt you to stay awake, just for a wee while?" he asked.

She pretended to think about it.

"Maybe just a little while, if you're very good."

Logan scooped her up into his arms.

"I'm always very good," he promised.

He walked her to the door but instead of opening it as she had expected he slid a key into the lock and turned it. She raised one eyebrow in question.

"I can't wait," he declared as he licked a seductive line down her neck. She shuddered, a wave of lust rushing through her. She had thought that she could make it through the night without any problems, but now she wasn't sure. She was distinctly aware that they had rushed out of the apartment earlier, and though they had snatched a few kisses on the stairs, they weren't nearly enough. She craved him with every fibre of her being and couldn't wait much longer. Logan's teeth nipped at her skin and she wriggled against him, heat pooling between her legs.

"Hungry, baby?" she purred, her voice dropping lower. While everyone else had seemed to have glasses filled with cocktails that she assumed were the ones with added extras, Logan had again drunk scotch. She recalled him telling her that he usually drank at the club, but since they had been together he had only drank from her as far as she knew.

Logan's eyes glittered gold as he looked at her, one eyebrow raised in question.

243

"You offering, darling?"

Nodding she rubbed her upper body against his like a cat.

"Oh, yes."

Logan wrapped his arms tighter around her waist and slammed his lips against hers, kissing the breath right out of her.

Before she could blink Logan dropped her to the ground and backed her up against his desk. His lips descended on hers as she wound her arms around his neck, her fingers tunnelling through his hair, trying to pull him even closer. She ground her hips against his and he groaned, pulling back to look at her.

"I love you," he purred, his voice low and seductive. She shuddered at his words and scored her nails down his back, being was rewarded with a shudder of his own.

"I love you too," she responded in a whisper.

His teeth nipped at her neck and she arched her back, pushing her aching breasts towards him. He accepted the invitation and yanked at her top, lifting it up and tossing it aside, exposing her breasts. Her bra went next, he flicked the clasp open with deft fingers and, helped by the lack of straps, pulled it off and tucked it into his back pocket. He bent his head and swept his tongue over one straining nipple, sucking it into the cool wetness of his mouth. She gasped at the sensation and arched against him, trying to get closer to the bulge in his jeans.

Topaz ran her hands up his chest and began to undo the buttons keeping his shirt closed. When she had bared his chest she gave into her body's urges and kissed his cool skin, sucking one nipple into her mouth and biting lightly. She heard him moan softly before he pulled away to look at her.

"I'm going to feast on you," he promised, his eyes glazed with lust.

"Take me," she answered.

244

Without further warning he lifted her up and laid her gently onto the desktop. He pulled his office chair round to face her and sat down, gripping her hips he pulled, sliding her lower body across the polished wood towards him. This sudden action caused her skirt to ride up, bunching around her hips.

"Mmm," he murmured. "Look what I have here." She gasped as his fingers slid into the waist band of her panties and slowly drew them down, over her hips and down her legs. She felt his lips on her skin and she shivered as he began to kiss his way up her thigh, heading higher.

"What are you up to?" she asked, suspiciously, lifting up onto her elbows she looked down at him.

He shot her a look that was pure wickedness.

"I'm feasting on you," he answered and bent his head a little closer, sweeping his tongue lightly over her flesh, hitting the spot that was crying out for attention.

Pleasure washed over her, throwing her body back onto the desk top, knocking a pen holder and a stack of papers onto the floor. Logan lifted one of her legs over his shoulder but left the other one dangling down to the floor.

Logan proceeded to do exactly as he had promised. He kissed and he licked, he sucked and he nipped, working her mercilessly, almost to breaking point before slowing down. Each sweep of his tongue had her writhing on the smooth polished wood, lifting her hips, her fingers gripping the edge of the desk.

Tension began to build again, rolling through her in one long wave.

"Logan, please," she begged, almost incoherent with need, desperate for him to let her finish.

Logan chuckled against her skin, licking slowly, drawing out the pleasure. She gasped as he slid one long finger inside her and rasped it over the spot deep inside, before sliding back out only to thrust deeper.

245

She moaned, as another finger joined the first. His tongue danced across her flesh as his fingers thrust in and out. She felt the beginnings of orgasm build within her as she lifted her hips, needing more.

Logan moved his head away and she whimpered at the loss, but his fingers kept up the relentless pace, moving faster inside her, catching that spot over and over again.

Logan kissed the soft flesh of her inner thigh and licked a wet path across her skin. She had a second to wonder what he was doing before she felt his fangs pierce her flesh and pleasure exploded, almost trebling in intensity.

She screamed his name, thrashing around on the desk, her nails clawing at the wood as pleasure continued to pour over her, each pull with his mouth seeming to zip straight to her clit, making it tingle and pulse, his fingers stroking and rubbing over that one perfect spot, her inner muscles clamping down on his invading fingers. His combined actions making her pant, writhe, thrust her hips closer as she rode the waves of orgasm past their ultimate peak. She felt his fangs withdraw and his tongue lick the wound closed, but she barely registered it, it was like her brain had detached from her body.

His tongue was back, licking her lightly as she finally came back down to earth, her breathing laboured and her skin slick with sweat. She dug her fingers into his hair and used her grip to raise his head, making him look at her.

"No more, baby, please. My heart won't take it." She collapsed back against the cool wood as he kissed his way up her body, stopping to pay homage to each breast in turn before finally reaching her lips.

"I'm still hungry," he whispered against her lips and, even though she felt so sated she doubted she could move for a month, her body responded. She reached down and cupped him through the thick material of his jeans, giving him a squeeze. Logan growled in response.

"What can I do for the second course?" she asked, kissing his neck.

"The main course, you mean," he corrected her and in a move too quick to see, he slipped his arms under her and flipped her over onto her front, pulling her close so she was able to stand on her own, her upper body bent over the desk. He ground his erection against her, the roughness of the denim rasping against her overly sensitive flesh.

She gasped and tried to pull away but Logan's hands found her hips and held her still. Once satisfied she would remain where he wanted her, he removed one hand from her hip. She heard the hiss of his zipper as he pulled it down, followed by the muffled thump of his jeans hitting the floor. She looked back over her shoulder as he kicked them aside and advanced on her, anticipation making her shiver.

Logan stood behind her and ran one hand over her butt, caressing and shaping the flesh. When he was done exploring her behind he slid his hand down lower, his fingers skimming through her wetness. She moaned and parted her legs to give him easier access.

"So eager," he purred, his fingers slipping inside her, making her buck against his hand.

"Please, Logan, please," she begged, needing him with such intensity she thought she might faint. His fingers slid back out and began to rub her in small tingling circles. She gasped and moaned as his skilled fingers quickly worked her towards another orgasm. Just as the pleasure reached its peak she felt him shift behind her and screamed his name as he thrust smoothly inside her. The feeling of being invaded pushed her over the edge and she bucked against him, ramming him into her hard.

His hands gripped her hips, his fingers biting into her flesh as he began to plunge in and out of her hot wetness.

"Oh, fuck," he moaned, "You feel so good." It was all she could do to nod in agreement, her head flopping down.

247

"Oh, no you don't," he wound the fingers of one hand into her hair and lifted her head up. "Don't quit on me now, we're not done." He bent forward, still thrusting in and out in a smooth flowing rhythm and kissed a path up her back, peppering her spine with light strokes of his tongue and little nips of his teeth.

She moaned and writhed under his lips, loving the feel of his touch. Trusting that she would hold herself up, he reached round and cupped her breasts gently in his hands, kneading them softly before pulling on her aching nipples. Jolts of pleasure shot through her and she pushed back on his groin, needing him deeper.

"More," she demanded with a groan.

Spurred on by her movements he took control again and sped up the pace of his thrusting, fairly pounded into her, gripping her hips once more. She leant forward a little, changing the angle slightly and gasped as he hit that spot deep inside her that was already so primed and ready from his skilled fingers. She felt the weight of another orgasm build inside her and turned her head to look at Logan.

His fabulous chest was framed by his shirt where it was hanging open. She could see his muscles quivering and flexing with each thrust. His head was thrown back, all that luscious hair flowing around his face, which was almost slack with pleasure.

The sight of him thrusting against her almost did her in.

"I'm close, baby," she whispered, knowing he could hear her. "So close. Please… together."

In response Logan wrapped his arms around her and lifted her up against his chest so she was almost standing upright. She gripped the edge of the desk with one trembling hand while sliding the other behind her to grab his butt, sinking her fingers into his tight flesh, and holding on to him like he was the only solid thing in her world.

Her breath was coming out in tiny gasps, little sounds of pleasure spilling from her lips in time to his movements.

248

Logan nipped and kissed at the skin on her neck and she knew what was coming, wanting it as much as he did.

"Yes… now," she moaned, feeling the muscles inside her tense around him. Logan grunted and thrust into her again before sinking his fangs into her neck. His arms held her tight against his chest as her legs gave way, pleasure crashing through her in waves.

She felt the same disconnection as she felt the night before, like something inside her broke away. She felt an answering shift inside Logan as he stilled, his cock pulsing as his seed pumped into her. She felt her soul reach out for his and when they joined the world seemed to melt away, leaving them with nothing but their combined pleasure.

She flopped forward, catching herself on her hands, Logan collapsed against her back, his mouth still working on her neck, drawing the blood from her veins, his tongue kneading her skin, pleasure accompanying each swallow.

Just when she couldn't stand any more he stopped and pulled away, his fangs sliding out, his tongue licking away the last drop of blood.

She felt boneless, her body sated beyond measure. She felt her eyelids droop and was pathetically grateful when Logan sat her in his chair.

He fetched their clothes and she donned her top and he his jeans. Her bra was still hanging out of his back pocket and he had told her that he was keeping her panties too. She was too tired to argue.

"Take me to bed, I'm done," she begged, holding out her arms to be picked up. "My legs won't work. I think you almost killed me."

Logan laughed at that, scooping her up into his arms making for the door.

"You do know that's impossible don't you?" he asked, his deep voice rumbling through his chest.

"What is?" she answered as he kicked open the door to his apartment and headed for the bedroom.

"It does not matter how much we make love, you're immortal now," he looked down at her. "I could make love to you all day, every day and it still would not be enough to satisfy me." He laid her gently down on the bed.

"I want you with every fibre of my being. I want you always by my side." He lay down next to her and pulled the covers over them before tucking her in under his arm. "You are mine."

"And you are mine," she agreed.

"I never want us to be parted again."

"We won't be," she promised.

They lay there in silence, Logan's hand playing over her skin in a loving caress as they waited for dawn. A thought struck her as sleep sucked her down. How could they be together when her life was back in London?

Chapter 23

Topaz had had a lot to think about over the past few days, her flight back to London was due to depart the next day, she had to make a choice.

She told Logan that she needed some time alone and he accepted this, leaving her in his apartment while he took care of some club business in his office downstairs.

She made herself a big pot of coffee and sat on the sofa, getting up now and then to refresh her cup.

She thought back over everything that had happened since she had touched down on Scottish soil. She made a mental list of pro's and con's, good and bad. Logan, of course, was very much on the pro list.

She looked back fondly, as much as she could now her memories were tainted, on the good times she had shared with Ronnie. She felt very sad about how that had turned out, but hey, she told herself, it wasn't her fault she was as batty as a belfry.

She still didn't fully understand all that had happened, even with Mason telling his side of the story. She just didn't get the reasons behind it. But she wanted to find out, the possibility of looking into Vampire culture further was just too good to pass up.

Topaz knew she didn't want to leave Logan, she *couldn't* leave Logan. She knew now that the sickness and headaches she had experienced when apart from him would only get worse. It wasn't even an option.

But she loved her job, couldn't imagine being away from everyone at Athena's, not permanently.

She puzzled it over for another hour, finishing off the coffee, but in the end her mind was made up.

The next night found them back in London, standing outside Andy and Clarissa's house.

Logan who was holding her hand gave it a little squeeze. She turned to look at him.

"Are you sure you want to do this?" he asked gently. "You don't have to, we can work something out."

She shook her head.

"No, I want to do this, I need to do this. My place is with you."

Logan smiled widely and gave her a modest kiss on the lips, mindful that they were on a public street.

She kissed him back then took a deep breath, steeling herself for what she was about to do. She rung the door bell and waited.

Almost instantly she could hear the sound of footsteps coming up the hall and seconds later Andy threw open the door. He caught sight of her and grinned, grabbing her up in a big hug.

"Topaz, hey, how's the trip been? You haven't called, you haven't written," he joked. She sighed, extracting herself from his enthusiastic hug. This was going to be so hard.

"Andy, we have to talk," she reached out and found Logan's hand, catching it up in a death grip, needing his strength.

252

"Uh oh, that sounds ominous. What's up? Nothing bad I hope? Come on inside and we'll have a chat."

He led the way down the hall into their comfy sitting room. Topaz waved to Clarissa who was sitting in one of the armchairs and took a seat on the sofa, pulling Logan down next to her. He slid his arm around her shoulders and hugged her close as she sank gratefully into his embrace.

Andy made himself comfortable in the last remaining arm chair.

"So, what happened? I can see that you definitely found something while you were away," he nodded to Logan, a bright smile on his face.

Topaz immediately realised that she hadn't introduced him to anyone.

"Oh, I'm sorry. Everyone I have seen in the last week knows Logan, I kinda forgot that you didn't. Andy, Logan, Logan, Andy." They both got up and politely shook hands. "And this is his lovely wife, Clarissa." Logan shook her hand too.

"It's lovely to meet you both," he said. "Topaz has told me so much about you, and your amazing work."

They both looked very pleased.

"Well it's great to meet you too," Clarissa said. "Any friend of Topaz's is a friend of ours."

"Well, we're a little more than friends," Topaz corrected.

She had already decided that she was going to tell them an edited version of the truth.

"So, are you going to tell us all about your trip?" Clarissa asked.

"OK, here goes. I checked into my hotel OK and that night I checked out the club where I was meeting Mason, but I wasn't allowed in because of the dress code."

"Dress code?" Andy asked, puzzled.

"Yeah, It's a goth place," Topaz made sure she said this with a kind of sneer, goths are not that popular with them.

Andy made a noise of agreement. Logan poked her gently in the side and she threw him an apologetic look.

Sorry, baby, she mentally sent to him. *We're not that fond of goths. They're all posers, not like us.*

You can make it up to me later.

Topaz narrowed her eyes at him as his hand crept lower down her back, but she wasn't really mad at him. He was just trying to ease her tension.

"So I went shopping the next day and went to the club," she continued, "Mason wasn't there, he hadn't shown up for work but I met his boss and he kept me company and we got on very well. That boss was Logan." She squeezed his hand and gave him a look of pure devotion, damn she loved him.

Logan took over the story.

"I took over the club a few years ago and decided the time was right to cash in on the renewed interest in Vampire culture. As you can see," he gestured to his clothes, faded blue jeans and a plain red t-shirt, "I'm not really into the goth thing, but there are plenty out there who are."

"I would have emailed you but my hotel room was broken into and my laptop was stolen," Topaz explained and they heard Andy's shocked intake of breath.

"Oh God, babe, are you OK?"

Topaz nodded.

"Yeah, I'm OK. We were out having dinner at the time. I let myself in and discovered the break in. I was so glad Logan was there. He comforted me and when the police closed off my room and I didn't have anywhere to stay, he offered me one of his guest rooms."

"Guest room huh? That was very generous of you," Andy didn't sound like he believed her, she knew when she was busted.

"I said he offered me his guest room, I didn't say I slept in there. Which brings me to the rest of our news."

"There's more?" he sounded intrigued.

"We got married," she almost squealed. It was so exciting, if a little nerve racking, to tell someone who knew her, and wasn't a Vampire, that they had gotten married.

Andy was silent and Clarissa looked like she had announced she had just slaughtered a goat.

"Come on guys, say something. You are happy for me, right?"

"Yeah," Andy finally said. "Of course we're happy for you. I mean, Clarissa and I got married almost straight away too." He smiled at his wife who smiled back, reaching over to take his hand.

"And look how well that turned out," Clarissa added.

"I know it sudden, but it feels right. I love Logan and he loves me, we were meant to be together, we're Soul Mates."

Andy let this sink in while giving Logan a more thorough, once over.

"What are you gonna do about work?" he finally asked. This was the bit Tope had been dreading.

"I'm gonna move and live with Logan. Obviously I can't continue working at Athena's and that has been one of the hardest decisions I have ever had to make. I love working with you guys and I am going to miss teaching my class, and I'm sorry to drop you in it and leave you without a teacher, but I have to do this."

"We understand that, and we are very sorry to lose you. We'll all miss you," Clarissa got up to give her a hug.

"Oh, you're not getting rid of me that easily."

"Why's that?" Andy asked.

"I want to go freelance. I still want to write my articles, go on my research trips and contribute to the web site. I know this trip was a bust, but I found something better," she smiled at Logan. "I know that Vampires are out there and I'll keep searching for tangible proof. I know in my gut that when the time is right I will be coming to you with an article that will prove it once and for all. Just not yet."

Topaz felt bad having left out the most important parts, of what she had discovered and what she could write about. But she knew that what she said was true, the Vampires would come out, maybe not in the near future but some day. And she would be right there, in the thick of it, ready to help.

Andy laughed looking relieved. "That's a great idea. It's the best of both worlds. Obviously we would love for you to keep working here, but you have to follow your heart."

Topaz nodded, agreeing.

"I do, and I am. We're going to clear out my flat tomorrow and then head back to Scotland. Logan has left his manager in charge of the club but we do need to get back."

"Is there anything we can do to help?" Andy asked. That's what Topaz loved about them; they were so accepting and ready to help.

"Well, I'm putting the flat up for sale. If it's not too much trouble, would you be able to keep an eye on the place and help with the arrangements? Obviously I'll come back to do the paperwork and everything when it sells."

"No problem at all love, we're happy to help. You leave it to us," Andy assured her.

An hour, and many hugs and congratulations, later, Topaz and Logan hopped into a cab, heading back to her flat.

She leaned back against the seat and closed her eyes.

Logan tentatively took her hand.

"Are you alright, darling?" he asked his voice warm and full of concern.

She opened her eyes and looked at him.

"I'm fine, baby, just a little sad. I don't want to be, but it's the end of an era for me."

Logan wrapped his arm around her and drew her onto his lap.

"I know, sweetheart, and I'm sorry. I know how much you are giving up for me. I'm so proud of you. You made a wonderful life for yourself, an amazing career and many good friends."

Topaz cupped his face gently in her hands and made him look at her.

"You don't have anything to be sorry for. I'm not giving anything up; I'm just changing it for the better. I love you, Logan and I want to be with you always." She kissed him soundly on the mouth, effectively cutting off any more protests he may have been about to make.

Logan pulled her closer and held her tight against his chest, she purred and ran her hands up between them, letting her fingers coast over the muscles under his shirt. She felt his muscles twitch under her touch and wriggled her butt against his crotch, loving the feel of him growing harder by the second.

"You're an evil Witch," he groaned against her lips. "We're in a taxicab and I can't have my wicked way with you."

She giggled and lifted her head to peer out of the window.

"Good job we're home then isn't it?" The cab pulled up to the kerb as she spoke.

Logan practically threw the money at the driver and grabbed her hand, pulling her up the path to the front door. They got inside in record time, kicking aside the moving boxes Logan had ordered so they could pack up her stuff.

"Care to show me your bedroom?" He asked, a suggestive look on his face.

She pointed in the general direction and squealed as Logan swept her up into his arms to carry her to the bedroom.

"I love you, wife," he said, kissing her nose.

"I love you too, husband," she replied, kissing him back. "Now take me to bed, I can't wait to find out just how wicked you can be."

257